GREG HILDEBRANDT'S FAVORITE FAIRY TALES

GREG HILDEBRANDT'S FAVORITE FAIRY TALES

Edited and
Illustrated by
Greg Hildebrandt

LITTLE SIMON
Published by Simon & Schuster, Inc.
New York

Published by LITTLE SIMON,
a division of Simon & Schuster, Inc.,
Simon & Schuster Building, Rockefeller Center,
1230 Avenue of the Americas, New York, New York 10020.
LITTLE SIMON and colophon are registered trademarks of Simon & Schuster, Inc.
Printed in U.S.A.

10 9 8 7 6 5 4 3 2 1
Library of Congress Cataloging in Publication Data

Hildebrandt, Greg.
Greg Hildebrandt's Favorite fairy tales.
Summary: Twenty fairy tales from various parts of the
world, including "Beauty and the Beast," "Aladdin and the
Magic Lamp," "Hansel and Gretel," "Andromeda and Perseus,"
and "Jack the Giant Killer."
1. Fairy tales. [1. Fairy tales. 2. Folklore]
I. Title.
PZ8.H5327Gr 1984   398.2'1   84–10048
ISBN 0-671-50327-8

CONTENTS

This collection is dedicated to my mother,
Germaine Hildebrandt,
for her belief in fantasy and fairy tales;
and for the inspiration and love
she has given to me.

Acknowledgments

I would like to extend my deepest thanks to the following friends and family members who gave their time and efforts to pose for the characters in this collection of some of my favorite fairy tales.

Josephine Paglia	Shoemaker's Wife
Lou Paglia	Shoemaker
Joe Varenelli	Elf
Gregory Hildebrandt	Jack The Giant Killer
Anthony Marcantuono	The Giant Blunderbore
William McGuire	Rip Van Winkle
Ron Wagner	Sigurd
Robert Irsay	Sindbad
Eric Shanower	Perseus
Stephanie Irsay	Andromeda
Donna Cole	Rapunzel
Pete Dominick	King's Son
	Aladdin
Fred Jones	Genie from Aladdin
Robert Port, MD	Prince Ahmed
Amy Port	Perie Banou
Gene O'Brien	Schaibar the Genie
	Eshirit
	Lepracaun Poet
Michael Resnick	Aed, Chief Poet of Ulster
Howard Gruder	King Iubdan
Marla Maier	Queen Bebo
Joseph D. Scrocco, Jr.	Rumpelstiltskin

	King Fergas Mac Leide
Dawn Felauer	Miller's Daughter
Daniel Slater	Marble Statue
Jean L. Scrocco	The Little Mermaid
	Freyja
	Snowdrop
	Witch
	Evil Fairy
Johnathan Kenny	Hansel
Amanda Eyrich	Grethel
Tanya Irsay	Seven Good Fairies
	Little Girl
Steve Giovanni	Dwarf
Erika Connell	Little Girl
Andrew Connell	Little Boy
Nicholas Kenny	Little Boy
Dina Rosenkrans	Elsa
	Clay Statue
Mary Hildebrandt	Beauty
Melvin Slater	Old Man of Magic
Bernice Slater	Fairy Mother
Greg Hildebrandt	The Ratcatcher
	Dwarf
Craig Maier	Polyphemus the Cyclopus
Adam Kubert	Greek Sailor
Andy Kubert	Odysseus
Bjorn Ousland	Greek Sailor
Jay Geldhof	Greek Sailor
Erin Lyons	Kisika

Greg Hildebrandt

Special thanks to Kate Klimo
for her personal involvement and guidance
throughout this fantasy series.

THE SECOND VOYAGE OF
SINDBAD THE SAILOR

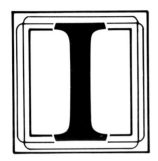

n the reign of the Caliph Haroun Al Raschid there lived in Bagdad a poor porter, whose name was Hindbad. It happened one day that he was carrying a heavy burden. The day was so hot that he was wearied by the load. In this state he passed by a fine house, before which the ground was swept and sprinkled and the air was cool. There came forth from the door a pleasant breeze laden with an exquisite odor. The porter was delighted and sat down upon the bench by the door to listen to the melodious sounds of stringed instruments and to joyous voices laughing and singing. He also heard the voices of nightingales warbling and praising Allah, whose name be exalted.

The porter was moved with curiosity, and he looked and saw within the house a lovely garden, wherein he beheld slaves and servants hurrying to and fro; from the charming melody and the smell of savory dishes he concluded there was a feast within. He asked the name of the owner of the house, and, learning that it was Sindbad, the famous voyager, he lifted up his eyes to Heaven and said, "Oh, Allah! Thou enrichest whom Thou wilt, and whom Thou wilt Thou abasest! Thou has bestowed wealth upon the owner of this palace, while I am wretched and weary, and spend the day carrying other people's burdens!" Scarcely had Hindbad finished lamenting when there came forth from the door a servant, who took the porter by the hand and said to him, "Enter! My master calleth for thee."

The porter entered the house with the servant and found himself in a grand chamber, in which he beheld noblemen and great lords. A feast was spread with all kinds of delicious viands and beverages. On both sides were beautiful slave girls performing upon instruments of music, and at the upper end of the chamber was a great and venerable man, who requested him to seat himself and placed before him delicious food.

THE SECOND VOYAGE OF SINDBAD THE SAILOR

So Hindbad advanced, and, having said, "In the name of Allah, the Compassionate, the Merciful," he ate until he was satisfied, said, "Praise be to Allah!" washed his hands, and thanked his host.

"Thou art welcome," said the master of the house. "What is thy name, and what trade dost thou follow?"

"O my master," the porter answered, "my name is Hindbad, and I am a porter."

At this the master of the house smiled and said, "I heard thy lamentation at my door, and I will now inform thee of all that happened to me and befell me before I attained this prosperity. My story is wonderful, for I have suffered severe fatigue and great troubles and many terrors."

Thereupon Sindbad related as follows:

Know, O my brothers, I lived most comfortably, until one day I felt a longing to travel again to lands of other peoples, and for the pleasure of seeing the countries and islands of the world. I decided to set forth at once, and, taking a large sum of money, I purchased with it goods and merchandise suitable for trade and packed them up. Then I went to the banks of the river, and found there a handsome new vessel, manned by a numerous crew. So I embarked my bales in it, as did also a party of merchants, and we set sail that day.

The voyage was pleasant; we passed from sea to sea and from island to island, and at every place where we cast anchor we sold, bought, and exchanged goods. Thus we continued to voyage until we arrived at a beautiful island, abounding with trees of ripe fruit, where there was not one single inhabitant. I landed with the rest and sat by a spring of pure water among the trees. Soon I fell asleep, enjoying the sweet shade and the fragrant air. When I awoke I found that the master had forgotten me; the vessel had sailed with all the passengers, leaving me alone on the island.

I had with me neither food, drink, nor worldly goods, and I was desolate and despairing of life. I began to weep and wail, and to blame myself for having undertaken the voyage and fatigue when I was reposing at ease in my home and country, in want of nothing. I repented of having gone forth from the city of Bagdad, and of having set out on a voyage over sea.

After a while I arose and walked about the island. I climbed a lofty tree and saw naught save sky and water, trees and birds, islands and sand. Looking attentively, I saw an enormous white object, indistinct in the distance. I descended from the tree and proceeded in that direction without stopping. And lo, it was a huge white dome, of great height

10

and immense circumference. I drew near to it and walked around it but found no door, and I could not climb it because of its excessive smoothness. I made a mark at the place where I stood and went around the dome measuring it, and lo, it was fifty full paces!

Suddenly the sky became dark, and the sun was hidden. I imagined a cloud had passed over it. I raised my head and saw a bird of enormous size, bulky body, and wide wings flying in the air, and this it was that concealed the sun and darkened the island. My wonder increased, and I remembered a story that travelers and voyagers had told me long before— how in certain islands there is a bird of enormous size called the roc, which feedeth its young ones with elephants. I was convinced, therefore, that the dome was the egg of a roc, and I wondered at the works of Allah, whose name be exalted!

The bird alighted upon the dome and, brooding over it with its wings, stretched out its legs behind upon the ground and slept over it. Thereupon I arose, unwound my turban from my head, and twisted it into a rope. I fastened it tightly about my waist and tied myself to one of the feet of the bird, saying to myself, Perhaps this bird will convey me to a land of cities and inhabitants, and that will be better than my remaining on this island.

I passed the night sleepless, and when the dawn came the bird rose from its egg, uttered a great cry, and flew up into the sky, drawing me with it. It soared higher and higher, and then it descended gradually, until it alighted with me upon the earth. When I reached the ground I hastily unbound myself from its foot, loosed my turban, shaking with fear as I did so, and walked away. The roc took something from the earth in its talons and soared aloft; I looked and saw that the bird had taken a serpent of enormous size and was carrying it off toward the sea.

I walked about the place and found myself in a large, deep, wide valley, shut in by a great mountain, whose summit I could not see because of its excessive height, and I could not ascend it because of its steepness. Seeing this, I blamed myself for what I had done. "Would that I had remained on the island," I cried aloud, "since it is better than this deserted place! For on that island are fruits that I might have eaten, and I might have drunk from its rivers, but in this place are neither trees, fruits, nor rivers! Verily every time I escape from one calamity I fall into another that is greater and more severe!" Then I arose and, encouraging myself, walked down the valley, and lo, its ground was covered with the most magnificent of diamonds, stones so hard that neither iron nor rock could have any effect upon it.

THE SECOND VOYAGE OF SINDBAD THE SAILOR

All that valley was likewise occupied by venomous serpents of enormous size, big enough to swallow an elephant. These serpents came out of their holes in the night, and during the day they hid themselves, fearing lest the rocs should carry them off and tear them to pieces. The day departed, and I began to search for a place in which to pass the night, fearing the serpents that were beginning to come forth. I found a cave nearby with a narrow entrance. I therefore entered, and, seeing a large stone, I pushed it and stopped up the mouth of the cave. I said to myself, I am safe in this cave, and when daylight cometh I will go forth and look for some means to escape from this valley.

I prepared to repose, when, looking toward the upper end of the cave, I saw a huge serpent sleeping over its eggs. At this my flesh quaked, and I raised my head and passed the night sleepless until dawn, when I removed the stone and went forth, giddy from sleeplessness and hunger and fear.

I walked along the valley, when all of a sudden the carcass of a great animal fell before me. I looked but could see no one, so I wondered extremely, and I remembered a story that I had heard long ago from merchants and travelers—how in the Valley of Diamonds are experienced great horrors, and that no one can gain access to the diamonds. To obtain these stones the merchants employ a stratagem. They take a sheep and slaughter it, skin it, and cut up its flesh, which they then throw down from the mountain to the bottom of the valley. The meat being fresh and moist, some of the diamonds stick to it. The merchants leave it until midday, when large birds descend to the valley and, taking the meat up in their talons, carry it to the top of the mountain, whereupon the merchants cry out and frighten away the birds. They then remove the diamonds sticking to the meat and carry them to their own country, leaving the flesh for the birds and wild beasts. No one can procure the diamonds but by this stratagem.

Therefore, when I beheld that slaughtered animal and remembered this story, I arose and selected a great number of large and beautiful diamonds, which I put into my pocket, wrapped carefully in my turban, and hid within my clothes. While I was doing this, behold, another great slaughtered animal fell before me. I bound myself to it with my turban and, lying down on my back, placed the meat upon my bosom and grasped it firmly. Immediately an enormous bird of prey descended upon it, seized it with its talons, and flew up with it into the air, with me attached to it. It soared to the summit of the mountain, where it alighted. Then a great and loud cry arose nearby, and a piece of wood fell clattering upon

13

the mountain; the bird, frightened by the noise, flew away.

I disengaged myself from the carcass and stood up by its side, when lo, the merchant who had cried out at the bird advanced and saw me standing there. He was very much terrified, and when he saw that there were no diamonds on the meat he uttered a cry of disappointment. "Who art thou," exclaimed he, "who hath brought this misfortune upon me?"

"Fear not, nor be alarmed," answered I, "for I am a human being, a merchant like thyself, and my tale is prodigious, and my story wonderful! I have with me an abundance of diamonds, and I will share them with thee to repay thee for those thou has lost." The man thanked me for this and conversed with me, and behold, the other merchants heard me talking with their companion, and they came and saluted me. I acquainted them with my whole story, relating to them all I had suffered upon the voyage. Then I gave the owner of the slaughtered animal to which I had attached myself a number of the diamonds that I had brought with me from the valley. And I passed the night with the merchants, full of utmost joy at my escape from the Valley of Diamonds.

When the next day came we arose and journeyed together until we arrived at a city, where I exchanged a part of my diamonds for merchandise and gold and silver. After which I journeyed from country to country, and from city to city, selling and buying, until I arrived at the city of Bagdad, the Abode of Peace. I entered my house, bringing with me a great quantity of diamonds and money and goods. I made presents to my family and relations, bestowed alms and gifts, and feasted with my friends and companions; and thus I forgot all that I had suffered.

When Sindbad had finished his story all the company marveled. They supped with him, and he presented to Hindbad a hundred pieces of gold.

RIP VAN WINKLE

hoever has made a voyage up the Hudson must remember the Kaatskill Mountains. They are a dismembered branch of the great Appalachian family, and are seen away to the west of the river, swelling up to a noble height and lording it over the surrounding country. Every change of season, every change of weather, indeed, every hour of the day, produces some change in the magical hues and shapes of these mountains, and they are regarded by all the good wives, far and near, as perfect barometers. When the weather is fair and settled, they are clothed in blue and purple and print their bold outlines on the clear evening sky; but sometimes, when the rest of the landscape is cloudless, they will gather a hood of gray vapors about their summits, which, in the last rays of the setting sun, will glow and light up like a crown of glory.

At the foot of these fairy mountains the voyager may have described the light smoke curling up from a village, whose shingle roofs gleam among the trees, just where the blue tints of the upland melt away into the fresh green of the nearer landscape. It is a little village, of great antiquity, having been founded by some of the Dutch colonists in the early times of the province, just about the beginning of the government of the good Peter Stuyvesant (may he rest in peace!). Some of the houses of the original settlers still stand, built of small yellow bricks brought from Holland, having latticed windows and gable fronts, and surmounted with weathercocks.

In that same village, and in one of these very houses (which, to tell the precise truth, was sadly time-worn and weather-beaten), there lived, many years since, while the country was yet a province of Great Britain, a simple, good-natured fellow, of the name of Rip Van Winkle. He was a descendant of the Van Winkles who figured so gallantly in the chivalrous days of Peter Stuyvesant, and accompanied him to the siege of Fort Christina. He inherited, however, but little of the martial character of his ancestors. I have observed that he was a simple, good-natured man; he was, moreover, a kind neighbor and an obedient, henpecked husband. Indeed, to the latter circumstance might be owing that meekness of spirit that gained him such universal popularity; for those men are most apt to be obsequious and conciliating abroad who are under the discipline of shrews at home. Their tempers, doubtless, are rendered pliant and malleable in the fiery furnace of domestic tribulation; and a curtain lecture is worth all the sermons in the world for teaching the virtues of patience and long-suffering. A termagant wife may, therefore, in some respects, be considered a tolerable blessing; and if so, Rip Van Winkle was thrice blessed.

Certain it is that he was a great favorite among all the good wives of the village, who, as is usual with the amiable sex, took his part in all family squabbles and never failed, whenever they talked those matters over in their evening gossipings, to lay all the blame on Dame Van Winkle. The children of the village, too, would shout with joy whenever he approached. He assisted at their sports, made their playthings, taught them to fly kites and shoot marbles, and told them long stories of ghosts, witches, and Indians. Whenever he went dodging about the village, he was surrounded by a troop of them, hanging on his skirts, clambering on his back, and playing a thousand tricks on him with impunity; and not a dog would bark at him throughout the neighborhood.

The great error in Rip's composition was an insuperable aversion to all kinds of profitable labor. It could not be from the want of assiduity or perseverance; for he would sit on a wet rock, with a rod as long and heavy as a Tartar's lance, and fish all day without a murmur, even though he should not be encouraged to a single nibble. He would carry a fowling piece on his shoulder for hours together, trudging through woods and swamps, up hill and down dale, to shoot a few squirrels or wild pigeons. He would never refuse to assist a neighbor in even the roughest toil and was a foremost man at all country frolics for husking Indian corn or building stone fences; the women of the village, too, used to employ him to run their errands and to do such little odd jobs as their less obliging husbands would not do for them. In a word, Rip was ready to attend to anybody's business but his own; but as to doing family duty, and keeping his farm in order, he found it impossible.

In fact, he declared it was of no use to work on his farm; it was the most pestilent little piece of ground in the whole country; everything about it went wrong, and would go wrong, in spite of him. His fences were continually falling to pieces; his cow would either go astray or get among the cabbages; weeds were sure to grow quicker in his fields than anywhere else; and the rain always made a point of setting in just as he had some outdoor work to do. Therefore, though his patrimonial estate had dwindled away under his management, acre by acre, until there was little more left than a mere patch of Indian corn and potatoes, yet it was the worst-conditioned farm in the neighborhood.

His children, too, were as ragged and wild as if they belonged to nobody. His son Rip, an urchin begotten in his own likeness, promised to inherit the habits, with the old clothes, of his father. He was generally seen trooping like a colt at his mother's heels, equipped in a pair of his father's cast-off galligaskins, which he had much ado to hold up with one hand, as a fine lady does her train in bad weather.

Rip Van Winkle, however, was one of those happy mortals, of foolish, well-oiled dispositions, who take the world easy, eat white bread or brown, whichever can be got with least thought or trouble, and would rather starve on a penny than work for a pound. If left to himself, he would have whistled life away in perfect contentment. But his wife kept continually dinning in his ears about his idleness, his carelessness, and the ruin he was bringing on his family. Morning, noon, and night her tongue was incessantly going, and everything he said or did was sure to produce a torrent of household eloquence. Rip had but one way of replying to all lectures of the kind, and that, by frequent use, had grown into a habit. He shrugged his shoulders, shook his head, cast up his eyes, but said nothing. This, however, always provoked a fresh volley from his wife; so that he was fain to draw off his forces and take to the outside of the house—the only side that, in truth, belongs to a henpecked husband.

Rip's sole domestic adherent was his dog Wolf, who was as much henpecked as his master. Dame Van Winkle regarded them as companions in idleness, and even looked upon Wolf with an evil eye, as the cause of his master's going so often astray. True it is, in all points of spirit befitting an honorable dog, he was as courageous an animal as ever scoured the woods; but what courage can withstand the ever-during and all-besetting terrors of a woman's tongue? The moment Wolf entered the house his crest fell, his tail dropped to the ground or curled between his legs, he sneaked about with a gallows air, casting many a sidelong glance at Dame Van Winkle, and at the least flourish of a broomstick or ladle he would fly to the door with yelping precipitation.

Times grew worse and worse with Rip Van Winkle as years of matrimony rolled on; a tart temper never mellows with age, and a sharp tongue is the only edged tool that grows keener with constant use. For a long while he used to console himself, when driven from home, by frequenting a kind of perpetual club of the sages, philosophers, and other idle personages of the village, which held its sessions on a bench before a small inn, designated by a rubicund portrait of His Majesty George the Third. Here they used to sit in the shade through a long, lazy summer's day, talking listlessly over village gossip, or telling endless sleepy stories about nothing. But it would have been worth any statesman's money to have heard the profound discussions that sometimes took place when by chance an old newspaper fell into their hands from some passing traveler. How solemnly they would listen to the contents, as drawled out by Derrick Van Bummel, the schoolmaster, a dapper learned little man who was not to be daunted by the most gigantic word in the dictionary; and how sagely they would deliberate upon public events some months after they had taken place.

The opinions of this junto were completely controlled by Nicholas Vedder, a patriarch of the village and landlord of the inn, at the door of which he took his seat from morning till night, just moving sufficiently to avoid the sun and keep in the shade of a large tree (in this fashion the neighbors could tell the hour by his movements as accurately as by a sundial). It is true he was rarely heard to speak but smoked his pipe incessantly. His adherents, however (for every great man has his adherents), perfectly understood him and knew how to gather his opinions. When anything that was read or related displeased him, he was observed to smoke his pipe vehemently and to send forth short, frequent, and angry puffs; when pleased, he would inhale the smoke slowly and tranquilly, and emit it in light and placid clouds; and sometimes, taking the pipe from his mouth and letting the fragrant vapor curl about his nose, he would gravely nod his head in token of perfect approbation.

From even this stronghold the unlucky Rip was at length routed by his termagant wife, who would suddenly break in upon the tranquillity of the assemblage and call the members all to naught. Not even that august personage Nicholas Vedder himself was spared the daring tongue of this terrible virago, who charged him outright with encouraging her husband in habits of idleness.

Poor Rip was at last reduced almost to despair. His only alternative, to escape from the labor of the farm and clamor of his wife, was to take gun in hand and stroll away into the woods. Here he would sometimes seat himself at the foot of a tree and share the contents of his wallet with Wolf, with whom he sympathized as a fellow sufferer in persecution.

"Poor Wolf," he would say, "thy mistress leads thee a dog's life of it; but never mind, my lad, whilst I live thou shalt never want a friend to stand by thee!" Wolf would wag his tail and look wistfully in his master's face. If dogs can feel pity, I verily believe he reciprocated the sentiment with all his heart.

In a long ramble of the kind on a fine autumnal day Rip had unconsciously scrambled to one of the highest parts of the Kaatskill Mountains. He was after his favorite sport of squirrel hunting, and the still solitudes had echoed and reechoed with the reports of his gun. Panting and fatigued, he threw himself, late in the afternoon, on a green knoll, covered with mountain herbage, that crowned the brow of a precipice. From an opening between the trees he could overlook all the lower country for many a mile of rich woodland. He saw at a distance the lordly Hudson, far, far below him, moving on its silent but majestic course, with the reflection of a purple cloud or the sail of a lagging bark here and there sleeping on its grassy bosom and at last losing itself in the blue highlands.

On the other side he looked down into a deep mountain glen, wild, lonely, and shagged, the bottom filled with fragments from the impending cliffs and scarcely lighted by the reflected rays of the setting sun. For some time Rip lay musing on this scene. Evening was gradually advancing; the mountains began to throw their long blue shadows over the valleys. He saw that it would be dark long before he could reach the village, and he heaved a heavy sigh when he thought of encountering the terrors of Dame Van Winkle.

As he was about to descend, he heard a voice from a distance, hallooing, "Rip Van Winkle! Rip Van Winkle!" He looked around but could see nothing but a crow winging its solitary flight across the mountain. He thought his fancy must have deceived him and turned again to descend, when he heard the same cry ring through the still evening air: "Rip Van Winkle! Rip Van Winkle!" At the same time Wolf bristled up his back and, giving a low growl, skulked to his master's side, looking fearfully down into the glen. Rip now felt a vague apprehension stealing over him; he looked anxiously in the same direction and perceived a strange figure slowly toiling up the rocks and bending under the weight of something he carried on his back. He was surprised to see any human being in this lonely and unfrequented place; but supposing it to be some one of the neighborhood in need of his assistance, he hastened down to yield it.

On nearer approach he was still more surprised at the singularity of the stranger's appearance. He was a short, square-built old fellow, with thick bushy hair and a grizzled beard. His dress was of the antique Dutch fashion—a cloth jerkin strapped around the waist, several pairs of breeches, the outer one of ample volume, decorated with rows of buttons down the sides and bunches at the knees. He bore on his shoulder a stout keg, which seemed full of liquor, and made signs for Rip to approach and assist him with the load. Though rather shy and distrustful of this new acquaintance, Rip complied with his usual alacrity. Mutually relieving one another, they clambered up a narrow gully, apparently the dry bed of a mountain torrent. As they ascended, Rip every now and then heard long, rolling peals, like distant thunder, that seemed to issue out of a deep ravine, or rather cleft, between lofty rocks, toward which their rugged path conducted. He paused for an instant, but supposing it to be the muttering of one of those transient thundershowers that often take place in mountain heights, he proceeded. Passing through the ravine, they came to a hollow like a small amphitheater, surrounded by perpendicular preci-pices, over the brinks of which impending trees shot their branches, so that you only caught glimpses of the azure sky and the bright evening cloud. During the whole time Rip and his companion had labored on in silence; for though the former marveled greatly what could be the object of carrying a keg of liquor up this wild mountain, yet there was something strange and incomprehensible about the unknown that inspired awe and checked familiarity.

On entering the amphitheater new objects of wonder presented them-selves. On a level spot in the center was a company of odd-looking per-sonages playing at ninepins. They were dressed in a quaint, outlandish fashion; some wore short doublets, others jerkins, with long knives in their belts, and most of them had enormous breeches, of similar style with that of the guide's. Their visages, too, were peculiar: one had a large beard, broad face, and small piggish eyes; the face of another seemed to consist entirely of nose, and was surmounted by a white sugar-loaf hat, set off with a red cock's tail. They all had beards of various shapes and colors. There was one who seemed to be the commander. He was a stout old gentleman, with a weatherbeaten countenance; he wore a laced doublet, broad belt and hanger, high-crowned hat and feather, red stockings, and high-heeled shoes with roses in them. The whole group reminded Rip of the figures in an old Flemish painting, in the parlor of Dominie Van Shaick, the village parson, which had been brought over from Holland at the time of the settlement.

What seemed particularly odd to Rip was that, though these folks were evidently amusing themselves, yet they maintained the gravest faces,

GREG HILDEBRANDT

the most mysterious silence, and were thus the most melancholy party of pleasure he had ever witnessed. Nothing interrupted the stillness of the scene but the noise of the balls, which, whenever they were rolled, echoed along the mountains like rumbling peals of thunder.

As Rip and his companion approached them, they suddenly desisted from their play and stared at him with such a fixed, statuelike gaze, and such strange, uncouth, lackluster countenances, that his heart turned within him and his knees smote together. His companion now emptied the contents of the keg into large flagons and made signs to him to wait upon the company. He obeyed with fear and trembling; they quaffed the liquor in profound silence and then returned to their game.

By degrees Rip's awe and apprehension subsided. He even ventured, when no eye was fixed upon him, to taste the beverage, which he found had much the flavor of excellent Hollands. He was naturally a thirsty soul and was soon tempted to repeat the draft. One taste provoked another; and he reiterated his visits to the flagon so often that at length his senses were overpowered, his eyes swam in his head, his head gradually declined, and he fell into a deep sleep.

On waking, he found himself on the green knoll where he had first seen the old man of the glen. He rubbed his eyes—it was a bright sunny morning. The birds were hopping and twittering among the bushes, and the eagle was wheeling aloft, breasting the pure mountain breeze. Surely, thought Rip, I have not slept here all night. He recalled the occurrences before he fell asleep. The strange man with a keg of liquor—the mountain ravine—the wild retreat among the rocks—the woebegone party at ninepins—the flagon— Oh! That flagon! That wicked flagon! thought Rip. What excuse shall I make to Dame Van Winkle?

He looked around for his gun, but in place of the clean, well-oiled fowling piece he found an old firelock lying by him, the barrel incrusted with rust, the lock falling off, and the stock worm-eaten. He now suspected that the grave roisterers of the mountain had played a trick upon him and, having dosed him with liquor, had robbed him of his gun. Wolf, too, had disappeared, but he might have strayed away after a squirrel or partridge. He whistled after him and shouted his name, but all in vain; the echoes repeated his whistle and shout, but no dog was to be seen.

He determined to revisit the scene of the last evening's gambol and, if he met with any of the party, to demand his dog and gun. As he rose to walk, he found himself stiff in the joints and wanting in his usual activity. These mountain beds do not agree with me, thought Rip, and if this frolic should lay me up with a fit of the rheumatism, I shall have a blessed time with Dame Van Winkle. With some difficulty he got down into the glen. He found the gully up which he and his companion had ascended the preceding evening; but to his astonishment a mountain stream was now foaming down it, leaping from rock to rock and filling the glen with babbling murmurs. He made shift to scramble up its sides, however, working his toilsome way through thickets of birch, sassafras, and witch hazel, and was sometimes tripped up or entangled by the wild grapevines that twisted their coils or tendrils from tree to tree and spread a kind of network in his path.

At length he reached to where the ravine had opened through the cliffs to the amphitheater; but no traces of such opening remained. The rocks presented a high, impenetrable wall, over which the torrent came tumbling in a sheet of feathery foam and fell into a broad deep basin, black from the shadows of the surrounding forest. Here, then, poor Rip was brought to a standstill. He again called and whistled after his dog, and was answered only by the cawing of a flock of idle crows, sporting high in the air about a dry tree that overhung a sunny precipice. Secure in their elevation, they seemed to look down and scoff at the poor man's perplexities. What was to be done? The morning was passing away, and Rip felt famished for want of his breakfast. He grieved to give up his dog and gun; he dreaded to meet his wife; but it would not do to starve among the mountains. He shook his head, shouldered the rusty firelock, and, with a heart full of trouble and anxiety, turned his steps homeward.

As he approached the village he met a number of people, but none whom he knew, which surprised him somewhat, for he had thought himself acquainted with everyone around the countryside. Their dress, too, was of a different fashion from that to which he was accustomed. They all stared at him with equal marks of surprise, and whenever they cast their eyes upon him they invariably stroked their chins. The constant recurrence of this gesture induced Rip, involuntarily, to do the same. To his astonishment, he found his beard had grown a foot long!

He now entered the skirts of the village. A troop of strange children ran at his heels, hooting after him and pointing at his gray beard. The dogs, too, not one of which he recognized for an old acquaintance, barked at him as he passed. The very village was altered; it was larger and more populous. There were rows of houses that he had never seen before, and those that had been his familiar haunts had disappeared. Strange names were over the doors—strange faces at the windows—everything was strange. His mind now misgave him; he began to doubt whether both he and the world around him were not bewitched. Surely this was his native village, which he had left but the day before. There stood the Kaatskill Mountains—there ran the silver Hudson at a distance—there was every hill and dale precisely as it had always been. Rip was sorely perplexed. That flagon last night, thought he, has addled my poor head sadly!

It was with some difficulty that he found the way to his own house, which he approached with silent awe, expecting every moment to hear the shrill voice of Dame Van Winkle. He found the house gone to decay—the roof fallen in, the windows shattered, and the doors off the hinges. A half-starved dog that looked like Wolf was skulking about it. Rip called him by name, but the cur snarled, showed his teeth, and passed on. This was an unkind cut indeed. My very dog, thought poor Rip with a sigh, has forgotten me!

He entered the house, which, to tell the truth, Dame Van Winkle had always kept in neat order. It was empty, forlorn, and apparently abandoned. This desolateness overcame all his connubial fears. He called loudly for his wife and children; the lonely chambers rang for a moment with his voice, and then all again was silence.

He now hurried forth and hastened to his old resort, the village inn—but it, too, was gone. A large rickety wooden building stood in its place, with great gaping windows, some of them broken and mended with old hats and petticoats. Over the door was painted THE UNION HOTEL, BY JONATHAN DOOLITTLE. Instead of the great tree that used to shelter the quiet little Dutch inn of yore, there now was reared a tall naked pole, with something on the top that looked like a red nightcap, and from it was fluttering a flag, on which was a singular assemblage of stars and stripes; all this was strange and incomprehensible. He recognized on the sign, however, the ruby face of King George, under which he had smoked so many a peaceful pipe; but even this was singularly metamorphosed. The red coat was changed for one of blue and buff, a sword was held in the hand instead of a scepter, the head was decorated with a cocked hat, and underneath was painted in large characters GENERAL WASHINGTON.

There was, as usual, a crowd about the door, but none that Rip recollected. The very character of the people seemed changed. There was a busy, bustling, disputatious tone about it, instead of the accustomed phlegm and drowsy tranquillity. He looked in vain for the sage Nicholas Vedder, with his broad face, double chin, and fair long pipe, uttering clouds of tobacco smoke instead of speeches; or Van Bummel, the schoolmaster, doling forth the contents of an ancient newspaper. In place of these, a lean, bilious-looking fellow, with his pockets full of handbills, was haranguing vehemently about rights of citizens—elections—members of Congress—liberty—Bunker Hill—heroes of seventy-six—and other words, which were a perfect Babylonian jargon to the bewildered Van Winkle.

The appearance of Rip, with his long, grizzled beard, his fowling piece, his uncouth dress, and an army of women and children at his heels, soon attracted the attention of the tavern politicians. They crowded around him, eyeing him from head to foot with great curiosity. The orator bustled up to him and, drawing him partly aside, inquired, "On which side ye voted?" Rip stared in vacant stupidity.

Another short but busy little fellow pulled him by the arm and, rising on tiptoe, inquired in his ear, "Are ye a Federal or Democrat?" Rip was equally at a loss to comprehend the question. Then a knowing, self-important old gentleman, in a sharp cocked hat, made his way through the crowd, putting them to the right and left with his elbows as he passed. Planting himself before Van Winkle, with one arm akimbo, the other resting on his cane, his keen eyes and sharp hat penetrating, as it were, into his very soul, he demanded in an austere tone, "What brought ye to the election with a gun on your shoulder, and a mob at your heels; do ye mean to breed a riot in the village?"

"Alas! Gentlemen," cried Rip, somewhat dismayed, "I am a poor quiet man, a native of the place, and a loyal subject of the king, God bless him!"

Here a general shout burst from the bystanders. "A Tory! A Tory! A spy! A refugee! Hustle him! Away with him!" It was with great difficulty that the self-important man in the cocked hat restored order; and, having assumed a tenfold austerity of brow, he demanded again of the unknown culprit what he came there for and whom he was seeking. The poor man humbly assured him that he meant no harm, but merely came there in search of his neighbors, who used to keep about the tavern.

"Well . . . who are they? Name them."

Rip bethought himself a moment, and inquired, "Where's Nicholas Vedder?"

There was a silence for a little while, when an old man replied, in a thin, piping voice, "Nicholas Vedder! Why, he is dead and gone these eighteen years! There was a wooden tombstone in the churchyard that used to tell all about him, but that's rotten and gone, too."

"Where's Brom Dutcher?"

"Oh, he went off to the army in the beginning of the war. Some say he was killed at the storming of Stony Point; others say he was drowned in a squall at the foot of Antony's Nose. I don't know—he never came back again."

"Where's Van Bummel, the schoolmaster?"

"He went off to the wars, too, was a great militia general, and is now in Congress."

Rip's heart died away at hearing of these sad changes in his home and friends, and finding himself thus alone in the world. Every answer puzzled him, too, by treating of such enormous lapses of time, and of matters that he could not understand: war, Congress, Stony Point. He had no courage to ask after any more friends, but cried out in despair, "Does nobody here know Rip Van Winkle?"

"Oh, Rip Van Winkle!" exclaimed two or three. "Oh, to be sure! That's Rip Van Winkle yonder, leaning against the tree."

Rip looked and beheld a precise counterpart of himself as he went up the mountain; apparently as lazy and certainly as ragged. The poor fellow was now completely confounded. He doubted his own identity and whether he was himself or another man. In the midst of his bewilderment, the man in the cocked hat demanded who he was and what was his name.

"God knows," exclaimed he, at his wit's end. "I'm not myself—I'm somebody else. That's me yonder. . . . No, that's somebody else got into my shoes. I was myself last night, but I fell asleep on the mountain, and they've changed my gun, and everything's changed, and I'm changed, and I can't tell what's my name, or who I am!"

The bystanders began to look at each other, nod, wink significantly, and tap their fingers against their foreheads. There was a whisper, also, about securing the gun and keeping the old fellow from doing mischief, at the very suggestion of which the self-important man in the cocked hat retired with some precipitation. At this critical moment a fresh, comely woman pressed through the throng to get a peep at the gray-bearded man. She had a chubby child in her arms which, frightened at his looks, began to cry. "Hush, Rip," cried she. "Hush, you little fool; the old man won't hurt you." The name of the child, the air of the mother, the tone of her voice, all awakened a train of recollection in his mind. "What is your name, my good woman?" asked he.

"Judith Gardenier."

"And your father's name?"

"Ah, poor man, Rip Van Winkle was his name, but it's twenty years since he went away from home with his gun and never has been heard of since. His dog came home without him; but whether he shot himself or was carried away by the Indians, nobody can tell. I was then but a little girl."

Rip had but one question more to ask; and he put it with a faltering voice:

"Where's your mother?"

"Oh, she, too, died but a short time since; she broke a blood vessel in a fit of passion at a New England peddler."

There was a drop of comfort, at least, in this intelligence. The honest man could contain himself no longer. He caught his daughter and her child in his arms. "I am your father!" cried he. "Young Rip Van Winkle once—old Rip Van Winkle now! Does nobody know poor Rip Van Winkle?"

All stood amazed, until an old woman, tottering out from among the crowd, put her hand to her brow and, peering under it in his face for a moment, exclaimed, "Sure enough! It is Rip Van Winkle—it is himself! Welcome home again, neighbor. Why, where have you been these twenty long years?"

Rip's story was soon told, for the whole twenty years had been to him but as one night. The neighbors stared when they heard it; some were seen to wink at each other and put their tongues in their cheeks. The self-important man in the cocked hat, who, when the alarm was over, had returned to the field, screwed down the corners of his mouth and shook his head—upon which there was a general shaking of the head throughout the assemblage.

It was determined, however, to take the opinion of old Peter Vanderdonk, who was seen slowly advancing up the road. He was a descendant of the historian of that name, who wrote one of the earliest accounts of the province. Peter was the most ancient inhabitant of the village, and well versed in all the wonderful events and traditions of the neighborhood. He recollected Rip at once, and corroborated his story in the most satisfactory manner. He assured the company that it was a fact, handed down from his ancestor the historian, that the Kaatskill Mountains had always been haunted by strange beings. It was affirmed that the great Henry Hudson, the first discoverer of the river and country, kept a kind of vigil there every twenty years with his crew of the *Halfmoon*. In this way he was permitted to revisit the scenes of his enterprise and keep a guardian eye upon the river and the great city called by his name. Peter Vanderdonk asserted that his father had once seen them in their old Dutch dresses playing at ninepins in a hollow of the mountain; and that he himself had heard, one summer afternoon, the sound of their balls like distant peals of thunder.

To make a long story short, the company broke up and returned to the more important concerns of the election. Rip's daughter took him home to live with her; she had a snug, well-furnished house and a stout, cheery farmer for a husband, whom Rip recollected as one of the urchins that used to climb upon his back. As to Rip's son and heir, who was the ditto of himself, seen leaning against the tree, he was employed to work on the farm; but he evinced an hereditary disposition to attend to anything else but his business.

Rip now resumed his old walks and habits. He soon found many of his former cronies, though all rather the worse for the wear and tear of time; and therefore he preferred making friends among the rising generation, with whom he soon grew into great favor.

Having nothing to do at home, and being arrived at that happy age when a man can be idle with impunity, he took his place once more on the bench at the inn door and was reverenced as one of the patriarchs of the village and a chronicle of the old times "before the war." It was some time before he could get into the regular track of gossip or could be made to comprehend the strange events that had taken place during his torpor—that there had been a revolutionary war; that the country had thrown off the yoke of old England; and that, instead of being a subject of His Majesty George the Third, he was now a free citizen of the United States. Rip, in fact, was no politician; the changes of states and empires made but little impression on him; but there was one species of despotism under which he had long groaned, and that was petticoat government. Happily that was at an end; he had gotten his neck out of the yoke of matrimony and could go in and out whenever he pleased, without dreading the tyranny of Dame Van Winkle. Whenever her name was mentioned, however, he shook his head, shrugged his shoulders, and cast up his eyes; which might pass either for an expression of resignation to his fate or joy at his deliverance.

He used to tell his story to every stranger who arrived at Mr. Doolittle's hotel. He was observed, at first, to vary on some points every time he told it, which was, doubtless, owing to his having so recently awakened. It at last settled down precisely to the tale I have related, and every man, woman, and child in the neighborhood knew it by heart. Some always pretended to doubt the reality of it and insisted that Rip had been out of his head, and that this was one point on which he always remained flighty. The old Dutch inhabitants, however, almost universally gave it full credit. Even to this day they never hear a thunderstorm of a summer afternoon about the Kaatskills but they say Henry Hudson and his crew are busy at their game of ninepins; and it is a common wish of all henpecked husbands in the neighborhood, when life hangs heavy on their hands, that they might momentarily put aside woe and have a quieting draft out of Rip Van Winkle's flagon.

THE LITTLE MERMAID

ar out in the ocean the water is as blue as the petals of the most beautiful cornflower and as clear as the purest glass. But it is very deep— much deeper, indeed, than any cable can sound. Many steeples would have to be piled one on top of the other to reach from the bottom to the surface of the water. Down there live the sea-folk.

Now you must not think that there is nothing but the bare white sand down at the bottom. No, there grow the strangest trees and plants, with such pliable stems and leaves that at the slightest movement of the water they stir as if they were alive. All the big and little fishes glide among their branches, as the birds do up above in the air. Where the ocean is deepest stands the sea-king's palace. Its walls are made of coral, and the high arched windows are of the clearest amber. The roof is made of mussel shells, which open and close in the current. It is very beautiful, for each of them is filled with gleaming pearls, a single one of which would make a fit jewel for a queen's crown.

The sea-king had been a widower for many years, but his old mother kept house for him. She was a clever woman, but very vain of her noble rank; so she wore twelve oysters on her tail, while other grand folk were only allowed to wear six. In other respects she deserved great praise, especially for her tender care of the little sea-princesses, her granddaughters. They were six lovely children, and the youngest was the most beautiful of all. Her skin was as clear and delicate as a rose petal, and her eyes were as blue as the deepest sea, but like all the others, she had no legs— her body ended in a silvery fishtail. All day long they used to play in the great halls of the palace, where living flowers grew out of the walls. The large amber windows were thrown open, and the fishes came swimming in to them, as the swallows fly in to us when we open our windows; but the fishes swam right up to the little princesses, and ate out of their hands, and let themselves be stroked and fondled like pet canaries.

In front of the palace was a large garden, in which bright-red and dark-blue trees were growing. The fruit glittered like gold, and the flowers looked like flames of fire, with their ever-moving stems and leaves. The ground was covered with the finest sand, as blue as the flame of sulfur. A strange blue light shone over everything; one would imagine oneself to be high up in the air, with the blue sky above and below, rather than at the bottom of the sea. When the sea was calm one could see the sun; it looked like a huge purple flower, from whose center the light streamed forth.

Each of the little princesses had her own little place in the garden, where she could dig and plant as she pleased. One gave her flower bed the shape of a whale; another liked better to make hers like a little mermaid; but the youngest made hers as round as the sun and only had flowers that shone red like it. She was a strange child, quiet and thoughtful. While her sisters made a great display of all sorts of curious objects that they found from wrecked ships, she only loved her rose-red flowers, like the sun above, and a beautiful marble statue of a handsome boy, carved out of clear white stone, which had sunk from some wreck to the bottom of the sea. She had planted by the statue a rose-colored weeping willow tree, which grew well, hanging over it with its fresh branches reaching down to the blue sand and casting a violet shadow that moved to and fro like the branches, so that it seemed as if the top and the roots of the tree were playing at kissing each other.

Nothing gave her greater pleasure than to hear stories about the world of men above, and her old grandmother had to tell her all she knew about ships and towns, men and animals. It seemed strangely beautiful to her that on earth the flowers were fragrant—for at the bottom of the sea they have no scent—and that the woods were green, and that the fish that one saw there among the branches could sing so loudly and beautifully that it was a delight to hear them. The grandmother called the little birds fishes; otherwise her granddaughter would not have understood her, as they had never seen a bird.

"When you are fifteen years old," said the grandmother, "you will be allowed to rise up to the surface of the sea and sit on the rocks in the moonlight, and see the big ships as they sail by. Then you will also see the forests and towns."

The following year one of the sisters would be fifteen; but the others— well, the sisters were each one year younger than the other; so the youngest had to wait fully five years before she could come up from the bottom of the sea and see what things were like on the earth above. But each promised to tell her sisters what she had seen and liked best on her first day; for their grandmother could not tell them enough—there were so many things about which they wanted to know. None of them, however, longed so much to go up as the youngest, who had the longest time to wait, and was so quiet and thoughtful. Many a night she stood at the open window and looked up through the dark-blue water, where the fishes splashed with their fins and tails. She could see the moon and the stars, which only shone faintly, but looked much bigger through the water than we see them. When something like a dark cloud passed under them and hid them for a while, she knew it was either a whale swimming overhead or a ship with many people, who had no idea that a lovely little mermaid was standing below stretching out her white hands toward the keel of their ship.

The eldest princess was now fifteen years old and was allowed to rise to the surface of the sea. When she came back she had hundreds of things to tell. But what pleased her most, she said, was to lie in the moonlight on a sandbank, in the calm sea, and to see near the coast the big town where the lights twinkled like many hundreds of stars; to hear music and the noise and bustle of carriages and people; and to see the many church towers and spires and listen to the ringing of the bells. Oh, how the youngest sister listened to all this! And when, later on in the evening, she again stood at the open window, looking up through the dark-blue water, she thought of the big town, with all its bustle and noise, and imagined she could hear the church bells ringing, even down where she was.

The year after, the second sister was allowed to go up to the surface, and swim about as she pleased. She came up just as the sun was setting, and this sight she thought the most beautiful of all she saw. The whole sky was like gold, she said, and the clouds—well, she could not find words to describe their loveliness. Rose and violet, they sailed by over her head; but, even swifter than the clouds, a flock of wild swans, like a long white veil, flew across the water toward the sun. She followed them, but the sun sank, and the rosy gleam faded from the sea and clouds.

The year after, the third sister went up. She was the boldest of them all and swam up a broad river that flowed into the sea. She saw beautiful green hills covered with vines, and houses and castles peeped out from magnificent woods. She heard the birds sing, and the sun shone so warmly that she often had to dive under the water to cool her burning face. In a little creek she came across a whole flock of little children, who were quite naked and splashed about in the water; she wanted to play with them, but they ran away terrified. Then a little black animal—it was a dog, but she had never seen a dog before—came out and barked so ferociously at her that she was frightened and hurried back as fast as she could to the open sea. But she could never forget the magnificent woods, the green hills, and the lovely children, who could swim even though they had no fishtails.

The fourth sister was not so daring; she stayed far out in the open sea and said that that was the loveliest place of all. There, she said, one could see for many miles around, and the sky above was like a great glass dome. She saw ships, but far away, and they looked to her like seagulls. The playful dolphins, she said, turned somersaults, and the big whales spouted out seawater through their nostrils, as if a hundred fountains were playing all around her.

Now the fifth sister's turn came, and, as her birthday was in winter, she saw on her first visit things the other sisters had not. The sea looked quite green; huge icebergs floated around her—they were like pearls, she said, and yet were much higher than the church steeples built by men. They were the strangest shapes and glittered like diamonds. She sat on one of the biggest, and all the passing sailors were terrified when they saw her sitting there, with the wind playing with her long hair. But toward evening the sky became overcast with black clouds; there was thunder and lightning, and the dark waves lifted up the big blocks of ice, which shone in each flash of lightning. On all the ships the sails were reefed, and there was anxiety and terror; but she sat quietly on her floating iceberg and watched the blue lightning dart in zigzags into the foaming sea.

The first time each one of the sisters came to the surface, all the new and beautiful things she saw charmed her. But now, when as grown-up girls they were allowed to come up whenever they liked, they became indifferent to them, longing for their home; and after a month they said that after all it was best down below, where one felt at home. On many an evening the five sisters would rise to the surface of the sea, arm in arm. They had beautiful voices, far finer than that of any human being; and when a storm was brewing, and they thought that some ships might be wrecked, they swam in front of them, singing beautifully of how lovely it was at the bottom of the sea and telling the people not to be afraid of coming down there. But the human beings could not understand the words and thought it was only the noise of the storm; and they never saw the wonders down below, for when the ship went down they were drowned and were dead when they came to the sea-king's palace. When her sisters went up arm in arm to the top of the sea there stood the little sister, all alone, looking after them and feeling as if she could cry; but mermaids have no tears, and so they suffer all the more.

"Oh, if only I were fifteen!" she said. "I know how much I shall love the world above, and the people who live in it."

At last she was fifteen years old.

"Well, now we have you off our hands," said her grandmother, the old dowager queen. "Come now! Let me adorn you like your other sisters!" She put a wreath of white lilies on her head, but every petal of the flowers was half a pearl; and the old lady had eight big oysters fixed to the princess's tail, to show her high rank.

"But it hurts so!" said the little mermaid.

"Yes, one must suffer to be beautiful," the old lady replied.

Oh, how gladly the little princess would have taken off all her ornaments and the heavy wreath! The red flowers in her garden would have suited her much better, but she dared not make any change now. "Good-bye!" she said and rose as lightly as a bubble through the water.

The sun had just set when she lifted her head out of the water, but the clouds gleamed with red and gold, and the evening star shone in the rosy sky. The air was mild and fresh, and the sea as calm as glass. Near her lay a big ship with three masts; only one sail was set, as not a breath of wind was stirring, and the sailors were sitting about on deck and in the rigging. There was music and singing on board, and when it grew dark many hundreds of colored lamps were lighted, and it looked as if the flags of all nations were floating in the air. The little mermaid swam up close to the cabin windows, and when the waves lifted her up she could see through the clear panes many richly dressed people. But the handsomest of them all was the young prince, with large black eyes— he could not have been older than sixteen; and it was his birthday that was the reason for all this celebration. The sailors were dancing on deck, and when the young prince came out, hundreds of rockets were sent off into the air, making the night as bright as day. The little mermaid was frightened and dived underwater. But soon she lifted up her head again, and then it seemed to her as if all the stars of heaven were falling down upon her. Never had she seen such fireworks! Great suns whirled around, gorgeous fiery fish flew through the blue air, and everything was reflected in the calm and glassy sea. The ship was so brilliantly lighted up that one could see everything distinctly, even to the smallest rope, and the people still better. Oh, how beautiful was the young prince! He shook hands with the people and smiled graciously, while the music sounded dreamily through the starry night.

It grew very late, but the little mermaid could not turn her eyes away from the ship and the handsome prince. The colored lamps were put out, no more rockets were sent off nor cannons fired. But deep down in the sea was a strange moaning and murmuring, and the little mermaid sitting on the waves was rocked up and down, so that she could look into the cabin. Soon the ship began to make greater headway, as one sail after another was unfurled. Then the waves rose higher and higher; dark clouds gathered; and flashes of lightning were seen in the distance. Oh, what a terrible storm was brewing! Then the sailors reefed all the sails, and the big ship rushed at flying speed through the wild sea. The waves rose as high as great black mountains, as if they would dash over the masts, but the ship dived like a swan between them, and then was carried up again to their towering crests. The little mermaid thought this was great fun; but not so the sailors. The ship creaked and groaned, her strong timbers bending under the weight of the huge waves. The sea broke over her; the mainmast snapped in two, like a reed; and the ship lay over on her side while the water rushed into her hold. The little mermaid then realized that the crew was in danger; she herself had to be careful of the beams and planks floating about in the water. For one moment it was so dark that not a thing could be seen, but flashes of lightning made everything visible, and she could see all on board. The little mermaid looked out for the young prince, and as the ship broke up she saw him sinking into the deep sea. At first she was very pleased, for now he would come down to her; but then she remembered that men cannot live in the water, and only if he were dead could he come to her father's palace. No, he must not die! Heedless of the beams and planks floating on the water, which might have crushed her, she dived down into the water and came up again in the waves, in search of the prince. At last she found him. His strength was failing him, and he could hardly swim any longer in the stormy sea; his arms and legs began to grow numb and his beautiful eyes closed; he would certainly have died if the little mermaid had not come to his assistance. She held his head above the water and let the waves carry them where they would.

Next morning the storm was over, but not a plank of the ship was anywhere to be seen. The sun rose red and brilliant out of the water, and seemed to bring new life to the prince's cheeks; but his eyes remained closed. The little mermaid kissed his beautiful high forehead, and smoothed back his wet hair; she thought he looked very much like the white marble statue in her little garden. She kissed him again and again, and prayed that he might live.

Then she saw before her eyes the mainland, where lay high, blue mountains on whose summits snow was glistening, so that they looked like swans. Down by the shore were beautiful green woods, and in front of them stood a church or convent—she did not know which, but it was some sort of building. Lemon trees and orange trees grew in the garden, and before the gate stood lofty palm trees. The sea formed a little bay here and was quite calm, though very deep. She swam straight to the cliffs, where the fine white sand had been washed ashore, and laid the handsome prince on the sand, taking special care that his head lay raised up in the warm sunshine. Then all the bells began to ring in the big white building, and many young girls came out into the garden. The little mermaid swam farther out and hid behind some rocks, covering her hair and breast with sea-foam, lest anybody should see her little face; and from there she watched to see who would come to the poor prince.

It was not long before a young girl came to the spot where he lay. At first she seemed very frightened, but only for a moment, and then she called some of the others. The little mermaid saw that the prince came back to life and smiled at all who stood around him; but at her he did not smile—he little knew who had saved him. She was very sad; and when they had taken him into the big building she dived sorrowfully down into the water, and so went back to her father's palace.

She had always been silent and thoughtful, and now she became still more so. Her sisters asked her what she had seen when she went up for the first time, but she told them nothing. Many a morning and many an evening she went back to the place where she had left the prince. She saw how the fruit in the garden ripened and was gathered, and how the snow melted on the high mountains, but she never saw the prince; and each time she returned home she was more sorrowful than before.

Her only comfort was to sit in her little garden and put her arms around the marble figure that was so like the prince. But she no longer looked after her flowers; her garden became a wilderness: the plants straggled over the paths and twined their long stalks and leaves around the branches of the trees, so that it became quite dark there.

At last she could bear the burden of her sorrow no longer and confided her troubles to one of her sisters, who, of course, told the others. These and a few other mermaids, who also told their intimate friends, were the only people in the whole of the ocean world who were in on the secret. One of them knew who the prince was and could tell them where

his kingdom lay. She also had watched the festivities on board the ship.

"Come, little sister!" said the other princesses, and arm in arm, in a long row, they rose to the surface of the sea, in front of where the prince's palace stood. It was built of bright-yellow stone and had broad marble staircases, one of which reached right down to the sea. Magnificent gilt cupolas surmounted the roof, and in the colonnades, which ran all around the building, stood lifelike marble statues. Through the clear panes of the high windows could be seen splendid halls, hung with costly silk curtains and beautiful tapestries, and on all the walls were paintings that were a joy to look at. In the center of the largest hall a big fountain was playing. Its jets rose as high as the glass dome in the ceiling, through which the sun shone on the water and on the beautiful plants that grew in the great basin.

Now she knew where he lived and came there many an evening and many a night across the water. She swam much closer to the shore than any of the others would have ventured, and she even went up the narrow channel under the magnificent marble terrace, which cast a long shadow over the water. Here she would sit and gaze at the young prince, who thought that he was all alone in the bright moonlight.

Many an evening she saw him sailing in his stately boat, with music on board and flags waving. She watched from behind the green rushes, and when the wind caught her long silvery-white veil, and people saw it, they thought it was a swan spreading its wings. Many a night when the fishermen were out at sea fishing by torchlight she heard them say many good things about the prince, and she was glad that she had saved his life when he was drifting half-dead upon the waves. She remembered how heavily his head had lain upon her breast and how passionately she had kissed him, but he knew nothing about it and did not even see her in his dreams.

More and more she grew to love the human beings, and more and more she longed to be able to live among them, for their world seemed to her so much bigger than hers. They could sail over the sea in great ships and climb mountains high above the clouds, and the lands that they owned stretched, in woods and fields, farther than her eyes could see. There were still so many things she wanted to know about, and her sisters could not answer all her questions; so she asked her grandmother, who knew the upper world very well, and rightly called it "the countries above the sea."

"If human beings are not drowned," asked the little mermaid, "can they live forever and ever? Don't they die as we do down here in the sea?"

"Yes," the old lady replied, "they also die, and their lives are even shorter than ours. We can live to be three hundred years old, but when we cease to exist we are turned into foam on the water, and have not even a grave down here among our dear ones. We have not got immortal souls, and can never live again. We are like the green rushes, which, when once cut down, can never grow again. Human beings, however, have a soul which lives forever, lives even after the body has become dust; it rises through the clear air up to the shining stars. As we rise out of the water and see all the countries of the earth, so they rise to unknown, beautiful regions which we shall never see."

"Why don't we also have an immortal soul?" asked the little mermaid sorrowfully. "I would gladly give all the hundreds of years I have yet to live if I could only be a human being for one day, and afterward have a share in the heavenly kingdom."

"You must not think about that," said the old lady. "We are much happier and better off than the human beings up there."

"So I must die, and float as foam on the sea, and never hear the music of the waves or see the beautiful flowers and the red sun! Is there nothing I can do to win an immortal soul?"

"No," the grandmother said. "Only if a man loved you so much that you were dearer to him than father or mother, and if he clung to you with all his heart and all his love, and let the priest place his right hand in yours, with the promise to be faithful to you here and to eternity—then would his soul flow into your body, and you would receive a share in the happiness of mankind. He would give you a soul and yet still keep his own. But that can never happen! What is thought most beautiful here below, your fishtail, they would consider ugly on earth—they do not know any better. Up there one must have two clumsy supports, which they call legs, in order to be beautiful."

The little mermaid sighed and looked sadly at her fishtail.

"Let us be happy!" said the old lady. "Let us hop and skip through the three hundred years of our life! That is surely long enough! And afterward we can rest all the better in our graves. This evening there is to be a court ball."

Such a splendid sight has never been seen on earth. The walls and ceiling of the big ballroom were of thick but transparent glass. Several hundred colossal mussel shells, red and grass-green, stood in rows down the sides, holding blue flames that illuminated the whole room and shone through the walls, so that the sea outside was brightly lit up. One could

THE LITTLE MERMAID

see innumerable fish, both big and small, swimming outside the glass walls; some with gleaming purple scales and others glittering like silver and gold. Through the middle of the ballroom flowed a broad stream, in which the mermen and mermaids danced to their own beautiful singing. No human beings have such lovely voices. The little mermaid sang most sweetly of all, and they all applauded her. For a moment she felt joyful at heart at the thought that she had the most beautiful voice on land or in the sea; but soon her mind returned to the world above, for she could not forget the handsome prince and her sorrow at not possessing an immortal soul like his. So she stole out of her father's palace, while all within was joy and merriment, and sat sorrowfully in her little garden.

Suddenly she heard the sound of a horn through the water, and she thought: Now he is sailing above, he whom I love more than father or mother, and into whose hands I would entrust my life's happiness. I will dare anything to win him and an immortal soul. While my sisters are dancing in my father's palace I will go to the sea-witch, whom I have always feared so much. Perhaps she may be able to give me advice and help.

Then the little mermaid left her garden and went out toward the roaring whirlpools where the witch lived. She had never been that way before; neither flowers nor seaweed grew there—only bare, gray sand stretching to the whirlpools, where the water swirled around like rushing mill wheels, dragging everything it got hold of down into the depths. She had to pass right through these dreadful whirlpools to reach the witch's territory. For a long way the only path led over bubbling mud, which the witch called the peat bog. Behind this her house stood, in a strange forest, for all the trees and bushes were polyps—half animals and half plants—which looked like hundred-headed snakes growing out of the ground. All the branches were slimy arms with fingers like wriggling worms, and they moved joint by joint from the root to the topmost branch. Everything that they could lay hold of in the sea they clutched and held fast, and never let go of again. The little mermaid stopped timidly in front of them. Her heart was beating with fear, and she nearly turned back; but then she thought of the prince and man's immortal soul, and took courage. She twisted her long flowing hair around her head, in case the polyps should seize her by it, and, crossing her hands on her breast, she darted through the water as fast as a fish, right past the hideous polyps, who stretched out their writhing arms and fingers after her. She saw that each one of them had seized something and held it tightly with hundreds of little arms like bands of iron. The bleached bones of men who had perished at sea and sunk into the depths were tightly grasped in the arms of some, while others clutched ships' rudders and sea chests, skeletons of land animals, and a little mermaid whom they had caught and strangled, which was the most terrifying sight of all to her.

She now came to a big marshy place in the forest, where big, fat water snakes were writhing about, showing their ugly yellow bellies. In the middle of this place stood a house built of the white bones of ship-wrecked men, and there sat the sea-witch, letting a toad eat out of her mouth, as we should feed a little canary with sugar. The ugly, fat water snakes she called her little chickens, and she allowed them to crawl all over her hideous bosom.

"I know quite well what you want!" said the sea-witch. "It is silly of you! But you shall have your way, for it is sure to bring you misfortune, my pretty princess! You want to get rid of your fishtail and have instead two stumps which human beings use for walking, so that the young prince may fall in love with you, and you may win him and an immortal soul!" As she said this the old witch laughed so loudly and horribly that the toad and the snakes fell to the ground, where they crawled about. "You have only just come in time," said the witch, "for if you had come after sunrise tomorrow I should not have been able to help you till another year had passed. I will make you a drink, and before sunrise you must swim ashore and sit on the beach and drink it. Then your tail will split in two and shrink into what human beings call legs; but it will hurt you, as if a sharp sword were running through you. Every one who sees you will say that you are the most beautiful child of man they have ever seen. You will keep your gracefulness, and no dancer will be able to move as lightly as you; but at each step you take you will feel as if you were treading on a sharp knife, and as if your blood must flow. Are you willing to suffer all this, and shall I help you?"

"Yes," said the little mermaid in a trembling voice, and she thought of the prince and of winning an immortal soul.

"But remember!" the witch said. "When once you have taken the human form you can never become a mermaid again. You will never again be able to dive down through the water to your sisters and your father's palace. And if you fail to win the prince's love, so that for your sake he will forget father and mother, and cling to you with body and soul, and make the priest join your hands as man and wife, you will not be given an immortal soul. On the first morning after he has married another your heart will break, and you will turn into foam on the water."

"I will do it," said the little mermaid, as pale as death.

"But you will have to pay me," the witch said, "and it is not a trifle that I ask. You have the most beautiful voice of all who live at the bottom of the sea, with which you probably think you can enchant the prince; but this voice you must give to me. I must have the best thing you possess in return for my precious drink, for I have to give you my own blood in it, so that the drink may be as sharp as a two-edged sword."

"But if you take away my voice," said the little mermaid, "what have I got left?"

"Your lovely figure," the witch replied, "your grace of movement, and your speaking eyes! With these surely you can capture a human heart. Well, have you lost your courage? Put out your little tongue, so that I may cut it off in payment, and you shall have the powerful drink."

"Do it," said the little mermaid, and the witch put her caldron on the fire to prepare the magic drink. "Cleanliness is a good thing," she said, and scoured the caldron with snakes that she had tied into a bundle. Then she pricked her breast and let her black blood drip into it, and the steam rose up in the weirdest shapes, so that one could not help being frightened and horrified. Every moment the witch threw some new thing into the caldron, and when it boiled the sound was like crocodiles weeping. At last the drink was ready, and it looked like the clearest water.

"Here it is!" said the witch, and she cut off the little mermaid's tongue, so that now she was dumb and could neither sing nor speak. "If the polyps should catch hold of you when you go back through my wood," the witch said, "you need only throw one drop of this liquid over them, and their arms and fingers will fly into a thousand pieces!" But the little mermaid had no need to do this, for the polyps shrank back from her in terror at the sight of the sparkling drink, which gleamed in her hand like a glittering star. So she came quickly through the forest and the bog and the roaring whirlpools.

She could see her father's palace: in the ballroom the lamps were all darkened, and every one was asleep; but she dared not go in to them, now that she was dumb and about to leave them forever. She felt as if her heart would break with sorrow. She stole into the garden, took a flower from each of her sisters' flower beds, kissed her hand a thousand times to the palace, and swam up through the dark-blue sea.

The sun had not yet risen when she came in sight of the prince's palace and reached the magnificent marble steps. The moon was shining bright and clear. The little mermaid drank the sharp, burning draft, and it felt as if a two-edged sword went through her tender body; she fainted and lay as if dead.

When the sun shone over the sea she awoke and felt a stabbing pain; but there before her stood the beautiful young prince. He fixed his black eyes on her, so that she cast hers down, and then she saw that her fishtail had disappeared and that she had the prettiest little white legs that any girl could possess. But she was quite naked, so she wrapped herself in her long thick hair. The prince asked her who she was and how she came there, and she looked at him tenderly and yet sadly with her deep-blue eyes, for she could not speak. Then he took her by the hand and led her into the palace. Every step she took felt, as the witch had warned her, as if she were trodding on pointed needles and sharp knives, but she bore it gladly and walked as lightly as a soap bubble by the side of the prince, who, with all the others, admired her grace of movement.

She was given wonderful dresses of silk and muslin to put on, and she was the greatest beauty in the palace; but she was dumb and unable either to sing or speak. Beautiful slaves, dressed in silk and gold, came to sing before the prince and his royal parents. One of them sang better than all the rest, and the prince clapped his hands and smiled at her. Then the little mermaid grew sad, for she knew that she had been able to sing far more beautifully; and she thought: Oh, if he only knew that to be with him I have given away my voice forever!

Now the slaves began to dance light, graceful dances to the loveliest music; and then the little mermaid lifted her beautiful white arms, rose on her toes, and glided across the floor, dancing as none of the others had danced. At every movement her beauty seemed to grow, and her eyes spoke more deeply to the heart than the songs of the slave girls. Everyone was charmed by her, especially the prince, who called her his little foundling, and she danced again and again, although every time her feet touched the ground she felt as if she were treading on sharp knives. The prince said that she should always be near him, and let her sleep on a velvet cushion before his door.

He had a man's dress made for her, so that she might ride with him. They rode through fragrant woods, where the green branches brushed her shoulders and the little birds sang among the fresh leaves. She climbed with the prince up the high mountains, and, though her tender feet bled so that even others could see it, she smiled and followed him, till they saw the clouds sailing beneath their feet, like a flock of birds flying to foreign lands.

At home, in the prince's palace, when all the others were asleep in their beds at night, she would go out onto the broad marble steps. It cooled her burning feet to stand in the cold seawater, and then she thought of times past and of those she had left far down below in the deep.

One night her sisters came up arm in arm, singing sorrowfully as they swam through the water, and she beckoned to them; they recognized her and told her how sad she had made them all. After that they came to see her every night, and one night she saw far out her old grandmother, who had not been up to the surface for many, many years, and the sea-king, with his crown on his head. They stretched out their hands toward her but did not venture as close to land as her sisters.

Day by day the prince grew fonder of her; he loved her as one would love a good, sweet child, but he never had the slightest idea of making her his queen. Yet his wife she must be, or she could not win an immortal soul, but on his wedding morning would turn into foam on the sea.

"Don't you love me more than them all?" the little mermaid's eyes seemed to say when the prince took her in his arms and kissed her beautiful forehead.

"Yes, you are the dearest to me," he said, "for you have the best heart of them all. You are the most devoted to me, and you are like a young girl whom I once saw, but whom I fear I shall never meet again. I was on board a ship which was wrecked, and the waves washed me ashore near a holy temple where several young maidens were serving in attendance. The youngest of them found me on the beach and saved my life. I only saw her twice. She is the only girl in the world I could love, but you are like her, and you almost drive her image from my heart. She belongs to the holy temple, and so by good fortune you have been sent to me, and we shall never be parted."

Alas! He doesn't know that it was I who saved his life! thought the little mermaid. I carried him across the sea to the wood where the temple stands; and I was hidden in the foam, watching to see if anyone would come to him. I saw the beautiful girl whom he loves better than me. She sighed deeply, for she could not weep. The girl belongs to the holy temple, he said. She will never come out into the world, and they will never meet again; but I am with him, and see him every day. I will care for him, love him, and give up my life for him.

But soon the rumor spread that the prince was to marry the beautiful daughter of a neighboring king, and that that was why they were fitting up such a magnificent ship. The prince is going to visit the neighboring king's country, they said, but really he is going to see his daughter, and a large suite is to accompany him. The little mermaid shook her head and smiled, for she knew the prince's thoughts much better than the others. "I must go," he said to her. "I must see the beautiful princess, for my parents wish it; but they will not force me to bring her home as my bride. I cannot love her. She will not be like the beautiful girl in the temple whom you are like. If one day I were to choose a bride I would rather have you, my dumb foundling with the eloquent eyes." And he kissed her red lips, played with her long hair, and laid his head on her heart, so that she began to dream of human happiness and an immortal soul.

"You are not afraid of the sea, my dumb child?" he said to her, when they were standing on board the stately ship that was to carry him to the neighboring king's country. He told her of the storm and of the calm, of the strange fish in the deep, and of the marvelous things that divers had seen down there. She smiled at his words, for she knew more about the things at the bottom of the sea than anyone else.

At night, in the moonlight, when all were asleep except the man at the helm, she sat by the ship's rail, gazing down into the clear water, and thought she could see her father's palace, and her grandmother, with her silver crown on her head, looking up through the swirling currents at the ship's keel. Then her sisters came up out of the water, looking sorrowfully at her and wringing their white hands. She beckoned to them and smiled, and wanted to tell them that she was well and happy, but a cabin boy came up to her, and her sisters dived under, so that he thought the white things he had seen were just foam on the sea.

The next morning the ship reached the harbor of the neighboring king's magnificent city. All the church bells were ringing, and from the high towers trumpets sounded, while soldiers paraded with flying colors and glittering bayonets. Every day there were festivities; balls and receptions followed one another. But the princess had not yet arrived. She was being brought up in a holy convent far away, they said, where she was learning every royal virtue. At last she came. The little mermaid was anxious to see her beauty, and she had to admit that she had never seen a lovelier being: her skin was clear and delicate, and behind her long dark lashes smiled a pair of deep-blue, loyal eyes.

"You are she!" said the prince. "She who saved me when I lay almost dead on the shore!" And he clasped his blushing bride in his arms.

"Oh, I am too happy!" he said to the little mermaid. "My greatest wish, which I have never dared to hope for, has come true. You will rejoice at my happiness, for you love me more than them all." The little mermaid kissed his hand and felt as if her heart were already breaking. His wedding morning, she knew, would bring death to her, and she would turn into foam on the sea.

THE LITTLE MERMAID

The church bells pealed, and heralds rode through the streets announcing the betrothal. On all the altars sweet-smelling oil was burning in costly silver lamps. The priests swung their censers, and the bride and bridegroom joined hands and received the bishop's blessing. The little mermaid, dressed in silk and gold, stood holding the bride's train, but her ears did not hear the joyous music, and her eyes saw nothing of the sacred ceremony—she was thinking of the night of her death, and of all that she had lost in this world.

That same evening the bride and bridegroom came on board the ship; cannons roared, flags were waving, and in the middle of the ship was erected a royal tent of purple and gold, with the most magnificent couch, where the bridal pair were to rest through the still, cool night.

The sails swelled in the wind, and the ship glided smoothly and almost without motion over the clear sea. When it grew dark, colored lamps were lighted, and the sailors danced merrily on deck. The little mermaid could not help thinking of the first time she had risen to the surface and had seen the same splendor and revelry. She threw herself among the dancers, darting and turning as a swallow turns when it is pursued, and they all applauded her, for she had never danced so wonderfully before. It was like sharp knives cutting her tender feet, but she did not feel it, for the pain in her heart was much greater. She knew that it was the last evening that she would be with him—him for whom she had left her family and her home, sacrificed her lovely voice, and daily suffered endless pain, of which he had not the slightest idea. It was the last night that she would breathe the same air as he, and see the deep sea and the starry sky. An unending night, without thoughts or dreams, was waiting for her, who had no soul and could not win one. On board the ship the rejoicing and revelry lasted till long past midnight, and she laughed and danced with the thought of death in her heart. The prince kissed his beautiful bride, and she played with his dark hair, and arm in arm they retired to rest in the magnificent tent.

Then everything grew quiet on board; only the steersman stood at the helm, and the little mermaid laid her white arms on the rail and looked toward the east for the rosy glimmer of dawn, for she knew that the first sunbeam would kill her.

Then she saw her sisters rising out of the waves; they were as pale as she was, and their beautiful hair no longer floated in the wind, for it had been cut off. "We have given it to the witch, to get her help, so that you need not die tonight. She has given us a knife: here it is. See how sharp it is! Before the sun rises you must thrust it into the prince's heart, and when the warm blood sprinkles your feet they will grow together again into a fishtail. Then you will be a mermaid again, and you can come down with us into the sea, and live your three hundred years before you turn into dead salt sea-foam. Hurry! For he or you must die before sunrise. Our old grandmother is so full of grief for you that her white hair has all fallen off, as ours fell under the witch's scissors. Kill the prince and come back to us! Hurry! Do you see that red streak in the sky? In a few moments the sun will rise, and then you must die!'' They gave a deep sigh and disappeared beneath the waves.

The little mermaid drew back the purple curtain of the tent and saw the lovely bride lying asleep with her head on the prince's breast, and she bent down and kissed him on his beautiful forehead. She looked up at the sky, where the rosy glow was growing brighter and brighter, and then at the sharp knife, and again at the prince, who murmured his bride's name in his dreams. Yes, she alone was in his thoughts, and for a moment the knife trembled in the little mermaid's hand. But suddenly she flung it far out into the waves, which shone red where it fell, so that it looked as if drops of blood were splashing up out of the water. Once more she looked with dimmed eyes at the prince, then she threw herself from the ship into the sea and felt her body dissolving into foam.

Now the sun rose out of the sea, and its rays fell with gentleness and warmth on the deathly cold sea-foam, and the little mermaid felt no pain of death. She saw the bright sun and, floating above her, hundreds of beautiful transparent beings, through whom she could see the white sails of the ship and the red clouds in the sky. Their voices were melodious, but so ethereal that no human ear could hear them, just as no earthly eye could see them, and without wings they floated through the air. The little mermaid saw that she had a body like theirs and was slowly rising up out of the foam.

''Where am I going to?'' she asked, and her voice sounded like that of the other spirits—so ethereal that no earthly music was like it.

''To the daughters of the air,'' answered the others. ''Mermaids have no immortal soul, and can never have one unless they win the love of a human being. Their eternal life must depend on the power of another. The daughters of the air have no immortal soul either, but by their own good deeds they can win one for themselves. We fly to the hot countries where the pestilent winds kill the human beings, and we bring them cool breezes. We spread the fragrance of the flowers through the air, and bring life and healing. When for three hundred years we have striven to do all the good we can we are given an immortal soul, and share the eternal happiness of mankind. You, poor little mermaid, have struggled with all your heart for the same goal, and have suffered and endured. Now you have risen to the spiritual world, and after three hundred years of good deeds you will win an immortal soul for yourself."

And the little mermaid lifted her eyes to the sun, and for the first time she felt tears in them.

On the ship there was life and noise once more. She saw the prince and his beautiful bride looking for her, gazing sadly at the gleaming foam as if they knew that she had thrown herself into the waves. Unseen, she kissed the bride's forehead and smiled at the prince. Then she rose with the other children of the air up to the rosy clouds that sailed across the sky.

"In three hundred years we shall float like this into the kingdom of God!"

"But we may get there sooner!" whispered one of them. "Unseen, we fly into houses where there are children, and for every day on which we find a good child that gives its parents joy and deserves their love, God shortens our time of probation. The child does not know when we fly through the room, and if we smile for joy one of the three hundred years is taken off; but if we see a naughty and wicked child we must shed tears of sorrow, and every tear adds a day to our time of probation."

THE STORY OF SIEGFRIED

(This is a very old story: the Danes who used to fight with the English in King Alfred's time knew this story. They have carved on the rocks pictures of some of the things that happen in the tale, and those carvings may still be seen. Because it is so old and so beautiful the story is told here again, but it has a sad ending—indeed it is all sad, and all about fighting and killing, as might be expected from the Danes.)

nce upon a time there was a king in the North who had won many wars, but now he was old. Yet he took a new wife, and then another prince, who wanted to have married her, came up against him with a great army. The old king went out and fought bravely, but at last his sword broke, he was wounded, and his men fled. In the night, when the battle was over, his young wife came out and searched for him among the slain; at last she found him and asked whether he might be healed. No, he replied, his luck was gone, his sword was broken, and he must die. He told her that she would have a son, and that son would be a great warrior and would avenge him on the other king, his enemy. He bade her keep the broken pieces of the sword and make a new sword for his son; that blade, he said, should be called Gram.

After his death, his wife called her maid to her and said, "Let us change clothes, and you shall be called by my name, and I by yours, lest the enemy finds us."

So this was done, and they hid in a wood; but there some strangers met them and carried them off in a ship to Denmark. And when they were brought before the king, he thought the maid looked like a queen, and the queen like a maid. So he asked the queen, "How do you know in the dark of night whether the hours are wearing to the morning?''

And she said:

"I know because, when I was younger, I used to have to rise before dawn and light the fires, and still I awaken each day at the same time."

A strange queen to light the fires, thought the king.

Then he asked the queen, who was dressed like a maid, "How do you know in the dark of night whether the hours are wearing near the dawn?''

"My father gave me a gold ring," said she, "and always, ere the dawning, it grows cold on my fingers."

"A rich house where the maids wore gold," said the king. "Truly you are no maid, but a king's daughter."

So he treated her royally, and as time went on she had a son called Siegfried, a beautiful boy and very strong. He had a tutor to be with him, and once the tutor bade him go to the king and ask for a horse.

"Choose a horse for yourself," said the king, and Siegfried went to the wood. There he met an old man with a white beard, to whom he said, "Come! Help me in horse choosing."

The old man said, "Drive all the horses into the river and choose the one that swims across."

So Siegfried drove them, and only one swam across. Siegfried chose him: his name was Grani; he came of Sleipnir's breed and was the best horse in the world. For Sleipnir was the horse of Odin, the god of the North, and was as swift as the wind.

But a day or two later the tutor said to Siegfried, "There is a great treasure of gold hidden not far from here, and it would become you to win it.''

But Siegfried answered, "I have heard stories of that treasure, and I know that the dragon Fafnir guards it, and he is so huge and wicked that no man dares to go near him."

"He is no bigger than other dragons," said the tutor, "and if you were as brave as your father, you would not fear him."

"I am no coward," said Siegfried. "Why do you want me to fight with this dragon?''

Then his tutor, whose name was Regin, told him that all this great hoard of red gold had once belonged to his own father. And his father had three sons—the first was Fafnir, the dragon; the next was Otter, who could put on the shape of an otter when he liked; and the third was himself, Regin, and he was a great smith and maker of swords.

Now there was at that time a dwarf called Andvari, who lived in a pool beneath a waterfall, and there he had hidden a great hoard of gold. One day Otter had been fishing there, had killed a salmon and eaten it, and was sleeping, like an otter, on a stone. Someone came by and threw a stone at the otter, killed it, flayed off the skin, and took it to the house of Otter's father. Then he knew his son was dead, and to punish the person who had killed him he said he must have the otter's skin filled with gold and covered all over with red gold, or it should go worse with him. Then the person who had killed Otter went down and caught the dwarf who owned all the treasure and took it from him.

Only one ring was left, which the dwarf wore, and even that was taken from him.

The poor dwarf was very angry, and he prayed that the gold might never bring any but bad luck to all the men who might own it, forever.

So the otter skin was filled with gold and covered with gold, all but one hair, and that was covered with the poor dwarf's last ring.

But it brought good luck to nobody. First Fafnir, the dragon, killed his own father; then he went and wallowed on the gold, and would let his brother have none, and no man dared go near it.

When Siegfried heard the story he said to Regin:

"Make me a good sword that I may kill this dragon."

So Regin made a sword, and Siegfried tried it with a blow on a lump of iron, and the sword broke.

Another sword he made, and Siegfried broke that, too.

Then Siegfried went to his mother and asked for the broken pieces of his father's blade, and these he gave to Regin. Regin hammered and wrought them into a new sword, so sharp that fire seemed to burn along its edges.

Siegfried tried this blade on the lump of iron, and it did not break but split the iron in two. Then he threw a lock of wool into the river, and when it floated down against the sword it was cut into two pieces. So Siegfried said that this sword would do. But before he went against the dragon, he led an army to fight the men who had killed his father, and he slew their king and took all his wealth; then he went home.

When he had been at home a few days, he rode out with Regin one morning to the heath where the dragon used to lie. He saw the track that the dragon made when he went to a cliff to drink, and the track was as if a great river had rolled along and left a deep valley.

Siegfried went down into that deep place and dug many pits in it, and in one of the pits he lay hidden with his sword drawn, readied for attack. There he waited, and presently the earth began to shake and tremble

GREG HILDEBRANDT

with the awesome weight of the dragon as he crawled to the water. And a great cloud of venom flew before him as he snorted and roared, so that it would have been certain and quick death to stand before him.

But Siegfried waited till half of him had crawled over the pit, and then he thrust the sword Gram right into his very heart.

The dragon lashed with his tail till stones broke and trees crashed about him.

Then he spoke, as he died, and said:

"Whoever thou art that hast slain me, this gold shall be thy ruin, and the ruin of all who own it."

Siegfried said:

"I would touch none of it if by losing it I should never die. But all men die, and no brave man lets death frighten him from his desire. Die thou, Fafnir." And then Fafnir died.

After that, Siegfried was called Fafnir's bane, and Dragonslayer.

Then Siegfried rode back and met Regin, and Regin asked him to roast Fafnir's heart and let him taste of it.

So Siegfried put the heart of Fafnir on a stake and roasted it. But it chanced that he touched it with his finger, and it burned him. Then he put his finger in his mouth, and so tasted the heart of Fafnir.

Immediately he understood the language of birds, and he heard the woodpeckers say:

"There is Siegfried roasting Fafnir's heart for another, when he should taste of it himself and learn all wisdom."

The next bird said:

"There lies Regin, ready to betray Siegfried, who trusts him."

The third bird said:

"Let him cut off Regin's head and keep all the gold to himself."

The fourth bird said:

"That let him do, and then ride over Hindfell, to the place where Brynhild sleeps."

When Siegfried heard all this, and how Regin was plotting to betray him, he cut off Regin's head with one blow of the sword Gram.

Then all the birds broke out singing:

> We know a fair maid,
> A fair maiden sleeping;
> Siegfried, be not afraid,
> Siegfried, win thou the maid.
> Fortune is keeping.

THE STORY OF SIEGFRIED

High over Hindfell
Red fire is flaming,
There doth the maiden dwell,
She that should love thee well,
Meet for thy taming.

There must she sleep till thou
Comest for her waking.
Rise up and ride, for now
Sure she will swear the vow,
Fearless of breaking.

Then Siegfried remembered how the story went that somewhere, far away, there was a beautiful lady enchanted. She was under a spell, so that she must always sleep in a castle surrounded by flaming fire; there she must sleep forever till there came a knight who would ride through the fire and awaken her. There he determined to go, but first he rode right down the horrible trail of Fafnir.

Fafnir had lived in a cave with iron doors, a cave dug deep down in the earth. There Siegfried found gold bracelets and crowns and rings. There, too, he found the Helm of Dread—a golden helmet that rendered its wearer invisible. All these he piled on the back of the good horse Grani, and then he rode south to Hindfell.

Now it was night, and on the crest of the hill Siegfried saw a red fire blazing up into the sky. Within the flame stood a castle, a banner on the topmost tower. He set the horse Grani at the fire, and he leaped through it lightly, as if it had been through the heather. So Siegfried went within the castle door, and there he saw someone sleeping, clad all in armor. He took the helmet off the head of the sleeper, and behold, she was a most beautiful lady. Awakening, she said, "Ah! Is it Siegfried, Sigmund's son, who has broken the curse, and comes here to waken me at last?"

This curse came upon her when the thorn of the tree of sleep ran into her hand long ago as a punishment because she had displeased the god Odin. Long ago, too, she had vowed never to marry a man who knew fear and dared not ride through the fence of flaming fire. For she, Brynhild, was a warrior maid herself and went armed into the battle like a man. But now she and Siegfried loved each other, and promised to be true to each other. He gave her a ring, the last ring taken from the dwarf Andvari. Then Siegfried rode away, and he came to the house

56

of a king who had a fair daughter. Her name was Gudrun, and her mother was a witch. Now Gudrun fell in love with Siegfried, but he was always talking of Brynhild, how beautiful she was and how dear. So one day Gudrun's witch mother put poppy and forgetful drugs in a magical cup, and she bade Siegfried drink to her health. He drank, and instantly he forgot poor Brynhild and fell in love with Gudrun, and they were married with great rejoicings.

Now the witch, the mother of Gudrun, wanted her son Gunnar to marry Brynhild; she bade him ride out with Siegfried and go and woo her. So forth they rode to her father's house, for Brynhild had quite gone out of Siegfried's mind by reason of the witch's wine; but Brynhild remembered Siegfried and loved him still. Thus, Brynhild's father told Gunnar that she would marry none but the man who could ride the flame in front of her enchanted tower; so thither they rode. Gunnar set his horse at the flame, but he would not face it; he tried Siegfried's horse Grani, but Grani would not move with Gunnar on his back. Then Gunnar remembered witchcraft that his mother had taught him, and by his magic he made Siegfried look exactly like himself, and he made himself look exactly like Siegfried. Then Siegfried, in the shape of Gunnar and in his mail, mounted on Grani, and Grani leaped the fence of fire, and Siegfried went in and found Brynhild, but he did not remember her yet, because of the forgetful medicine in the cup of the witch's wine.

Now Brynhild had no recourse but to promise she would be his wife— the wife of Gunnar, she supposed, as Siegfried wore Gunnar's shape— for she had sworn to wed whoever should ride the flames. He gave her a ring, and she gave him back the ring he had given her before in his own shape as Siegfried, and it was the last ring of that poor dwarf Andvari.

Then he rode out again, and he and Gunnar changed shapes; each was himself again, and they went home to the witch queen's, where Siegfried gave the dwarf's ring to his wife, Gudrun.

Meanwhile Brynhild went to her father and told him that a king called Gunnar had come and had ridden the fire, and she must marry him. "Yet I thought," she said, "that no man could have done this deed but Siegfried, Fafnir's bane, who was my true love. But he has forgotten me, and my promise I must keep."

So Gunnar and Brynhild were married, though it was not Gunnar, but Siegfried in Gunnar's shape, who had ridden the fire.

When the wedding ceremony and feast were over, then the magic of the witch's wine went out of Siegfried's brain, and he remembered all. He remembered how he had freed Brynhild from the spell, how she was his own true love, how he had forgotten and had married another woman, and how he had won Brynhild to be the wife of another man.

But he was brave, and he spoke not a word of it to the others to make them unhappy. Still he could not keep away the curse that was to come on everyone who owned the treasure and golden ring of the dwarf Andvari.

And the curse soon came upon all of them. For one day, when Brynhild and Gudrun were bathing, Brynhild waded far out into the river and said she did that to show she was Gudrun's superior. For her husband, she said, had ridden through the flame when no other man dared face it.

Gudrun became very angry and told her that it was Siegfried, not Gunnar, who had ridden through the flame and had received from Brynhild that fatal ring, the ring of the dwarf Andvari.

Then Brynhild saw the ring that Siegfried had given to Gudrun, and she knew it and knew all. She turned as pale as a dead woman and went home. All that evening she never spoke. Next day she told Gunnar, her husband, that he was a coward and a liar, for he had never ridden through the flame but had sent Siegfried to do it for him and pretended that he had done it himself. And she said he would never see her glad in his hall, never drinking wine, never playing chess, never embroidering with golden thread, never speaking words of kindness. Then she rent all her needlework asunder and wept aloud, so that everyone in the house heard her. For her heart and her pride had been broken in the same hour. She had lost her true love, Siegfried, the slayer of Fafnir, and she was married to a man who was a liar.

Then Siegfried came and tried to comfort her, but she would not listen and said she wished the sword stood fast in his heart.

"Not long to wait," he said, "till the bitter sword stands fast in my heart, and thou will not live long when I am dead. But, dear Brynhild, live and be comforted, and love Gunnar thy husband, and I will give thee all the gold, the treasure of the dragon Fafnir."

Brynhild said:

"It is too late."

Siegfried was so grieved and his heart so swelled in his breast that it burst the steel rings of his shirt of mail.

Siegfried went out and Brynhild determined to slay him. She mixed serpent's venom and wolf's flesh, and gave them in one dish to her husband's younger brother; when he had tasted them he was driven mad, and he went into Siegfried's chamber while he slept and pinned him to the bed with a sword. But Siegfried awoke, caught the sword Gram, and threw it at the man as he fled, and the sword cut him in twain.

Thus died Siegfried, Fafnir's bane, whom no ten men could have slain in fair fight.

Then Gudrun awakened and saw him dead, and she moaned aloud. Brynhild heard her and laughed; but the kind horse Grani lay down and died of grief. And then Brynhild fell aweeping till her heart broke.

So they attired Siegfried in all his golden armor and built a great pile of wood on board his ship; and at night they laid on it the dead Siegfried and the dead Brynhild, and the good horse, Grani, set fire to it, and launched the ship. And the wind bore it blazing out to sea, flaming into the dark. So there were Siegfried and Brynhild burned together, and the curse of the dwarf Andvari was fulfilled.

SNOWDROP

nce upon a time, in the middle of winter when the snowflakes were falling like feathers on the earth, a queen sat at a window framed in black ebony and sewed. As she sewed and gazed out to the white landscape, she pricked her finger with the needle; three drops of blood fell on the snow outside, and because the red showed out so well against the white, she thought to herself:

Oh! What wouldn't I give to have a child as white as snow, as red as blood, and as black as ebony!

And her wish was granted, for not long after a little daughter was born to her, with skin as white as snow, lips and cheeks as red as blood, and hair as black as ebony. They called her Snowdrop, and not long after her birth the queen died.

After a year the king married again. His new wife was a beautiful woman but so proud and overbearing that she couldn't stand any rival to her beauty. She possessed a magic mirror, and when she used to stand before it, gazing at her own reflection, and ask:

> Mirror, mirror, hanging there,
> Who in all the land's most fair?

it always replied:

> You are most fair, my Lady Queen,
> None fairer in the land, I ween.

Then she was quite happy, for she knew the mirror always spoke the truth.

But Snowdrop was growing prettier and prettier every day, and when she was seven years old she was as beautiful as she could be, and fairer even than the queen herself. One day when the latter asked her mirror the usual question, it replied:

> My Lady Queen, you are fair, 'tis true,
> But Snowdrop is fairer far than you.

Then the queen flew into the most awful passion and turned every shade of green in her jealousy. From this hour she hated poor Snowdrop like poison, and every day her envy, hatred, and malice grew, for envy and jealousy are like evil weeds that spring up and choke the heart. At last she could endure Snowdrop's presence no longer, and, calling a huntsman to her, she said:

"Take the child out into the wood, and never let me see her face again. You must kill her, and bring me back her lungs and liver, that I may know for certain she is dead."

The huntsman did as he was told and led Snowdrop out into the wood, but as he was in the act of drawing out his knife to slay her, she began to cry, and said:

"Oh, dear huntsman, spare my life, and I will promise to fly forth into the wide wood and never to return home again."

And because she was so young and pretty the huntsman had pity on her, and said:

"Well, run along, poor child." For he thought to himself, The wild beasts will soon eat her up.

His heart thus felt lighter because he hadn't had to do the deed himself. As he turned away, a young boar came running past, so he shot it and brought its lungs and liver home to the queen as proof that Snowdrop was really dead. The wicked woman had them stewed in salt and ate them up, thinking she had made an end of Snowdrop forever.

Now when the poor child found herself alone in the big wood, the very trees around her seemed to assume strange shapes, and she felt so frightened she didn't know what to do. Then she began to run over the sharp stones, and through the bramble bushes, and the wild beasts ran past her, but they did her no harm. She ran as far as her legs would carry her, and as evening approached she saw a little house, and she stepped inside to rest. Everything was very small in the little house, but cleaner and neater than anything you can imagine. In the middle of the room there stood a little table, covered with a white tablecloth, and seven little plates and forks and spoons and knives and tumblers. Side by side against the wall there were seven little beds, covered with snow-white counterpanes. Snowdrop felt so hungry and so thirsty that she ate a bit of bread and a little porridge from each plate, and drank a drop of wine out of each tumbler. Then, feeling tired and sleepy, she lay down on one of the beds, but it wasn't comfortable; she tried all the others in turn, but one was too long and another too short, and it was only when she got to the seventh that she found one to suit her exactly. So she lay down upon it, said her prayers like a good child, and fell fast asleep.

When it got quite dark, the masters of the little house returned. They were seven dwarfs who worked in the mines, right down deep in the heart of the mountain. They lighted their seven little lamps, and as soon as their eyes got accustomed to the glare, they saw that someone had been in the room, for all was not in the same order as they had left it.

The first said:

"Who's been sitting on my little chair?"

The second said:

"Who's been eating my little loaf?"

The third said:

"Who's been tasting my porridge?"

The fourth said:

"Who's been eating out of my little plate?"

The fifth said:

"Who's been using my little fork?"

The sixth said:

"Who's been cutting with my little knife?"

The seventh said:

"Who's been drinking out of my little tumbler?"

Then the first dwarf looked around and saw a little hollow in his bed, and he asked again:

"Who's been lying on my bed?"

The others came running and, when they saw their beds, cried:

"Somebody has lain on ours, too."

But when the seventh came to his bed, he started back in amazement, for there he beheld Snowdrop fast asleep. Then he called the others, who turned their little lamps full on the bed, and when they saw Snowdrop lying there they nearly fell down with surprise.

"Goodness gracious!" they cried. "What a beautiful child!"

And they were so completely enchanted by her beauty that they did not wake her, but let her sleep on in the little bed the night long. The seventh dwarf slept with his companions in turn one hour in each bed, and in this way he managed to pass the night.

In the morning Snowdrop awoke, but when she saw the seven little dwarfs she felt very frightened. They were very friendly, however, and they asked her what her name was in such a kind way that she replied:

"I am Snowdrop."

"Why did you come to our house?" continued the dwarfs.

Then she told them how her stepmother had wished her put to death, and how the huntsman had spared her life, and how she had run the whole day until she had come to their little house. When they had heard her sad story, the dwarfs asked her:

"Will you stay and keep house for us, cook, make the beds, do the washing, sew, and knit? And if you give satisfaction and keep everything neat and clean, you shall want for nothing."

"Yes," answered Snowdrop, "I will gladly do all you ask."

And so she took up her abode with them. Every morning the dwarfs went into the mountain to dig for gold, and in the evening, when they returned home, Snowdrop always had their supper ready for them. But during the day the girl was left quite alone, so the good dwarfs warned her, saying:

"Beware of your stepmother. She will soon find out you are here; and whatever you do don't let anyone into the house."

Now after she thought she had eaten Snowdrop's lungs and liver, the queen never dreamed but that she was once more the most beautiful woman in the world; so, stepping before her mirror one day, she said:

> Mirror, mirror, hanging there,
> Who in all the land's most fair?

And the mirror replied:

> My Lady Queen, you are fair, 'tis true,
> But Snowdrop is fairer far than you.
> Snowdrop, who dwells with the seven little men,
> Is as fair as you, as fair again.

When the queen heard these words she was nearly struck dumb with horror, for the mirror always spoke the truth, and she knew now that the huntsman must have deceived her and that Snowdrop was still alive. She pondered day and night how she might destroy her, for as long as she felt she had a rival in the land her jealous heart left her no rest. At

last she hit upon a plan. She stained her face and dressed herself up as
an old peddler's wife, so that she was quite unrecognizable. In this guise,
she went over the seven hills until she came to the house of the seven
dwarfs. There she knocked at the door, calling out at the same time:

"Fine wares to sell, fine wares to sell!"

Snowdrop peeped out of the window and called out:

"Good day, mother, what have you to sell?"

"Good wares, fine wares," she answered. "Laces of every shade and
description." And she held one up that was made of some gay-colored
silk.

Surely I can let the honest woman in, thought Snowdrop; so she un-
barred the door and bought the pretty lace.

"Good gracious! Child," said the old woman, "what a figure you've
got. Come! I'll lace you up properly for once."

Snowdrop, suspecting no evil, stood before her and let her lace her
bodice up, but the old woman laced her so quickly and so tightly that it
took Snowdrop's breath away, and she fell down dead.

"Now you are no longer the fairest," said the wicked old woman,
and then she hastened away.

In the evening the seven dwarfs came home, and you may think what
a fright they got when they saw their dear Snowdrop lying on the floor,
as still and motionless as a dead person. They lifted her up tenderly,
and when they saw how tightly laced she was, they cut the lace in two,
and she began to breathe a little and gradually came back to life. When
the dwarfs heard what had happened, they said:

"Depend upon it, the old peddler's wife was none other than the
queen. In future you must be sure to let no one in, if we are not at
home."

As soon as the wicked queen got home, she went straight to her mirror
and said:

> Mirror, mirror, hanging there,
> Who in all the land's most fair?

And the mirror answered as before:

> My Lady Queen, you are fair, 'tis true,
> But Snowdrop is fairer far than you.
> Snowdrop, who dwells with the seven little men,
> Is as fair as you, as fair again.

SNOWDROP

When she heard this, she became as pale as death, because she saw at once that Snowdrop must be alive again.

This time, she said to herself, I will think of something that will make an end of her once and for all.

And by the witchcraft that she understood so well she made a poisonous comb; then she dressed herself up and assumed the form of another old woman. So she went over the seven hills until she reached the house of the seven dwarfs, and knocking at the door she called out:

"Fine wares for sale."

Snowdrop looked out of the window and said:

"You must go away, for I may not let anyone in."

"But surely you are not forbidden to look out?" said the old woman, and she held up the poisonous comb for her to see.

It pleased the girl so much that she let herself be taken in and opened the door. When they had settled their bargain the old woman said:

"Now I'll comb your hair properly for you, for once in the way."

Poor Snowdrop thought no evil, but hardly had the comb touched her hair than the poison worked and she fell down unconscious.

"Now, my fine lady, you're really done for this time," said the wicked woman, and she made her way home as fast as she could.

Fortunately it was now near evening, and the seven dwarfs returned home. When they saw Snowdrop lying dead on the ground, they at once suspected that her wicked stepmother had been at work again; so they searched until they found the poisonous comb, and the moment they pulled it out of her head Snowdrop came to herself again and told them what had happened. They warned her once more to be on her guard, and to open the door to no one.

As soon as the queen got home she went straight to her mirror, and asked:

> Mirror, mirror, hanging there,
> Who in all the land's most fair?

And it replied as before:

> My Lady Queen, you are fair, 'tis true,
> But Snowdrop is fairer far than you.
> Snowdrop, who dwells with the seven little men,
> Is as fair as you, as fáir again.

66

SNOWDROP

When she heard these words, she literally trembled and shook with rage.

"Snowdrop shall die!" she cried. "Yes, though it cost me my own life."

Then she went to a little secret chamber, which no one knew of but herself, and there she made a poisonous apple. Outwardly it looked beautiful, white with red cheeks, so that everyone who saw it longed to eat it, but anyone who might do so would certainly die on the spot. When the apple was quite finished, she stained her face and dressed herself up as a peasant, and so she went over the seven hills to the seven dwarfs. She knocked at the door, as usual, but Snowdrop put her head out of the window and called out:

"I may not let anyone in; the seven dwarfs have forbidden me to do so."

"Are you afraid of being poisoned?" asked the old woman. "See, I will cut this apple in half. I'll eat the white cheek and you can eat the red."

But the apple was so cunningly made that only the red cheek was poisonous. Snowdrop longed to eat the tempting fruit, and when she saw that the peasant woman was eating it herself, she couldn't resist the temptation any longer, and stretching out her hand she took the poisonous half. But hardly had the first bite passed her lips than she fell down dead on the ground. Then the eyes of the cruel queen sparkled with glee, and, laughing aloud, she cried:

"As white as snow, as red as blood, and as black as ebony, this time the dwarfs won't be able to bring you back to life."

When she got home she asked the mirror:

> Mirror, mirror, hanging there,
> Who in all the land's most fair?

And this time it replied:

> You are most fair, my Lady Queen,
> None fairer in the land, I ween.

Then her jealous heart was at rest—at least, as much at rest as a jealous heart can ever be.

When the little dwarfs came home in the evening they found Snowdrop lying on the ground, and she neither breathed nor stirred. They lifted her up and looked around everywhere to see if they could find anything poisonous about. They unlaced her bodice, combed her hair, washed her with water and wine, but all in vain; the child was dead and remained dead. Then they placed her on a bier, and all the seven dwarfs sat around it, weeping and sobbing for three whole days. At last they made up their minds to bury her, but she looked as blooming as a living being, and her cheeks were still such a lovely color, so they said:

"We can't hide her away in the black ground."

They had a coffin made of transparent glass, and they laid her in it and wrote on the lid in golden letters that she was a royal princess. Then they put the coffin on the top of the mountain, and one of the dwarfs always remained beside it and kept watch over it. And the very birds of the air came and bewailed Snowdrop's death, first an owl, then a raven, and last of all a little dove.

Snowdrop lay a long time in the coffin, and she always looked the same, just as if she were fast asleep, and she remained as white as snow, as red as blood, and her hair as black as ebony.

Now it happened one day that a prince came to the wood and passed by the dwarfs' house. He saw the coffin on the hill, with the beautiful Snowdrop inside it, and when he had read what was written on it in golden letters, he said to the dwarf:

"Give me the coffin. I'll pay you whatever you like for it."

But the dwarf said: "No; we wouldn't part with it for all the gold in the world."

"Well, then," he replied, "give it to me, because I can't live without Snowdrop. I will cherish and love it as my dearest possession."

He spoke so sadly that the good dwarfs had pity on him and gave him the coffin, and the prince made his servants bear it away on their shoulders. Now it happened that as they were going down the hill they stumbled over a bush and jolted the coffin so violently that the poisonous bit of apple Snowdrop had swallowed fell out of her throat. She gradually opened her eyes, lifted up the lid of the coffin, and sat up alive and well.

"Oh! Dear me, where am I?" she cried.

The prince answered joyfully, "You are with me." And he told her all that had happened, adding, "I love you better than anyone in the whole wide world. Will you come with me to my father's palace and be my wife?"

Snowdrop consented and went with him, and the marriage was celebrated with great pomp and splendor, and the merriment lasted all through

the day and night.

Now Snowdrop's wicked stepmother was one of the guests invited to the wedding feast. When she had dressed herself very gorgeously for the occasion, she went to the mirror, and said:

> Mirror, mirror, hanging there,
> Who in all the land's most fair?

And the mirror answered:

> My Lady Queen, you are fair, 'tis true,
> But Snowdrop is fairer far than you.

When the wicked woman heard these words she uttered a curse and was beside herself with rage and mortification. At first she didn't want to go to the wedding at all, but at the same time she felt she would never be happy till she had seen the young queen. As she entered, Snow-drop recognized her and nearly fainted with fear; but red-hot iron shoes had been prepared for the wicked queen, and she was made to get into them and dance till she fell down dead!

THE STORY OF ALADDIN,
OR
THE WONDERFUL LAMP

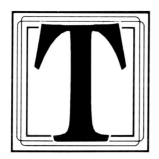here lived in ancient times in the capital of China a tailor named Mustapha, who was so poor that he could scarcely support his wife and son. Now his son, whose name was Aladdin, was idle and careless and disobedient to his father and mother, and he played from morning till night in the streets with other bad and idle lads. Mustapha chastised him, but Aladdin remained incorrigible, and his father was so much troubled that he became ill and died in a few months. His mother, finding that Aladdin would not work, did all she could by spinning cotton to maintain herself and him.

Now Aladdin, who was no longer restrained by fear of a father, gave himself over entirely to his idle habits. As he was one day playing according to custom with his vagabond associates, a stranger, passing by, stood and regarded him earnestly. This stranger was a sorcerer, an African magician. By means of his magic he saw in Aladdin's face something necessary for the accomplishment of a deed in which he was engaged. And the wily magician, taking Aladdin aside from his companions, said, "Boy, is not thy father called Mustapha the tailor?"

"Yes," answered the boy, "but he has been dead a long time."

At these words the African magician threw his arms about Aladdin's neck and kissed him several times, with tears in his eyes. "Alas, O my son," he cried, "I am thine uncle. I have been abroad for many years, and now I am come home with the hope of seeing thy father, but thou tellest me that he is dead! I knew thee at first sight, because thou art so like him, and I see that I was not deceived!" Then, putting his hand into his pocket, he asked Aladdin where his mother lived and gave him a small handful of money, saying, "Go, O my son, to thy mother. Give her my love and tell her that I will visit her tomorrow!"

As soon as the African magician had departed Aladdin ran to his mother, overjoyed at the reunion. "Mother," he said, "I have met my uncle!"

"No, my son," answered his mother, "thou hast no uncle by thy father's side or mine." Then Aladdin related to her all that the African magician had told him.

The next day Aladdin's mother made ready a repast, and when night came someone knocked upon the door. Aladdin opened it, and the African magician entered, laden with wine and various fruits. He saluted Aladdin's mother, shed tears, and lamented that he had not arrived in time to see his brother Mustapha. "I have been forty years absent from my country," said the wily magician, "traveling in the Indies, Persia, Arabia, Syria, and Egypt. At last I was desirous of seeing and embracing my dear brother, so I immediately prepared for the journey and set out. Reaching this city, I wandered through the streets, where I observed my brother's features in the face of my nephew, thy son."

The African magician, perceiving that the widow began to weep at these words, turned to Aladdin and asked him what trade or occupation he had chosen. At this question Aladdin hung down his head, blushing and abashed, while his mother replied that he was an idle fellow, living on the streets. "This is not well," said the magician. "If thou hast no desire to learn a handicraft, I will take a shop for thee and furnish it with fine linens and rich stuffs." This plan greatly flattered Aladdin, for he knew that the owners of such shops were much respected; so he thanked the African magician, saying that he preferred such a shop to any trade or handicraft. Aladdin's mother, who had not until then believed that the magician was the brother of her husband, now could no longer doubt. She thanked him for his kindness to Aladdin, and exhorted the lad to repay his uncle with good behavior.

The next day, early in the morning, the African magician came again and took Aladdin to a merchant, who provided the lad with a rich and handsome suit, after which the magician took him to visit the principal shops, where they sold the richest stuffs and linens. He showed him also the largest and finest mosques and entertained him at the most frequented inns. Then the magician escorted Aladdin to his mother, who, when she saw her son so magnificently attired, bestowed a thousand blessings upon his benefactor.

Aladdin rose early the next morning and dressed himself in his elegant new garments. Soon after this the African magician approached the house and entered it, and, caressing him, he said, "Come, my dear son, and I will show thee fine things today!" He then led the lad out of the city, through magnificent parks and gardens, past fine palaces and buildings, enticing him beyond the gardens, across the country, until they arrived at some mountains. He amused Aladdin all the way by relating to him pleasant stories, and by feasting him with cakes and fruit.

When at last they arrived at a valley between two mountains of great height the magician said to Aladdin, "We will go no farther. I will now show thee some extraordinary things. While I strike a light do thou gather up loose sticks for a fire." Aladdin collected a pile of sticks, and the African magician set fire to them, and when they began to burn he muttered several magical words and cast a perfume upon the fire. Immediately a great smoke arose, and the earth, trembling, opened and uncovered a stone with a brass ring fixed in the middle.

Aladdin became so frightened at what he saw that he would have run away, but the magician caught hold of him and gave him such a box on the ear that he knocked him down. Aladdin rose up trembling, and with tears in his eyes inquired what he had done to merit such a punishment. "I have my reasons," answered the magician harshly. "Thou seest what I have just done! But, my son," continued he, softening, "know that under this stone is hidden a treasure destined to be thine. It will make thee richer than the greatest monarch in the world. Fate decrees that no one but thou mayest lift the stone or enter the cave, but to do this successfully thou must promise to obey my instructions."

Aladdin was amazed at all he saw, and, hearing that the treasure was to be his, his anger was appeased, and he said quickly, "Command me, Uncle, for I promise to obey." The magician then directed him to take hold of the ring and lift the stone, and to pronounce at the same time the names of his father and grandfather. Aladdin did as he was bidden, raised the heavy stone with ease and laid it on one side. When the stone was pulled up there appeared a cave several feet deep, with a little door and steps to go farther down.

"Observe, my son," said the African magician, "what I direct. Descend, and at the bottom of these steps thou wilt find a door open. Beyond the door are three great halls, in each of which thou wilt see four large brass chests, full of gold and silver. Take care that thou dost not touch any of the wealth. Before thou enterest the first hall tuck up thy vest, and pass through the first and the second and the third hall without stopping. Above all things do not touch the walls, not even with thy clothing, for if thou do so, thou wilt die instantly.

"At the end of the third hall thou wilt find a door which opens into a garden planted with fine trees, loaded with fruits. Walk directly across the garden by a path that will lead thee to five steps, which will bring thee to a terrace, where thou wilt see a niche, and in that niche a lighted lamp. Take down the lamp, extinguish the flame, throw away the wick, pour out the oil, put the lamp into thy bosom, and bring it to me. If thou shouldst wish for any of the fruits of the garden, thou mayest gather as much as thou pleasest.''

The magician then took a ring from his finger and placed it upon Aladdin's hand, telling him that it would preserve him from all evil. Aladdin sprang into the cave, descended the steps, and found the three halls just as the African magician had described. He passed through, taking care not to touch the walls, crossed the garden without stopping, took down the lamp from the niche, threw away the wick, poured out the oil, and placed the lamp in his bosom.

But as he came down from the terrace he stopped to observe the fruits. All the trees were loaded with extraordinary fruits of different colors. Some trees bore fruit entirely white, and some as clear and transparent as crystal; some were red, some green, blue, purple, and others yellow. In short, there were fruits of all colors. The white were pearls, the clear and transparent diamonds, the red rubies, the green emeralds, the blue turquoises, the purple amethysts, and those that were yellow sapphires. Aladdin was altogether ignorant of their worth and would have preferred figs and grapes, or any other fruits. But though he took them for colored glass of little value, yet he was so pleased with the variety of bright colors and with the beauty and extraordinary size of the seeming fruits that he gathered some of every sort, filled the two new purses his uncle had given him, and crammed his bosom as full as it could hold.

Aladdin, having thus loaded himself with riches he knew not the value of, returned through the three halls to the mouth of the cave, where the magician was expecting him with the utmost impatience. Now the African magician intended, as soon as he should receive the lamp from Aladdin, to push the lad back into the cave, so that there should remain no witness of the affair. But as soon as Aladdin saw him he cried out, ''Pray, Uncle, lend me thy hand to help me out.''

''Give me the lamp first,'' said the magician. ''It will be troublesome to thee.''

''Indeed, Uncle,'' answered Aladdin, ''I am unable to give it to thee now, but I will do so as soon as I am up.''

But the magician was obstinate and insisted on having the lamp; and Aladdin, whose bosom was so stuffed with the fruits that he could not well get at it, refused to give up the lamp until he was out of the cave. The magician, provoked at this refusal, flew into a rage, threw some incense into the fire, and pronounced two magical words; instantly the stone that had covered the mouth of the cave moved back into its place. Then the African magician, having lost all hope of obtaining the wonderful lamp, returned that same day to Africa.

When Aladdin found himself thus buried alive he cried and called out to his uncle that he was ready to give him the lamp, but in vain, since his cries could not be heard. He descended to the bottom of the steps, desiring to enter the garden, but the door, which had been open before by enchantment, was now closed by the same means. He then redoubled his cries and tears, and sat down upon the steps, without any hope of ever seeing the light again.

Aladdin remained in this state for two days, without eating or drinking. On the third day, clasping his hands in despair, he accidentally rubbed the ring that the magician had placed upon his finger. Immediately a genie of enormous size and frightful aspect rose out of the earth, his head reaching the roof of the cave, and said to him, "What wouldst thou have? I will obey thee as thy slave, and the slave of all who may possess the ring on thy finger, I and the other slaves of that ring!"

At any other time Aladdin would have been frightened at the sight of so extraordinary a figure, but the danger that he was in made him answer without hesitation, "Whoever thou art, deliver me from this place!" He had no sooner spoken these words than he found himself on the very spot where the magician had caused the earth to open.

Thankful to find himself safe, he quickly made his way home. When he reached his mother's door the joy at seeing her and the weakness due to lack of food made him faint, and he remained for a long time as dead. His mother did all she could to bring him to himself, and the first words he spoke were, "Pray, Mother, give me something to eat." His mother brought what she had and set it before him.

Aladdin then related to his mother all that had happened to him, and he showed her the transparent fruits of different colors that he had gathered in the garden. But though these fruits were precious stones, as brilliant as the sun, the mother was ignorant of their worth, and she laid them carelessly aside.

Aladdin slept very soundly until the next morning, but on waking he found that there was nothing to eat in the house, nor any money with which to buy food.

"Alas, my son," said his mother, "I have not a bit of bread to give thee, but I have a little cotton which I have spun, and I will go and sell it, that I may provide you with food to restore your strength."

75

"Mother," replied Aladdin, "keep thy cotton for another time, and give me the lamp I brought home with me yesterday. I will go and sell it, and the money I shall get for it will serve both for breakfast and dinner, and perhaps for supper also."

Aladdin's mother brought the lamp, and as it was very dirty she took some fine sand and water to clean it, but she no sooner began to rub than in an instant a hideous genie of gigantic size appeared before her and said in a voice like thunder, "What wouldst thou have? I am ready to obey thee as thy slave, and the slave of all those who hold the lamp in their hands, I and the other slaves of the lamp!"

Aladdin's mother, terrified at the sight of the genie, fainted, but Aladdin snatched the lamp out of her hand and said to him, "I am hungry. Bring me something to eat." The genie disappeared immediately and in an instant returned with a large silver tray holding twelve covered dishes of the same metal, which contained the most delicious viands, six large white bread cakes, two flagons of wine, and two silver cups. All these he placed upon a carpet and disappeared. This was done before Aladdin's mother recovered from her swoon.

Aladdin fetched some water and sprinkled it on her face, and she recovered. Great was her surprise to see the silver tray, twelve dishes, six loaves, the two flagons and cups, and to smell the savory odor that exhaled from the dishes. When, however, Aladdin informed her that they were brought by the genie whom she had seen, she was greatly alarmed and urged him to sell the enchanted lamp and have nothing to do with the genie. "With thy leave, Mother," answered Aladdin, "I will keep the lamp, as it has been of service to us. Thou mayest be sure that my false and wicked uncle would not have taken so much pains and undertaken such a long journey if he had not known that this wonderful lamp was worth more than all the gold and silver which were in those three halls. He knew too well the worth of this lamp not to prefer it to so great a treasure. Let us make profitable use of it, without exciting the envy and jealousy of our neighbors. However, since the genie frightens thee I will take the lamp out of thy sight, and put it where I may find it when I want it." His mother, convinced by his arguments, said he might do as he wished, but for herself she would have nothing to do with genies.

The mother and son then sat down to breakfast, and when they were satisfied they found that they had enough food left for dinner and supper, and also for two meals for the next day. By the following night they had eaten all the provisions the genie had brought; so the next day Aladdin, putting one of the silver dishes under his vest, went to the silver market and sold it. Before returning home he called at the baker's and bought bread, and on his return he gave the rest of the money to his mother, who went and purchased provisions enough to last for some time.

In this manner they lived, until Aladdin had sold all the dishes and the silver tray. When the money was spent he turned once again to the lamp. He took it in his hand, rubbed it, and immediately the genie appeared and said, "What wouldst thou have? I am ready to obey thee as thy slave, and the slave of all those who hold that lamp in their hands, I and the other slaves of the lamp!"

"I am hungry," said Aladdin. "Bring me something to eat."

The genie immediately disappeared and returned instantly with a tray containing the same number of dishes as before, and he set them down and vanished. And when the provisions were gone Aladdin sold the tray and dishes as before. Thus he and his mother continued to live for some time, and though they had an inexhaustible treasure in their lamp they dwelt quietly with frugality.

Meanwhile Aladdin frequented the shops of the principal merchants, where they sold cloths of gold and silver, linens and silk stuffs, and jewelry, and, oftentimes joining in their conversation, he acquired a knowledge of the world and a polished manner. By his acquaintance among the jewelers he came to know that the fruits that he had gathered in the subterranean garden, instead of being colored glass, were jewels of inestimable value.

One day as Aladdin was walking about the town he heard an order proclaimed, commanding the people to close their shops and houses and to keep within doors while Princess Badroulboudour, the sultan's daughter, went to the baths and returned. When Aladdin heard this he became filled with curiosity to see the face of the princess. So he placed himself behind the outer door of the bath, which was so situated that he could not fail to see her.

He had not long to wait before the princess came, and he could see her plainly through a chink in the door without being discovered. She was attended by a great crowd of ladies, slaves, and eunuchs, who walked on each side and behind her. When she came near to the door of the bath she took off her veil, and Aladdin saw her face.

The princess was the most beautiful brunette in the world. Her eyes were large, lively, and sparkling, her looks sweet and modest, her nose without a fault, her mouth small, and her lips vermilion red. It was not surprising that Aladdin, who had never before seen such a blaze of charms, was dazzled and that his heart became filled with admiration and love.

THE STORY OF ALADDIN, OR THE WONDERFUL LAMP

After the princess had passed by, Aladdin returned home in a state of great dejection, which he could not conceal from his mother, who was surprised to see him thoughtful and melancholy. She inquired the cause of this, and Aladdin told her all that had occurred, saying, "This, my mother, is the cause of my melancholy! I love the princess more than I can express, I cannot live without the beautiful Badroulboudour, and I am resolved to ask her in marriage of the sultan, her father."

Aladdin's mother listened in surprise to what her son told her, but when he spoke of asking the princess in marriage she burst into a loud laugh. "Alas, my son," she said, "what art thou thinking of? Thou must be mad to talk thus!"

"I assure thee, my mother," replied Aladdin, "that I am not mad, but I am resolved to demand the princess in marriage, and thy remonstrances shall not prevent me; instead I will expect thee to use thy persuasion with the sultan."

"I go to the sultan?" answered his mother, amazed and surprised. "I assure thee I cannot undertake such an errand. And who art thou, my son," she continued, "to think of the sultan's daughter? Hast thou forgotten that thy father was one of the poorest tailors in the city? How can I open my mouth to make such a proposal to the sultan? His majestic presence and the luster of his court would confound me! There is another reason, my son, which thou dost not think of, which is that no one ever asks a favor of the sultan without taking him a fitting present."

Aladdin heard very calmly all that his mother had to say; then he replied, "I love the princess, or rather I adore her, and shall always persevere in my design to marry her. Thou sayest that it is not customary to go to the sultan without a present. Would not those fruits that I brought home from the subterranean garden make an acceptable present? For what thou and I took for colored glass are really jewels of inestimable value, and I am persuaded that they will be favorably received by the sultan. Thou hast a large porcelain dish fit to hold them; fetch it, and let us see how the stones will look when we have arranged them according to their different colors."

Aladdin's mother brought the porcelain dish, and he arranged the jewels on it according to his fancy. But the brightness and luster they emitted in daylight and the variety of colors so dazzled the eyes of both mother and son that they were astonished beyond measure. After they had admired the beauty of the jewels Aladdin said to his mother, "Now thou canst not excuse thyself from going to the sultan under the pretext of not having a present for him!" His mother did not believe in the beauty and value of the stones, however, and she used many arguments to make her son change his mind. Aladdin, however, could not be changed from his purpose and continued to persuade her, until out of tenderness she complied with his request.

The next morning Aladdin's mother took the porcelain dish, in which were the jewels, and, wrapping it in two fine napkins, she set out for the sultan's palace. She entered the audience chamber and placed herself just before the sultan, the grand vizier, and the great lords of the court, who sat in council, but she did not venture to declare her business; and when the audience chamber closed for the day she returned home. The next morning she again repaired to the audience chamber and left it when it closed without having dared to address the sultan. She continued to do this daily, until at last one morning the chief officer of the court approached her, and at a sign from him she followed him to the sultan's throne, where he left her.

Aladdin's mother saluted the sultan and, kissing the ground before him, bowed her head down to the carpet that covered the steps of the throne and remained in that posture until he bade her rise, which she had no sooner done than he said to her, "My good woman, I have observed thee to stand for a long time from the opening to the closing of the audience chamber. What business brings thee thither?"

When Aladdin's mother heard these words she prostrated herself a second time, and when she arose she said, "O King of Kings, I will indeed tell thee the incredible and extraordinary business that brings me, but I presume to beg of thee to hear what I have to say in private." The sultan ordered all but the grand vizier to leave the audience chamber, and then directed her to proceed with her tale.

Thus encouraged, Aladdin's mother humbly entreated the sultan's pardon for what she was about to say. She then told him faithfully how Aladdin had seen the Princess Badroulboudour, and of the love that the fatal sight had inspired him with. She ended by formally demanding the princess in marriage for her son; then she took the porcelain dish, which she had set down at the foot of the throne, unwrapped it, and presented it to the sultan.

The sultan's amazement and surprise were inexpressible when he saw so many large, beautiful, and valuable jewels. He remained for some time motionless with admiration. At length, when he had recovered himself, he received the present from the hand of Aladdin's mother, crying out in a transport of joy, "How rich, how beautiful!" After he had admired and handled all the jewels one by one he turned to his grand vizier and, showing him the dish, said, "Behold, admire, wonder! Confess that thine eyes never beheld precious stones so rich and beautiful before! What sayest thou to such a present? Is it not worthy of the princess my daughter?"

These words agitated the grand vizier, for the sultan had for some time intended to bestow the princess his daughter upon the vizier's son. Therefore, going to the sultan, the vizier whispered in his ear and said, "I cannot but own that the present is worthy of the princess, but I beg thee to grant me three months' delay, and before the end of that time I hope that my son may be able to make a nobler present than Aladdin, who is an entire stranger to Thy Majesty."

The sultan granted his request, and, turning to Aladdin's mother, he said to her, "My good woman, go home and tell thy son that I agree to the proposal thou hast made me, but that I cannot marry the princess my daughter until the end of three months. At the expiration of that time come again." Aladdin's mother, overjoyed at these words, hastened home and informed Aladdin of all the sultan had said. Aladdin thought himself the most happy of all men at hearing this news. He waited with great impatience for the expiration of the three months, counting not only the hours, days, and weeks, but every moment.

One evening when two of the three months had passed, his mother, finding no oil in the house, went out to purchase some. She found in the city a general rejoicing. The shops were decorated with foliage, silks, and gay carpets; the streets were crowded with officers, magnificently dressed, mounted on horses richly caparisoned, each attended by numerous footmen. Aladdin's mother asked the oil merchant what was the meaning of all this festivity. "Whence comest thou, my good woman?" he answered. "Know that tonight the grand vizier's son is to marry Princess Badroulboudour, the sultan's daughter!"

Aladdin's mother hastened home and related all the news to Aladdin. He was thunderstruck on hearing her words, and, hastening to his chamber, he closed the door, took the lamp in his hand, and rubbed it in the same place as before; immediately, the genie appeared and said to him, "What wouldst thou have? I am ready to obey thee as thy slave, and the slave of all those who hold that lamp in their hands, I and the other slaves of the lamp!"

"Genie," said Aladdin, "I have demanded the Princess Badroulboudour in marriage of the sultan her father. He promised her to me, only requiring three months' delay. But instead of keeping his word he has this night married her to the grand vizier's son. What I require of thee is this: As soon as the bride and bridegroom are alone bring them both hither."

"Master," said the genie, "I hear and obey!" The genie then disappeared, flew to the palace, took up the bed with the bride and bridegroom in it, returned, and set it down in Aladdin's room. The genie then took up the bridegroom, who was trembling with fear, and shut him up in a dark closet. Aladdin then approached the princess and said most respectfully, "Adorable Princess, thou art here in safety! The sultan thy father promised thee in marriage to me, and as he has now broken his word I am thus forced to carry thee away, in order to prevent thy marriage with the grand vizier's son. Sleep in peace until morning, when I will restore thee to the sultan thy father." Having thus reassured the princess, Aladdin laid himself down and slept until morning.

Aladdin had occasion the next morning to summon the genie, who appeared instantly. He brought the bridegroom from the closet and, placing him beside the princess, bid the genie transport the bed to the royal palace. The bridegroom, pale and trembling with fear, sought the sultan, related to him all that had happened, and implored him to break off his marriage with the princess. The sultan did so and commanded all rejoicings to cease.

Aladdin waited until the three months were completed, and the next day he sent his mother to the palace to remind the sultan of his promise. The sultan no sooner saw her than he remembered her business, and as he did not wish to give his daughter to a stranger, he thought to put her off by a request impossible to fulfill. "My good woman," he said, "it is true that sultans should keep their promises, and I am willing to do so as soon as thy son shall send me forty trays of massy gold, full of the same sort of jewels thou hast already made me a present of. The trays must be carried by a like number of black slaves, who shall be led by as many young and handsome white slaves magnificently dressed."

Aladdin's mother prostrated herself a second time before the sultan's throne and retired. She hastened home, laughing within herself at her son's foolish ambition. She then gave him an exact account of what the sultan had said to her and the conditions on which he consented to the marriage. Aladdin immediately retired to his room, took the lamp, and rubbed it. The genie appeared and, with the usual salutation, offered his services. "Genie," said Aladdin, "the sultan gives me the princess his daughter in marriage, but demands first forty large trays of massy gold, full of the fruits of the subterranean garden; these he expects to be carried by as many black slaves, each preceded by a young and handsome white slave, richly clothed. Go and fetch me this present as soon as possible." The genie told him that his command should be instantly obeyed and disappeared.

In a short time the genie returned with forty black slaves, each bearing upon his head a heavy tray of pure gold, full of pearls, diamonds, rubies, emeralds, and every sort of precious stone, all larger and more beautiful than those already presented to the sultan. Each tray was covered with silver tissue, richly embroidered with flowers of gold. These, together with the white slaves, quite filled the house, which was but a small one, as well as the little court before it and a small garden behind. The genie, having thus fulfilled his orders, disappeared.

Aladdin found his mother in great amazement at seeing so many people and such vast riches. "Mother," he said, "I would have you return to the palace with this present as a dowry, that the sultan may judge by the rapidity with which I fulfill his demands of the ardent and sincere love I have for the princess his daughter." And, without waiting for his mother's reply, Aladdin opened the door into the street and made the slaves walk out, each white slave followed by a black with a tray upon his head. When they were all out his mother followed the last black slave, and Aladdin shut the door and retired to his chamber, full of hopes.

The procession of slaves proceeded through the streets, and the people ran together to see so extraordinary and magnificent a spectacle. The dress of each slave was rich in stuff and decorated with jewels, and the noble air and fine shape of each was unparalleled. Their grave walk, at an equal distance from each other, the luster of the jewels curiously set in their girdles of gold, the aigrettes of precious stones in their turbans, all filled the spectators with wonder and amazement. At length they arrived at the sultan's palace, and the first slave, followed by the rest, advanced into the audience chamber, where the sultan was seated on his throne, surrounded by his viziers and the chief officers of the court. After all the slaves had entered, they formed a semicircle before the sultan's throne, the black slaves laid the golden trays upon the carpet, and all the slaves prostrated themselves, touching the ground with their foreheads. They then arose, the black slaves uncovering the trays, and stood with their arms crossed over their breasts.

In the meantime Aladdin's mother advanced to the foot of the throne and prostrated herself before the sultan. When he cast his eyes on the forty trays filled with the most precious and brilliant jewels and gazed upon the fourscore slaves so richly attired, he no longer hesitated, as the sight of such immense riches and Aladdin's quickness in satisfying his demand easily persuaded him that the young man would make a most desirable son-in-law. Therefore he said to Aladdin's mother, "Go and tell thy son that I wait with open arms to embrace him, and the more haste he makes to come and receive the princess my daughter the greater pleasure he will do me."

Aladdin's mother hastened home and informed her son of this joyful news. He, enraptured at the prospect of his marriage with the princess, retired to his chamber. Again he rubbed the lamp, and again the obedient genie appeared as before. "Genie," said Aladdin, "provide me with the richest and most magnificent raiment ever worn by a king, and with a charger that surpasses in beauty the best in the sultan's stable, with a saddle, bridle, and other caparisons worth a million gold pieces. I want also twenty slaves, richly clothed, to walk by my side and follow me, and twenty more to go before me in two ranks. Besides these, bring my mother six female slaves to attend her, as richly dressed as any of Princess Badroulboudour's, each carrying a dress fit for a sultan's wife. I want also ten thousand pieces of gold in ten purses. Go, and make haste."

As soon as Aladdin had given these orders the genie disappeared, returning instantly with the horse, the forty slaves—ten of whom each carried a purse containing ten thousand pieces of gold—and six female slaves, each carrying on her head a dress for Aladdin's mother, wrapped in silver tissue. The genie presented all these to Aladdin and disappeared.

Of the ten purses Aladdin took four, which he gave to his mother; the other six he left in the hands of the slaves who brought them, with an order to throw the gold by handfuls among the people as they journeyed to the sultan's palace. The six slaves who carried the purses he ordered likewise to march before him, three on the right hand and three on the left.

Aladdin then clad himself in his new garments, and, mounting his charger, he began the march to the sultan's palace. The streets through which he passed were instantly filled with a vast concourse of people, who rent the air with their acclamations. When he arrived at the palace everything was prepared for his reception. He was met at the gate by the grand vizier and the chief officers of the empire. The officers formed themselves into two ranks at the entrance to the audience chamber, and their chief led Aladdin to the sultan's throne.

When the sultan perceived Aladdin he was surprised at the elegance of his attire, at his fine shape and air of dignity, very different from the meanness of his mother's late appearance. Rising quickly from the throne, the sultan descended two or three steps and prevented Aladdin from throwing himself at his feet. He embraced him with demonstrations of joy, held him fast by the hand, and obliged him to sit close to the throne.

The marriage feast was begun, and the sultan ordered that the contract of marriage between the Princess Badroulboudour and Aladdin should be immediately drawn up. Then he asked Aladdin if he wished the ceremony solemnized that day. Aladdin answered, "Though great is my impatience, I beg leave to defer it until I have built a palace fit to receive the princess; therefore, I pray thee, give me a spot of ground near thy palace where I may build."

"My son," said the sultan, "take what ground thou thinkest proper." And he embraced Aladdin, who took his leave with as much politeness as though he had always lived at court.

As soon as Aladdin reached home he dismounted, retired to his own chamber, took the lamp, and called the genie as before, who in the usual manner offered him his services. "Genie," said Aladdin, "I would have thee build me as soon as possible a palace near the sultan's fit to receive my wife, the Princess Badroulboudour. Build it of porphyry, jasper, lapis lazuli, or the finest marbles of various colors. On the terraced roof build me a large hall, crowned with a dome. Let the walls be of massy gold and silver. On each of the four sides of this hall let there be six windows. Leave one window lattice unfinished, but enrich all the others with diamonds, rubies, and emeralds. I would have also a spacious garden and a treasury full of gold and silver. There must be kitchens, offices, storehouses, and stables full of the finest horses. I want also male and female slaves and equerries and grooms. Come and tell me when all is finished."

The next morning before break of day the genie presented himself to Aladdin and said, "Master, thy palace is finished. Come and see if it pleaseth thee." Aladdin had no sooner signified his consent than the genie transported him thither in an instant and led him through richly furnished apartments, and Aladdin found nothing but what was magnificent. Officers, slaves, and grooms were busy at their tasks, the treasury was piled to the ceiling with purses of gold, and the stables were filled with the finest horses in the world. When Aladdin had examined the palace from top to bottom, and particularly the hall with four and twenty windows, he found all beyond anything he had imagined. "Genie," he said, "there is only one thing wanting, which I forgot to mention. That is a carpet of fine velvet for the princess to walk upon, between my palace and the sultan's." The genie disappeared, and instantly a carpet of fine velvet stretched across the park to the door of the sultan's palace.

THE STORY OF ALADDIN, OR THE WONDERFUL LAMP

When the porters of the sultan's palace came to open the gates they were amazed to see a carpet of velvet stretching from the grand entrance across the park to a new and magnificent palace. The grand vizier, who arrived soon after the gates were opened, being no less amazed than the others, hastened to acquaint the sultan with the wonderful news. The hour of going to the audience chamber put an end to their conjectures, but scarcely were they seated before Aladdin's mother arrived, dressed in her most sumptuous garments and attended by the six female slaves, who were clad richly and magnificently. She was received at the palace with honor and introduced into Princess Badroulboudour's apartment by the chief of the eunuchs. As soon as the princess saw her she arose and saluted her, and desired her to sit beside her upon a sofa. A collation was served, and then the slaves finished dressing the princess and adorning her with the jewels that Aladdin had presented to her.

The sultan immediately ordered bands of trumpets, cymbals, drums, fifes, and hautbois, placed in different parts of the palace, to play, so that the air resounded with concerts, which inspired the city with joy. The merchants began to adorn their shops and houses with fine carpets and silks, and to prepare illuminations for the coming festival.

When night arrived the princess took tender leave of her father and, accompanied by Aladdin's mother, set out across the velvet carpet, amid the sound of trumpets and lighted by a thousand torches. Aladdin received her with joy and led her into the large, illuminated hall, where was spread a magnificent repast. The dishes were of massy gold and contained the most delicious viands, and after the supper there was a concert of the most ravishing music, accompanied by graceful dancing, performed by a number of female slaves.

The next morning Aladdin mounted and went in the midst of a large troop of slaves to the sultan's palace. The sultan received him with honors, embraced him, placed him upon the throne near him, and ordered a collation. Aladdin then said, "I entreat thee to dispense with my eating with thee this day, as I came to invite thee to partake of a repast in the princess's palace, attended by thy grand vizier and all the lords of thy court." The sultan consented with pleasure, rose up immediately and, followed by all the officers of his court, accompanied Aladdin.

The nearer the sultan approached Aladdin's palace the more he was struck with its beauty, but he was much more amazed when he entered it and could not forbear breaking out into exclamations of wonder. But when he came into the hall of the four and twenty windows enriched with diamonds, rubies, and emeralds, all large and perfect stones, he was so much surprised that he remained for some time motionless. "This palace," he exclaimed at length, "is surely one of the wonders of the world, for where in all the world besides shall we find walls built of massy gold and silver, and diamonds, pearls, and rubies adorning the windows!"

The sultan examined and admired all the windows, but on counting them he found that there were but three and twenty so richly adorned, and that the four and twentieth was left imperfect. In great astonishment he inquired the reason of this. "It was by my orders that the workmen left it thus," said Aladdin, "since I wished that thou shouldst have the glory of finishing this hall." The sultan was much pleased with this compliment and immediately ordered his jewelers and goldsmiths to complete the four and twentieth window. When the sultan returned to his palace he ordered his jewels to be brought out, and the jewelers took a great quantity, which they soon used without making any great advance in their work. They worked steadily for a whole month, but could not finish half the window, although they used all the jewels the sultan had and borrowed off the vizier.

Aladdin, who knew that all the sultan's endeavors to complete the window were in vain, sent for the jewelers and goldsmiths and commanded them not only to desist but to undo the work they had done and to return the jewels to the sultan and to the grand vizier. They undid in a few hours what they had accomplished in a month, and retired, leaving Aladdin alone in the hall. He took the lamp, which he carried about with him, and rubbed it, and the genie appeared. "Genie," said Aladdin, "I order thee to complete the four and twentieth window." And immediately the window became perfect like the others.

Scarcely was the window completed before the sultan arrived to question Aladdin as to why the jewelers and goldsmiths had desisted from their work. Aladdin received him at the door and conducted him directly to the hall, where he was amazed to see the window perfect like the rest. "My son," exclaimed the sultan, embracing him, "what a man thou art to do all this in the twinkling of an eye! Verily, the more I know thee the more I admire thee!" And the sultan returned to his palace content.

After this Aladdin lived in great state. He visited mosques, attended prayers, and returned the visits of the principal lords of the court. Every time he went out he caused two slaves, who walked by the side of his horse, to throw handfuls of money among the people as he passed through the streets and the squares; and no one came to his palace gates to ask alms but returned satisfied with his liberality, which gained him the love and blessings of the people.

Aladdin had conducted himself in this manner for several years when the African magician, who had undesignedly been the instrument of Aladdin's prosperity, became curious to know whether he had perished in the subterranean garden. He employed his magic arts to discover the truth, and he found that Aladdin, instead of having perished miserably in the cave, had made his escape and was living splendidly, and that he was in possession of the wonderful lamp and had married a princess. The magician no sooner learned this than his face became inflamed with anger, and he cried out in a rage, "This miserable tailor's son has discovered the secret and the virtue of the lamp! I will, however, prevent his enjoying it long!"

The next morning he mounted a horse, set forward, and never stopped until he arrived at the capital of China, where he alighted and took up his residence at an inn. The next day his first object was to inquire what people said of Aladdin, and, taking a walk through the town, he heard them talking of the wonderful palace and of Aladdin's marriage to the princess. He went instantly and viewed the palace from all sides, and he doubted not but that Aladdin had made use of the lamp to build it, for none but genies, the slaves of the lamp, could have performed such wonders. Piqued to the quick at Aladdin's happiness and splendor, he returned to the inn where he lodged.

As soon as he entered his chamber he ascertained by the means of his magic arts that Aladdin was absent on the hunt, and that the lamp was in the palace. He then went to a coppersmith's and bought a dozen copper lamps. These he placed in a basket, which he bought for the purpose, and with the basket on his arm he went directly to Aladdin's palace. As he approached he began crying, "Who will change old lamps for new ones? Who will change old lamps for new ones?" And all who passed by thought him a madman or a fool to offer to change new lamps for old.

Now the Princess Badroulboudour, who was in the hall with the four and twenty windows, heard a man crying, "Who will change old lamps for new ones?" Remembering the old lamp that Aladdin had laid upon a shelf before he went to the chase, the princess, who knew not the value of the lamp, commanded a eunuch to take it and make the exchange for a new lamp. The eunuch did as the princess bade him to, and the African magician, as soon as he saw the lamp, snatched it eagerly from his hand and gave him a new one in its place.

The magician then hastened away until he reached a lonely spot in the country, when he pulled the lamp out of his bosom and rubbed it. At that summons the genie appeared and said, "What wouldst thou have? I am ready to obey thee as thy slave, and the slave of all those who hold that lamp in their hands, I and the other slaves of the lamp!"

"I command thee," replied the magician, "to transport me immediately, and the palace which thou and the other slaves of the lamp have built in this city, with all the people in it, to Africa." The genie disappeared, and immediately the magician, the palace, and all its inhabitants were lifted up and transported from the capital of China and set down in Africa.

As soon as the sultan arose the next morning he went, according to his custom, to the window to contemplate and admire Aladdin's palace. When he looked that way, instead of a palace he saw an empty space. He thought that he was mistaken and looked again—in front, to the right, and to the left—and beheld only empty space where formerly had stood the palace. His amazement was so great that he remained for some time turning his eyes toward the spot, and at last, convinced that no palace stood opposite his own, he returned to his apartment and ordered his grand vizier to be sent for with expedition.

The grand vizier came with much precipitation. "Tell me," said the sultan, "what has become of Aladdin's palace."

"His palace!" exclaimed the vizier. "Is it not in its usual place?"

"Go to my window," answered the sultan, "and tell me if thou canst see it."

The grand vizier went to the window, where he was struck with no less amazement than the sultan had been. When he was well assured that there was not the least appearance of the palace he returned to the sultan.

"Well," said the sultan, "hast thou seen Aladdin's palace?"

"Alas," answered the grand vizier, "it has vanished completely! I have always thought that the edifice, which was the object of thy admiration, with all its immense riches, was only the work of magic and a magician."

At these words the sultan flew into a pasion. "Where is that imposter, that wicked wretch," cried he, "that I may have his head taken off immediately? Go thou, bring him to me loaded with chains!" The grand vizier hastened to obey these orders and commanded a detachment of horse to meet Aladdin returning from the chase and to arrest him and bring him before the sultan.

The detachment pursued their orders, and about five or six leagues from the city they met Aladdin returning from the chase. Without explanation they arrested him and fastened a heavy chain about his neck and one around his body, so that both his arms were pinioned to his sides. In this state they carried him before the sultan, who ordered him to be put to death immediately. But a multitude of people had followed Aladdin as he was led in chains through the city, and they threatened a riot if any harm should befall him. The sultan, terrified at this menace, ordered the executioner to put up his scimitar and to unbind Aladdin; at the same time he commanded the porters to declare unto the people that the sultan had pardoned him, and that they might retire.

When Aladdin found himself at liberty he turned toward the sultan and said, "I know not what I have done to lose thy favor. Wilt thou not tell me what crime I have committed?"

"Your crime, perfidious wretch!" answered the sultan. "Dost thou not know it? Where is thy palace? What has become of the princess my daughter?"

Aladdin looked from the window and, perceiving the empty spot where his palace had stood, was thrown into such confusion and amazement that he could not return one word of answer. At length, breaking the silence, he said, "I know not whither my palace has vanished. Neither can I tell thee where it may be. Grant me but forty days in which to make inquiry, and if at the end of that time I have not the success I wish, I will offer my head at the foot of thy throne, to be disposed of at thy pleasure."

"Go," said the sultan. "I give thee the forty days thou askest for, but if thou dost not find my daughter thou shalt not escape my wrath. I will find thee out in whatsoever part of the world thou mayest conceal thyself, and I will cause thy head to be struck off!"

Aladdin went out of the sultan's presence in great humiliation, filled with confusion. For three days he wandered about the city making inquiries, but all in vain: he could find no trace of the vanished palace. At last he wandered into the country, and at the approach of night came to the banks of a river, where he sat down to rest. Clasping his hands in despair, he accidentally rubbed the ring that the African magician had placed upon his finger before he went down into the subterranean abode to fetch the precious lamp. Immediately the same genie appeared whom he had seen in the cave where the magician had left him. "What wouldst thou have?" said the genie. "I am ready to obey thee as thy slave, and the slave of all those who have that ring on their fingers, I and the other slaves of the ring!"

Aladdin, agreeably surprised at an apparition he so little expected, replied, "Save my life, genie, by showing me the place where the palace I caused to be built now stands, or immediately transport it back where

"What thou commandest is not in my power," answered the genie. "I am only the slave of the ring. Thou must address thyself to the slave of the lamp."

"If that be the case," replied Aladdin, "I command thee by the power of the ring to transport me to the spot where my palace stands, in whatever part of the world it may be, and set me down under the window of the Princess Badroulboudour."

These words were no sooner out of his mouth than the genie transported him into Africa, to the middle of a large plain, where his palace stood, and, placing him exactly under the window of Princess Badroulboudour's apartment, he left him there. The next morning when the princess looked out of her window she perceived Aladdin sitting beneath it. Scarcely believing her eyes, she opened the window and motioned to him to come up. Aladdin hastened to her apartment, and it is impossible to express the joy of both at seeing each other after so cruel a separation.

After embracing and shedding tears of joy they sat down, and Aladdin said, "I beg of thee, Princess, both for thine own sake and the sultan thy father's and mine, tell me what became of an old lamp which I left upon a shelf in my robing room when I departed for the chase?"

"Alas, dear husband," answered the princess, "I was afraid our misfortune might be owing to that lamp, and what grieves me most is that I have been the cause of it!"

"Princess," replied Aladdin, "do not blame thyself, but tell me what has happened, and into whose hands it has fallen."

The princess then related how she had changed the old lamp for a new, and how the next morning she had found herself in an unknown country, which she was told was Africa by the traitor who had transported her hither by his magic arts. She also told how the wicked magician visited her daily, forcing upon her his unwelcome attentions, and how he daily tried to persuade her to take him for a husband in the place of Aladdin. "And," added the princess, "he carries the wonderful lamp carefully wrapped in his bosom, and this I can assure thee of, because he pulled it out before me and showed it to me in triumph."

"Princess," said Aladdin, "this magician is a most perfidious wretch, and I have here the means to punish him, and to deliver thee from both thine enemy and mine. To accomplish this thou must obey my direction most carefully. When the African magician comes tonight place this powder in his cup of wine. Offer him the cup, and he will esteem it so great a favor that he will not refuse, but will eagerly quaff it off. No sooner will he have drunk than thou wilt see him fall backward." After the princess had agreed to the measures proposed by Aladdin he took his leave and spent the rest of the day in the neighborhood of the palace till it was night and he might safely return by a private door.

When the evening arrived the magician came at the usual hour, and as soon as he was seated the princess handed him a cup of wine, in which the powder had been dissolved. The magician reclined his head back to show his eagerness, drank the wine to the very last drop, turned his eyes in his head, and fell to the floor dead. At a signal from the princess, Aladdin entered the hall, and he requested her to retire immediately to her own apartment.

When the princess, her women, and the eunuchs were gone out of the hall Aladdin shut the door, and, going to the magician, he opened his vest, took out the lamp, which was carefully wrapped up, unfolded it, and rubbed it, whereupon the genie immediately appeared. "Genie," said Aladdin, "transport this palace instantly to China, to the place from whence it was brought hither."

The genie bowed his head in token of obedience and disappeared. Immediately the palace was lifted up and transported to China.

The morning of the return of Aladdin's palace the sultan stood at his window absorbed in grief. He cast his eyes toward the spot where the palace had once stood, and which he now expected to find vacant, but to his surprise and amazement there stood Aladdin's palace in all its former grandeur. He immediately ordered a horse to be saddled and bridled and brought to him without delay, which he mounted that instant, thinking that he could not make haste enough to reach the palace.

Aladdin received the sultan at the foot of the great staircase, helped him to dismount, and led him into the princess's apartment. The happy father embraced her with his face bathed in tears of joy, and the princess related to him all that had happened to her from the time the palace was transported to Africa to the death of the African magician.

Aladdin ordered the magician's body to be removed, and in the meantime the sultan commanded the drums, trumpets, cymbals, and other instruments of music to announce his joy to the public, and a festival of ten days to be proclaimed for the return of the princess and Aladdin.

THE NECKLACE
OF THE BRISINGS

he night was almost over; the sky was green and gray in the east, and snowflakes were ghosting around Asgard.

Loki and only Loki saw Freyja leave Sessrumnir. Her cats slept undisturbed by the hearth; her chariot lay unused; in the half-light she set off on foot toward Bifrost. Then the Sly One's mind was riddled with curiosity; he wrapped his cloak around him and followed her.

The goddess seemed not to walk so much as drift over the ground. She glided through sleeping Asgard, her hips swaying as she made her way over the rainbow that trembled and danced around her.

The snow veils of Midgard beneath were dazzling in the rising sun. Dreaming of gold, lusting after gold, Freyja crossed a barren plain (and Loki hurried behind her). She picked her way across a twisting river, silenced by ice; she passed the base of a great glacier, chopped and bluish and dangerous; and at the end of the short hours of daylight she came to a group of huge rounded boulders, jostling under the shoulder of an overhanging cliff.

Freyja found the string-thin path that led in and down. Her eyes streamed from the cold and her tears fell as a small shower of gold in front of her. The path became a passage between rock and rock and she followed it until it led into a large dank cavern. There the goddess stood motionless; she could hear water dripping into rock pools and the movement of a small stream coursing over rock; she listened again and then she heard the sound of distant tapping, and her own heart began to beat faster, to hammer with longing.

The goddess sidled through the dismal cave. The sound of the tapping, insistent yet fitful, grew stronger and stronger with each of her footsteps. Freyja stopped, listened again, moved on; at last she stopped, eased her way down a narrow groin, and stepped into the sweltering and glowing

93

smithy of the four dwarfs, Alfrigg and Dvalin, Berling and Grerr.

For a moment Freyja was dazzled by the brilliance of the furnace. She rubbed her eyes, and then she gasped as she saw the breathtaking work of the dwarfs—a necklace, a choker of gold incised with wondrous patterns, a marvel of fluid metal twisting and weaving and writhing. She had never seen anything so beautiful nor had she so desired anything before.

The four dwarfs, meanwhile, stared at the goddess—she shimmered in the warm light of the forge. Where her cloak had fallen apart, the gold brooches and jewels on her dress gleamed and winked. They had never seen anyone so beautiful nor had they so desired anyone before.

Freyja smiled at Alfrigg and Dvalin and Berling and Grerr. "I will buy that necklace from you," she said.

The four dwarfs looked at each other. Three shook their heads and the fourth said, "It's not for sale."

"I want it," said Freyja.

The dwarfs grimaced.

"I want it. I'll pay you with silver and gold—a fair price and more than a fair price," Freyja said, her voice rising. She moved closer to the bench where the necklace was lying. "I'll bring you other rewards."

"We have enough silver," said one dwarf

"And we have enough gold," said another.

Freyja gazed at the necklace. She felt a great longing for it, a painful hunger.

Alfrigg and Dvalin and Berling and Grerr huddled in one corner of the forge. They whispered and murmured and nodded.

"What is your price?" the goddess asked.

"It belongs to us all," said one dwarf.

"So what each has must be had by the others," said the second, leering.

"There's only one price," the third said, "that will satisfy us."

The fourth dwarf looked at Freyja. "You," he said.

The goddess flushed, and her breasts began to rise and fall.

"Only if you will lie one night with each of us will this necklace ever lie around your throat," said the dwarfs.

Freyja's distaste for the dwarfs—their ugly faces, their pale noses, their misshapen bodies, and their small greedy eyes—was great, but her desire for the necklace was greater. Four nights were but four nights; the glorious necklace would adorn her for all time. The walls of the forge were red and flickering; the dwarfs' eyes were motionless.

"As you wish," murmured Freyja shamelessly. "As you wish. I am

94

in your hands for four nights, and four nights only."

Four days passed; four nights passed. Freyja kept her part of the bargain. Then the dwarfs, too, kept their word. They presented the necklace to Freyja and jostled her and fastened it around her throat. The goddess hurried out of the cavern and across the bright plains of Midgard, and her shadow followed her. She crossed over Bifrost and returned in the darkness to Sessrumnir. And under her cloak, she wore the necklace of the Brisings.

The Sly One made straight for Odin's hall. He found the Terrible One, the Father of Battle, sitting alone in Valaskjalf. His ravens perched on his shoulders and his two wolves lay beside him.

"Well?" said Odin.

Loki smirked.

"I can read your face—"

"Ah!" interrupted Loki, his eyes gleaming wickedly. "But did you see hers?"

"Whose?" Odin said.

"Did it escape you? Didn't you see it all from Hlidskjalf?"

"What?" insisted Odin.

"Where were you, Odin, when the goddess you love, the goddess you lust after, slept with four dwarfs?"

"Enough!" Odin shouted.

Loki ignored him altogether and Odin was possessed with such jealousy that he found it impossible not to listen. With unfeigned delight at shaming Freyja and angering Odin at the same time, Loki launched into his story. He left out nothing and he saw no need to add anything.

"Get that necklace for me," said Odin coldly, when Loki had at last brought Freyja home to Asgard.

Loki smiled and shook his head.

"You do nothing that is not vile," Odin cried. "You set us all at one another's throats. Now I set you at her throat: get that necklace."

The Sly One sniffed. "You know as well as I—indeed, surely far better than I—that there's no way into that hall against her wishes."

"Get that necklace!" shouted Odin. His face was contorted; his one eye was burning. "Until you get it, let me never see your face again."

Then Loki looked at the Terrible One. Odin's face was a mask now, grim and sinister. The Sly One's arrogance turned to cold fear; he recognized the danger.

THE NECKLACE OF THE BRISINGS

Then Odin's wolves got up, and so did Loki. He ran out of the hall, howling.

Later that same night, the Sly One walked across the shining snowfield to the hall Sessrumnir. Boldly he made his way up to the door. It was locked.

He drew his cloak more closely around him; he shivered as the night wind picked up snow and grazed his face with it. He felt the cold working its way into his body and into his blood.

Loki remembered Sif—her locked bedchamber, her shorn shining hair, his own lips pierced with an awl. He scowled and inspected the door again. The Shape Changer shook his head; he muttered the words and turned himself into a fly.

Sessrumnir was so well built that he was still unable to find a way into the hall—a chink between wood and plaster or plaster and turf. He buzzed around the keyhole, but that was no good; he examined the top and bottom of the door, and they were no good; he flew up to the eaves and they were no good; then he flitted to one gable end and there, at the top, right under the roof, he found an opening little larger than a needle's eye. Loki, the Shape Changer, squirmed and wriggled his way through. He was at large and inside Sessrumnir. After making sure that Freyja's daughters and serving maids were asleep, he flew to Freyja's bedside, but the sleeping goddess was wearing the necklace and its clasp lay under her neck; it was out of sight and out of reach.

So Loki changed shape again, this time becoming a flea. Then he amused himself crawling over Freyja's breast, across the necklace, and up onto one cheek. There he sat down; he gathered his strength and stung her pale skin.

Freyja started. She moaned and turned onto her side and settled again. But now the clasp of the necklace was exposed just as the Shape Changer had intended.

As soon as he was certain that Freyja was sleeping soundly once more, Loki resumed his own form. He looked swiftly around and then with light fingers released the clasp and gently drew the necklace from Freyja's throat. No thief in the nine worlds was as nimble and skillful as he. With no movement that was not necessary and without making a sound, he stole to the hall doors, slid back the bolts, turned the lock, and disappeared into the night.

Freyja did not wake until morning. And as soon as she opened her eyes she put her fingers to her throat . . . she felt the back of her neck . . .

The goddess looked around her; she leaped up and her face colored in anger. When she saw the doors of Sessrumnir were open and had not been forced, she knew that only Loki could have entered the hall, and knew that not even he would have risked such an undertaking and such a theft unless Odin himself had sanctioned it. What she did not know and could not fathom was how her secret—her greed and her guilt and her gain—had been discovered.

Freyja hurried to Valaskjalf and confronted Odin. "Where is that necklace?" she demanded. "You've debased yourself if you've had any part in this."

Odin scowled at Freyja. "Who are you," he said, "to speak of debasement? You've brought shame on yourself and shame on the gods. Out of nothing but sheer greed you sold your body to four foul dwarfs."

"Where is my necklace?" repeated Freyja. She stormed at Odin; she took his rigid arm and pressed herself against him; she wept showers of gold.

"You'll never see it again," said the Terrible One, Father of the Battle, "unless you agree to one condition. There is only one thing that will satisfy me."

Freyja looked at Odin quickly. And whatever it was that passed through her mind, she bit her tongue.

"You must stir up hatred. You must stir up war. Find two kings in Midgard and set them at each other's throats; ensure that they meet only on the battlefield, each of them supported by twenty vassal kings." The Father of Battle looked grimly at the goddess. "And you must use such charms as give new life to corpses. As soon as each warrior is chopped down, bathed in blood, he must stand up unharmed and fight again."

Freyja stared at Odin.

"Those are my conditions. Whether they wish it or not, let men rip one another to pieces."

Freyja inclined her head. "Then give me my necklace," she said.

THE SLEEPING BEAUTY

here was once a king and queen who were very sorrowful because they had no children. When at last, after a long wait, a daughter was born the king showed his delight by giving a christening feast, the likes of which had never been known before. He invited all the fairies in the land—there were seven altogether—to become the little princess's godmothers, hoping that each one would bestow a gift upon her.

After the christening all the guests returned to the palace, where a grand feast was prepared. Before each fairy was placed a splendid cover, with a spoon and knife and fork of pure gold studded with diamonds and rubies. As they were all sitting down at the table a very old fairy came into the hall. She had not been invited, because for more than fifty years she had not been heard of.

The king ordered a cover to be placed for her, but he could not give her one of gold as he had the others, for he had had only seven made. The old fairy thought herself slighted and muttered some angry threats that were overheard by one of the young fairies who chanced to sit beside her.

Thinking that some harm might be done to the pretty baby, the young fairy hid herself behind the curtains in the hall. She did this so that all the others might speak first. Then if any evil gift were bestowed upon the child she might be able to counteract it.

The six fairies now began to make their gifts to the princess. She was to grow up the fairest person in the world. She was to have a temper as sweet as that of an angel. She was to be graceful in every way. She was to sing like a nightingale, to dance like a leaf fluttering in the breeze, and she was to be able to play upon all kinds of musical instruments with perfection.

Then came the turn of the old fairy. Shaking her head spitefully, she uttered the wish that when the baby grew up she might prick her finger with a spindle and die of the wound.

At this terrible prophecy all the guests shuddered, and some of them began to weep. The parents, who till then had been so happy, were now almost beside themselves with grief. Just then the young fairy appeared from behind the curtains and said in a cheerful tone, "Your Majesties may comfort yourselves; the princess shall not die. I have not the power to change entirely the ill fortune just wished her by my ancient sister. The princess must indeed pierce her finger with a spindle, though she will not die but sink instead into a deep sleep that will last a hundred years. At the end of that time a king's son shall come and awaken her."

As soon as these words were spoken all the fairies vanished.

The king, in the hope of warding off the evil, issued a command forbidding all persons to spin, or even to have spinning wheels in their houses, on pain of instant death.

But it was in vain.

One day, when she was just fifteen years of age, the princess was left by her parents in one of the castles. Wandering about idly she came to a room at the top of a tower, where she found a very old woman—so deaf that she had never heard of the king's command—busy with her wheel.

"What are you doing, my good woman?" asked the princess.

"I'm spinning, my pretty child," was the answer.

"Ah, how charming! How do you do it? Do let me try."

She had no sooner taken the spindle than, being hasty and a little awkward, she pierced her finger with the point. Though it was but a small wound, she immediately fainted and fell to the floor. The poor old woman, thoroughly frightened, called for help, and there soon came ladies-in-waiting, who tried their best to restore the young princess. They threw water upon her face, loosened her clothing, smacked the palms of her hands, and bathed her temples; but all their efforts were in vain. There she lay, as beautiful as an angel, with the color still lingering in her lips and cheeks, but her eyes were tightly closed.

When the king and queen saw her thus they knew that all regrets were idle and that their daughter was beyond their help. This was the fulfillment of the cruel fairy's wish. But they also knew that the princess would not sleep forever, though it was not likely that they would behold her awakening. So they determined to let her sleep in peace. They sent away all the physicians and attendants, and laid her upon a bed in the finest apartment of the palace, where she slept like an angel.

THE SLEEPING BEAUTY

While this was happening the good young fairy who had saved the life of the princess by changing her sleep of death into this sleep of a hundred years was twelve thousand leagues away, in the kingdom of Matakin. As soon as she heard the news she left the kingdom immediately and arrived at the palace about an hour after in a chariot drawn by dragons. The king was rather startled by the sight, but nevertheless he went to the door and handed the fairy out of her chariot.

She sympathized with His Majesty and approved of all that he had done. Then, being a fairy of great common sense and foresight, she thought that the princess, awakening after a long sleep of one hundred years in this ancient castle, might find it irksome and awkward to find herself all alone. Accordingly, without asking anyone's permission, she waved her magic wand over everybody and everything in the palace—except the king and queen. Governesses, kitchen maids, pages, footmen, the horses in the stables, and the grooms that attended them—all received the magic touch. Even the princess's little spaniel, who had lain down beside his mistress, fell asleep in a moment. The very spits before the kitchen fire ceased turning, the fire went out, and everything became as silent as in the dead of night.

The king and queen, having kissed their daughter, went sorrowfully from the castle and gave orders that no one should come near it. The command was unnecessary, for in a quarter of an hour there grew up around the castle a wood of thorny briers so thick and close that neither beasts nor men could get through it. All that could be seen of the building was the top of the high tower where the lovely princess slept.

Many things happen in a hundred years. The king, who never had a second child, died, and his throne passed to another family. The story of the poor princess was quite forgotten, and one day the son of the reigning king when out hunting asked what wood this was and what tower it was that appeared over the tops of the trees. Nobody could give him an answer, until an old peasant was found who remembered hearing his grandfather tell his father that in this tower was a beautiful princess who was doomed to sleep there for one hundred years until awakened by the king's son, her destined bridegroom.

When the young prince heard this he determined to find out the truth for himself. He immediately leapt from his horse and began to force his way through the thick wood. This seemed as if it would be most difficult, but to his astonishment the stout branches all gave way, the ugly thorns sheathed themselves so as not to hurt him, and the brambles buried themselves in the ground to let him pass. But they closed again

103

behind him, so that he alone was able to pass that way without receiving any hurt.

The first thing he saw was enough to fill the heart of the bravest man with dread. On the ground before him were the bodies of men and horses. They appeared to be dead, but the rosy faces of the men and the goblets beside them, half-filled with wine, showed that they had gone to sleep while in the act of drinking. Then the prince entered a large court paved with marble, where there stood rows of guards presenting arms, but quite motionless, as if they had been carved out of stone. He passed through room after room, where ladies and gentlemen, all dressed in the clothes that were worn a hundred years before, were soundly sleeping. Some were sitting, and some were standing. In the corners pages were lurking, the ladies of honor were stooping over their embroidery frames or appeared to be listening very attentively to the gentlemen of the court, but all were as silent and as motionless as statues. What was most strange was that their clothes appeared as fresh and new as ever. There was not a speck of dust upon the furniture, and not a spider's web to be seen anywhere, though neither duster nor broom had been used for a hundred years.

At last the prince came to an inner chamber, where was the fairest sight his eyes had ever beheld. In an embroidered bed a young girl of surpassing beauty lay asleep. She looked as if she had only just closed her eyes. Trembling and filled with admiration, the prince approached the bed and knelt beside it. Some say he kissed her, but as nobody saw it and she never told, we can never be quite sure. Be that as it may, the end of the enchantment had come, and the princess awakened immediately. Looking at him very tenderly, she said, in a drowsy tone, "Is that you, my prince? I have waited for you very long."

Charmed with these words, and still more with the manner in which they were uttered, the prince answered that he loved her more than his life. Nevertheless he was more embarrassed than she was, for she had had plenty of time to dream of him during her long sleep of a hundred years, whereas he had never heard of her before. For a long time they sat talking together, and still they had not said half enough. The only interruption came from the princess's spaniel, who had also awakened and was very jealous because his mistress did not notice him as much as she had formerly.

Meanwhile all the attendants had had their enchantments broken, and as they were not in love they were ready to die of hunger after their fast of a hundred years. A lady of honor ventured to intimate that dinner was served, and, the prince giving the princess his arm, they at once proceeded to the great hall. There was no need for the princess to wait to dress for dinner, as she was already magnificently attired, though in a style that was somewhat out-of-date. The prince was polite enough not to tell her of this, or to point out that she was dressed exactly like his grandmother, whose portrait hung upon the palace walls.

During dinner the musicians gave a concert, and, considering that they had not touched their instruments for a hundred years, they played extremely well. They ended with a wedding march, for that very evening the marriage of the prince and princess was celebrated, and though the bride was nearly one hundred years older than the bridegroom nobody would ever have imagined it.

After a few days they left the castle and the enchanted wood, and immediately both of these vanished, never again to be beheld by mortal eyes. The princess was restored to her ancestral kingdom, but her history was kept secret. During a hundred years people had become so much wiser that they would not have believed the story if they had been told. So nothing was explained, and nobody presumed to ask any questions about her, for a prince could marry whom he pleased.

THE STORY OF POLYPHEMUS,
THE CYCLOPS

n days of yore, before the reign of mighty Zeus, a multitude of monstrous creatures were brought into existence—hundred-headed beings, giants, and the like. When at last they had all been cast from the face of the earth, only the Cyclopes were permitted to return. Before long, they were to bask in the favor of Zeus himself and become the forgers of his mighty thunderbolts.

In the beginning, there had been only three Cyclopes; soon they had multiplied to such numbers that Zeus provided them with a homeland of their own—a lush acre blessed with vineyards and cornlands that produced their fruits uncoaxed by human or Cyclopean hand, and flocks of sheep and goats that fed off the tender grasses. Here the monstrous race lived a life of ease and plenty, albeit a lawless one, for theirs was a fierce and savage nature, untempered by either morality or the restrictions of law. Strangers were heedful never to roam in this beautiful but dangerous country.

During the age in which man had learned the lesson of civilization and developed the skill to build sailing ships, a Greek prince by the name of Odysseus ventured unknowingly into the land of the Cyclopes. He was returning from the Trojan War by sea and had run his boat upon the coast of the monsters' dominion. Unbeknownst to Odysseus, dangers lay ahead of him and his crew that mocked the rigors of Troy's bloodiest battles.

Close to the spot where Odysseus had beached his boat, there was an open cave facing the sea, imposing in its loftiness. No doubt it served as home for some equally impressive creature; a sturdy fence guarded its entrance. Odysseus decided to explore the cavern with twelve of his bravest men, for they were in need of food. With them they brought a goatskin full of wine to offer the inhabitant of the cave in return for favor and kindly treatment. However, as Odysseus soon discovered, the master was not home. But there was much for a crew of sea-weary, hungry voyagers to feast their tired eyes upon: pens of fattened lambs and kids lined the walls of the cave; wooden racks displayed a marvelous variety of cheese; and fresh milk brimmed in pails.

No doubt the prosperous keeper of these goods wouldn't mind if we indulged more than our hungry eyes on his bounty, reasoned Odysseus; so the men helped themselves to the food and drink while they awaited their host's return.

Hours passed, and finally the master of the cave approached, herding his flock before him. Struck with awe and fear, the prince and his crew looked up to see a towering representative of the Cyclopean tribe, as hideous as he was huge, enter the cave and barricade its entrance with a gigantic boulder. Then, casting his single eye about the dwelling, he caught sight of Odysseus and his men, and thundered in a voice as mighty in strength as Zeus' own thunderbolts, "Identify yourselves, intruders to the house of Polyphemus. Be you traders or thieves?"

The others were struck dumb with fear; only Odysseus was made of stronger mettle. "We are shipwrecked warriors returning from the battles of Troy, and we beseech you to afford us food and shelter in the name of Zeus, god of the suppliant," answered the noble prince swiftly.

Polyphemus was equally quick to answer, and his thundering voice shook the cavern walls. "I care not for Zeus, mortal, for I am mightier than even the thunderbolt-thrower himself. It is I who am the forger of the flaming bolt, and no god holds sway over me."

And upon saying that, the Cyclops reached out and seized two of Odysseus' men, holding each firmly in his mighty fists. Then, to the horror of the onlookers, the monster broke their skulls upon the floor like wine goblets and hungrily gobbled up the spilt brains. His hunger sated, Polyphemus lay down upon the floor of the cavern and slept, leaving his captors to bemoan their cruel fate. Escape was impossible, for even if the crew could muster the courage and strength to cut down the giant, the stone blocking the entranceway was immovable, and they would be forever trapped in the cave.

Odysseus spent the long and arduous night that followed searching for a solution to their seemingly insurmountable problem, but with no success; the dawn heralded a new day of uncertainty and the death of yet two more of Odysseus' company, for the night's rest had left Polyphemus hungry for breakfast.

When the morning sun was high, the flock, desiring to graze, gathered at the mouth of the cave; Odysseus watched as the giant pushed away the great boulder from the entranceway with the ease of a farmer's wife removing an egg from a hen's nest, and herded the flock out of the cave.

As the day wore tediously on, all hope seemed to perish with the sun's dying rays. Just as the men were prepared to resign themselves to their odious fate, Odysseus thought of a plan. The prince had spied an enormous log, as large as the trunk of a mighty oak, lying near one of the goat pens. Rallying his men on, he and his crew sawed off a portion of the log and whittled it down to a sharp point on one end. Then they tempered the point in the giant's hearth till it was as strong as steel and hid the enormous weapon from view.

At dusk, Polyphemus returned to the cave and selected two more men for his evening meal. When he was through, Odysseus poured a generous portion of his wine into the giant's cup and offered it to the giant. The Cyclops was delighted with the draft and drained his cup, demanding more. Odysseus accommodated him until his keg was drained and Polyphemus had succumbed to intoxication and sleep. Taking full advantage of the monster's temporary incapacity, Odysseus and his men hauled out the sharpened log and heated its point in the hearth until it glowed as red as an ember. Calling upon the gods to imbue them with the courage required of their task, the men plunged the point into the Cyclops' eye, blinding him with a single thrust.

The cavern echoed with the giant's screams of pain; he leaped up, pulled the spike from his eye, and flailed about the cave, arms outstretched, in search of his prisoners, but to no avail, for they managed to hide themselves from his wrath. Finally Polyphemus pushed aside the great boulder and planted himself in the entranceway, hoping to lay hold of Odysseus and the crew as they attempted to sneak past him. Once again the giant had underestimated the noble warrior-prince. Odysseus instructed each of his men to secure three fleecy rams together with ropes of bark and quietly await the coming day. At that time the flock, as was its custom, would gather at the entrance to be let out, and the men could make their escape.

All came to pass just as Odysseus had foretold: early in the morning, the sightless giant pushed aside the great boulder from the mouth of the cave and allowed the herd to pass, but not before he had felt the fleecy back of each member of the flock to be certain that none of his prisoners were using the great beasts for their escape. Foolish oaf that he was, it never once occurred to him that as the sheep exited the cave three abreast, so did every last one of the remaining crew, each hidden

from the monster's notice under the ample belly of the middle sheep!

Having escaped the Cyclops at last, the men wasted no time launching their ship into the open sea. Once safely aboard and beyond reach of the giant's wrath, Odysseus gave vent to his anger and called out, "Great Polyphemus, forger of Zeus' thunderbolt, has your great strength so deserted you that you have allowed us mortal weaklings to escape you? You deserve your cruel fate, monster, for the crueler way in which you treated us, your guests!"

But Odysseus would come to regret his impetuousness, for his words so infuriated the giant that he ripped off a portion of an overhanging cliff bare-handed and hurled it toward the boat, narrowly missing the prow. The backwash, however, would have succeeded in tossing the craft back to shore had it not been for the rowing skills of the crew. When at last the prince was certain that Polyphemus could effect no destruction to his boat or crew, he ventured one last parting insult. "Be you not as deaf as you are blind, Cyclops, hear and remember this: Odysseus, victor over Troy, stole your vision, should you be asked of the culprit."

But the once mighty Polyphemus was powerless to exact retribution and could only sit dejectedly by the shore, his great eye orbiting, sightless, in its socket.

THE PIED PIPER

A very long time ago the town of Hamel in Germany was invaded by bands of rats, the likes of which had never been seen before nor ever will be again.

They were great black creatures that ran boldly in broad daylight through the streets, and swarmed so, all over the houses, that people at last could not put their hands or feet down anywhere without touching one. When dressing in the morning they found them in their breeches and petticoats, in their pockets and in their boots; and when they wanted a morsel to eat, the voracious horde had swept away everything from cellar to garret. The night was even worse. As soon as the lights were out, these untiring nibblers set to work. And everywhere—in the ceilings, in the floors, in the cupboards, at the doors—there was a chase and a rummage, and so furious a noise of gimlets, pincers, and saws, that a deaf man could not have rested for one hour together.

Neither cats nor dogs, neither poison nor traps, neither prayers nor candles burnt to all the saints—nothing would do any good. The more they killed the more came. And the inhabitants of Hamel began to go to the dogs (not that *they* were of much use), when one Friday there arrived in the town a man with a queer face, who played the bagpipes and sang this refrain:

> Qui vivra verra:
> Le voilà,
> Le preneur des rats.

He was a great gawky fellow, dry and bronzed, with a crooked nose, a long rattail mustache, and two great yellow piercing and mocking eyes under a large felt hat set off by a scarlet cock's feather. He was dressed in a green jacket with a leather belt and red breeches, and on his feet were sandals fastened by thongs passed around his legs in the gypsy fashion.

That is how he may be seen to this day, painted on a window of the cathedral of Hamel.

He stopped in the great marketplace before the town hall, turned his back on the church, and went on with his music, singing:

> Who lives shall see:
> This is he,
> The ratcatcher.

The town council had just assembled to consider once more this plague of Egypt, from which no one could save the town.

The stranger sent word to the counselors that, if they would make it worth his while, he would rid them of all their rats before night, down to the very last.

"Then he is a sorcerer!" cried the citizens with one voice, "We must beware of him."

The town counselor, who was considered clever, reassured them.

He said: "Sorcerer or no, if this bagpiper speaks the truth, it was he who sent us this horrible vermin that he wants to rid us of today for money. Well, we must learn to catch the devil in his own snares. You leave it to me."

"Leave it to the town counselor," said the citizens to one another.

And the stranger was brought before them.

"Before night," said he, "I shall have despatched all the rats in Hamel if you will but pay me a *gros* a head."

"A *gros* a head!" cried the citizens. "But that will come to millions of florins!"

The town counselor simply shrugged his shoulders and said to the stranger:

"A bargain! To work; the rats will be paid one *gros* a head as you ask."

The bagpiper announced that he would operate that very evening when the moon rose. He added that the inhabitants should at that hour leave the streets free and content themselves with looking out of their windows at what was passing, and that it would be a pleasant spectacle. When the people of Hamel heard of the bargain, they, too, exclaimed: "A *gros* a head! But this will cost us a deal of money!"

"Leave it to the town counselor," said the town council maliciously.

THE PIED PIPER

And the good people of Hamel repeated with their counselors, "Leave it to the town counselor."

Toward nine at night the bagpiper reappeared at the marketplace. He turned, as at first, his back to the church, and the moment the moon rose on the horizon, the bagpipes resounded: "Trarira, trari!"

It was first a slow, caressing sound, then more and more lively and urgent, and so sonorous and piercing that it penetrated as far as the farthest alleys and retreats of the town.

Soon, from the bottoms of the cellars, the tops of the garrets, from under all the furniture, from all the nooks and corners of the houses, out came the rats, searching for the doors, flinging themselves into the street, and trip, trip, trip, running in file toward the front of the town hall, so squeezed together that they covered the pavement like the waves of a flood torrent.

When the square was quite full, the bagpiper faced about and, still playing briskly, turned toward the river that runs at the foot of the walls of Hamel.

Arrived there, he turned around; the rats were following.

"Hop! Hop!" he cried, pointing with his finger to the middle of the stream, where the water whirled and was drawn down as if through a funnel. And hop! hop! Without hesitating, the rats took the leap, swam straight to the funnel, plunged in headfirst, and disappeared.

The plunging continued thus without ceasing till midnight.

At last, dragging himself with difficulty, came a big rat, white with age; he stopped on the bank.

He was the king of the band.

"Are they all there, friend Blanchet?" asked the bagpiper.

"They are all there," replied friend Blanchet.

"And how many were they?"

"Nine hundred and ninety thousand, nine hundred and ninety-nine."

"Well reckoned?"

"Well reckoned."

"Then go and join them, old sire, and *au revoir.*"

Then the old white rat sprang in his turn into the river, swam to the whirlpool, and disappeared.

When the bagpiper had thus concluded his business he went to bed at his inn. And for the first time in three months the people of Hamel slept quietly through the night.

The next morning, promptly at nine o'clock, the bagpiper returned to the town hall, where the town council awaited his arrival.

THE PIED PIPER

"All your rats took a jump into the river yesterday," said he to the counselors, "and I guarantee that not one of them will come back. There were nine hundred and ninety thousand, nine hundred and ninety-nine, at one *gros* a head. Reckon!"

"Let us reckon the heads first. One *gros* a head is one head the *gros*. Where are the heads?"

The ratcatcher did not expect this treacherous stroke. He paled with anger and his eyes flashed fire.

"The heads!" cried he. "If you care about them, go and find them in the river."

"So," replied the town counselor, "you refuse to hold to the terms of your agreement? We ourselves could refuse you all payment. But you have been of use to us, and we will not let you go without recompense." And he offered him fifty crowns.

"Keep your recompense for yourself," replied the ratcatcher proudly. "If you do not pay me, I will be paid by your heirs."

Thereupon he pulled his hat down over his eyes, went hastily out of the hall, and left the town without speaking to a soul.

When the Hamel people heard how the affair had ended they rubbed their hands, and with no more scruple than their town counselor, they laughed over the ratcatcher, who, they said, was caught in his own trap. But what made them laugh above all was his threat of getting himself paid by their heirs. Ha! They wished that they only had such creditors for the rest of their lives.

Next day, which was a Sunday, they all went gaily to church, thinking that after Mass they would at last be able to eat some good thing that the rats had not tasted before them.

They never suspected the terrible surprise that awaited them on their return home. No children anywhere; they had all disappeared!

"Our children! Where are our poor children?" was the cry that was soon heard in all the streets.

Then through the east door of the town came three little boys, who cried and wept, and this is what they told:

While the parents were at church, a wonderful music had resounded. Soon all the little boys and all the little girls that had been left at home had gone out, attracted by the magic sounds, and had rushed to the great marketplace. There they found the ratcatcher playing his bagpipes at the same spot as the evening before. Then the stranger had begun to walk quickly, and they had followed, running, singing, and dancing, to the sound of the music, as far as the foot of the mountain that one sees on entering Hamel. At their approach the mountain had opened a little, and the bagpiper had gone in with them, after which it had closed again. Only the three little ones who told the adventure had remained outside, as if by a miracle. One was bandy-legged and could not run fast enough; the other, who had left the house in haste, one foot shod, the other bare, had hurt himself against a big stone and could not walk without difficulty; the third had arrived in time, but in hurrying to go in with the others he had struck violently against the wall of the mountain and had fallen backward at the moment it had closed upon his comrades.

At this story the parents redoubled their lamentations. They ran with pikes and mattocks to the mountain, and searched till evening to find the opening by which their children had disappeared, without being able to find it. At last, the night falling, they returned desolate to Hamel.

But the most unhappy of all was the town counselor, for he lost three little boys and two pretty little girls, and to crown it all, the people of Hamel overwhelmed him with reproaches, forgetting that the evening before they had all agreed with him.

What had become of all these unfortunate children?

The parents always hoped they were not dead, and that the ratcatcher, who certainly must have come out of the mountain, would have taken them with him to his country. That is why for several years they sent in search of them to different countries, but no one ever came upon a trace of the poor little ones.

It was not until much later that anything was to be heard of them.

About one hundred and fifty years after the event, when there was no longer one left of the fathers, mothers, brothers, or sisters of that day, there arrived one evening in Hamel some merchants of Bremen returning from the east, who asked to speak with the citizens. They told that they, in crossing Hungary, had sojourned in a mountainous country called Transylvania, where the inhabitants only spoke German, while all around them nothing was spoken but Hungarian. These people also declared that they came from Germany, but they did not know how they chanced to be in this strange country. "Now," said the merchants of Bremen, "these Germans cannot be other than the descendants of the lost children of Hamel."

The people of Hamel did not doubt it; and since that day they regard it as certain that the Transylvanians of Hungary are their countryfolk, whose ancestors, as children, were brought there by the ratcatcher. There are more difficult things to believe than that.

BEAUTY
AND THE BEAST

here was once a very rich merchant who had six children, three boys and three girls, for whose education he very wisely spared no expense. The three daughters were all handsome, but the youngest was so particularly beautiful that in her childhood everyone called her Beauty. Being equally lovely when she was grown-up, nobody called her by any other name, which made her sisters very jealous of her. This youngest daughter was not only more handsome than her sisters but also was better tempered. The others were vain of their wealth and position. They gave themselves a thousand airs and refused to visit other merchants' daughters; nor would they condescend to be seen except with persons of quality. They went every day to balls, plays, and public places, and always made sport of their youngest sister, who often spent her leisure in reading or other useful work. As it was well known that these young ladies would have large fortunes, many great merchants wished to get them for wives; but the two eldest always answered that, for their parts, they had no thought of marrying anyone below a duke or an earl at least. Beauty had quite as many offers as her sisters, but she always answered, with the greatest civility, that though she was much obliged to her lovers she would rather live some years longer with her father, as she thought herself too young to marry.

It happened that by some unlucky accident the merchant suddenly lost all his fortune and had nothing left but a small cottage in the country. Upon this he said to his daughters, while the tears ran down his cheeks, "My children, we must now go and dwell in the cottage, and try to get a living by labor, for we have no other means of support."

The two eldest replied that they did not know how to work and would not leave town, for they had lovers enough who would be glad to marry them, though they had no longer any fortune. But in this they were mistaken, for when the lovers heard what had happened they said that as the girls were so proud and ill-tempered they were not sorry at all to see their pride brought down. They could now show off to their cows and sheep. But everybody pitied poor Beauty because she was so sweet-tempered and kind to all, and several gentlemen offered to marry her, though she had not a penny; but Beauty still refused and said she could not think of leaving her poor father in this trouble. At first Beauty could not help sometimes crying in secret for the hardships she was now obliged to suffer; but in a very short time she said to herself, All the crying in the world will do me no good, so I will try to be happy without a fortune.

When they had removed to their cottage the merchant and his three sons employed themselves in ploughing and sowing the fields and working in the garden. Beauty also did her part, for she rose by four o'clock every morning, lighted the fires, cleaned the house, and got ready the breakfast for the whole family. At first she found all this very hard; but she soon grew quite used to it and thought it no hardship. Indeed, the work greatly benefited her health and made her more beautiful still, and when she had done all that was necessary she used to amuse herself with reading, playing her music, or singing while she spun. But her two sisters were at a loss what to do to pass the time away. They had their breakfast in bed and did not rise till ten o'clock. Then they commonly walked out but always found themselves very soon tired, when they would often sit down under a shady tree and grieve for the loss of their carriage and fine clothes, saying to each other, "What a mean-spirited, poor, stupid creature our young sister is to be so content with this low way of life!" But their father thought differently, and loved and admired his youngest child more than ever.

After they had lived in this manner about a year, the merchant received a letter that informed him that one of his richest ships, which he thought was lost, had just come into port. This news made the two eldest sisters almost mad with joy, for they thought they would now leave the cottage and have all their finery again. When they found that their father must take a journey to the ship, the two eldest begged that he not fail to bring them back some new gowns, caps, rings, and all sorts of trinkets. But Beauty asked for nothing; for she thought in herself that all the ship was worth would hardly buy everything her sisters wished for. "Beauty," said the merchant, "how comes it that you ask for nothing? What can I bring you, my child?"

"Since you are so kind as to think of me, dear Father," she answered, "I should be so very glad if you would bring me a rose, for we have none in our garden and of all the flowers, I love roses the best."

Now Beauty did not indeed wish for a rose, nor anything else, but she only said this that she might not affront her sisters; otherwise they would have said she wanted her father to praise her for desiring nothing.

The merchant took his leave of them and set out on his journey. But when he got to the ship some persons went to law with him about the cargo, and after a deal of trouble and several months' delay he started back to his cottage as poor as he had left it. When he was within thirty miles of his home, in spite of the joy he felt at again meeting his children, he could not help thinking of the presents he had promised to bring them, particularly of the rose for Beauty, which, as it was now midwinter, he could by no means have found for her. It rained hard, and then it began to snow, and before long he had lost his way.

Night came on, and he feared he would die of cold and hunger or be torn to pieces by the wolves that he heard howling around him. All at once he cast his eyes toward a long avenue and saw at the end a light, but it seemed a great way off. He made the best of his way toward it and found that it came from a splendid palace, the windows of which were all blazing with light. It had great bronze gates, standing wide open, and fine courtyards, through which the merchant passed; but not a living soul was to be seen. There were stables, too, which his poor, starved horse entered at once, making a good meal of oats and hay. His master then tied him up and walked toward the entrance hall, but still without seeing a single creature. He went on to a large dining parlor, where he found a good fire and a table covered with some very appetizing dishes, but only one plate with a knife and fork. As the snow and rain had wetted him to the skin, he went up to the fire to dry himself. I hope, said he to himself, the master of the house or his servants will excuse me, for it surely will not be long now before I see them. He waited some time, but still nobody came; at last the clock struck eleven, and the merchant, being quite faint for the want of food, helped himself to a chicken and to a few glasses of wine, all the time trembling with fear. He sat till the clock struck twelve, and then, taking courage, he began to think he might as well look about him, so he opened a door at the end of the hall and went through it into a very grand room, in which there was a fine bed; and as he was feeling very weary, he shut the door, took off his clothes, and got into it.

It was ten o'clock in the morning before he awoke, when he was amazed to see a handsome new suit of clothes laid ready for him, instead of his own, which were all torn and spoiled. To be sure, said he to himself, this place belongs to some good fairy who has taken pity on my ill luck. He looked out of the window, and though far away there were the snow-covered hills and the wintry wood where he had lost himself the night before within the palace grounds, he saw the most charming arbors covered with all kinds of summer flowers blooming in the sunshine. Returning to the hall where he had supped, he found a breakfast table, ready prepared. "Indeed, my good fairy," said the merchant aloud, "I am vastly obliged to you for your kind care of me." He then made a hearty breakfast, took his hat, and was going to the stable to pay his horse a visit; but as he passed under one of the arbors, which was loaded with roses, he thought of what Beauty had asked him to bring back to her, and so he took a bunch of roses to carry home. At that same moment he heard a loud noise and saw coming toward him a creature so frightful to look at that he was ready to faint with fear.

"Ungrateful man!" said the Beast in a terrible voice. "I have saved your life by admitting you into my palace, and in return you steal my roses, which I value more than anything I possess. But you shall atone for your fault: you shall die in a quarter of an hour."

The merchant fell on his knees and, clasping his hands, said, "Sir, I humbly beg your pardon. I did not think it would offend you to gather a rose for one of my daughters, who had entreated me to bring her one home. Do not kill me, my lord!"

"I am not a lord, but a beast," replied the monster. "I hate false compliments, so do not fancy that you can coax me by any such ways. You tell me that you have daughters; now I will suffer you to escape if one of them will come and die in your stead. If not, promise that you will yourself return in three months, to be dealt with as I may choose."

The tenderhearted merchant had no thoughts of letting any one of his daughters die for his sake; but he knew that if he seemed to accept the Beast's terms he should at least have the pleasure of seeing them once again. So he gave his promise and was told he might then set off as soon as he liked. "But," said the Beast, "I do not wish you to go back empty-handed. Go to the room you slept in and you will find a chest there; fill it with whatsoever you like best, and I will have it taken to your own house for you."

When the Beast had said this he went away. The good merchant, left to himself, began to consider that as he must die—for he had no thought of breaking a promise, even one made to a monster—he might as well have the comfort of leaving his children provided for. He returned to the room he had slept in and found there heaps of gold pieces lying about. He filled the chest with them to the very brim, locked it, and, mounting his horse, left the palace and the garden full of flowers as sorrowful as he had been glad when he first beheld it.

The horse took a path across the snowy forest of his own accord, and in a few hours they reached the merchant's house. His children came running to meet him, but, instead of kissing them with joy, he could not help weeping as he looked at them. He held in his hand the bunch of roses, which he gave to Beauty, saying, "Take these roses, Beauty; but little do you think how dear they have cost your poor father." Then he gave them an account of all that he had seen or heard in the palace of the Beast.

The two eldest sisters now began to shed tears and to lay the blame upon Beauty, who, they said, would be the cause of her father's death. "See," said they, "what happens from the pride of the little wretch. Why did she not ask for such things as we did? But of course, she could not be like other people, and though she will be the cause of her father's death, yet she does not shed a tear."

"It would be useless," replied Beauty, "for my father shall not die. As the Beast will accept one of his daughters, I will give myself up, and be only too happy to prove my love for the best of fathers."

"No, sister," said the three brothers with one voice, "that cannot be; we will go in search of this monster, and either he or ourselves shall perish."

"Do not hope to kill him," said the merchant. "His power is far too great. But Beauty's young life shall not be sacrificed. I am old, and cannot expect to live much longer, so I shall but give up a few years of my life, and shall only grieve for the sake of my children."

"Never, Father!" cried Beauty. "If you go back to the palace, you cannot hinder my going after you. Though young, I am not overfond of life; and I would much rather be eaten up by the monster than die of grief for your loss."

The merchant in vain tried to reason with Beauty, who still obstinately kept to her purpose. This, in truth, made her two sisters glad, for they were jealous of her because everybody loved her.

The merchant was so grieved at the thought of losing his child that he never once thought of the chest filled with gold; but at night, to his great surprise, he found it standing by his bedside. He said nothing about his riches to his eldest daughters, for he knew very well it would at once make them want to return to town; but he told Beauty his secret. She then said that while he was away two gentlemen had been on a visit at their cottage and had fallen in love with her two sisters. She entreated her father to marry them without delay, for she was so sweet-natured she only wished them to be happy.

Three months went by, only too fast, and then the merchant and Beauty got ready to set out for the palace of the Beast. Upon this the two sisters rubbed their eyes with an onion, to make believe they were crying, but both the merchant and his sons cried in earnest. Only Beauty shed no tears. They reached the palace in a very few hours, and the horse, without bidding, went into the same stable as before. The merchant and Beauty walked toward the large hall, where they found a table covered with every dainty and two plates laid ready. The merchant had very little appetite; but Beauty, that she might the better hide her grief, placed herself at the table and helped her father. She then began to eat herself and thought all the time that to be sure the Beast had a mind to fatten her before he ate her up, since he had provided such good cheer for her. When they had done their supper they heard a great noise, and the good old man began to bid his poor child farewell, for he knew it was the Beast coming to them. When Beauty first saw that frightful form she was very much terrified but tried to hide her fear. The creature walked up to her and eyed her all over, then asked her in a dreadful voice if she had come quite of her own accord.

"Yes," said Beauty.

"Then you are a good girl, and I am very much obliged to you."

This was such an astonishingly civil answer that Beauty's courage rose; but it sank again when the Beast, addressing the merchant, desired him to leave the palace next morning and never return to it again. "And so good night, merchant. And good night, Beauty."

"Good night, Beast," she answered as the monster shuffled out of the room.

"Ah, my dear child," said the merchant, kissing his daughter, "I am half-dead already at the thought of leaving you with this dreadful Beast; you shall go back and let me stay in your place."

"No," said Beauty boldly, "I will never agree to that; you must go home tomorrow morning."

They then wished each other good night and went to bed, both of them thinking they should not be able to close their eyes; but they immediately fell into a deep sleep and did not wake till morning. Beauty dreamt that a lady came up to her and said, "I am very pleased, Beauty, that you have been willing to give your life to save that of your father. Do not be afraid; you shall not go without a reward."

As soon as Beauty awoke she told her father this dream; but though it gave him some comfort it was a long time before he could be persuaded to leave the palace. At last Beauty succeeded in getting him safely away.

When her father was out of sight poor Beauty began to weep sorely; still, having naturally a courageous spirit, she soon resolved not to make her sad case still worse by useless sorrow, but to wait and be patient. She walked through the rooms of the palace, and the elegance of every part of it charmed her.

But imagine her surprise when she came to a door on which was written BEAUTY'S ROOM! When she opened it her eyes were dazzled by the splendor and taste of the apartment. What made her wonder more than all the rest was a large library filled with books, a harpsichord, and many pieces of music. "The Beast surely does not mean to eat me up immediately," said she aloud, "since he takes care I shall not be at a loss how to amuse myself." She opened the library and saw these verses written in letters of gold on the back of one of the books:

> Beauteous lady, dry your tears;
> Here's no cause for sighs or fears.
> Command as freely as you may,
> For you command, and I obey."

"Alas," said she, sighing, "I wish I could only command a sight of my poor father and know what he is doing at this moment." Just then, by chance, she cast her eyes on a looking glass that stood near her, and in it she saw a picture of her old home and her father riding mournfully up to the door. Her sisters came out to meet him, and although they tried to look sorry it was easy to see that in their hearts they were very glad. In a short time all this picture disappeared, but it caused Beauty to think that the Beast, besides being very powerful, was also very kind. About the middle of the day she found a table laid ready for her, and sweet music was played all the time she was dining, although she could not see anybody. But at supper, when she was going to seat herself at table, she heard the noise of the Beast and could not help trembling with fear.

"Beauty," said he, "will you give me leave to see you sup?"

"That is as you please," answered she, very much afraid.

"Not in the least," said the Beast. "You alone command in this place. If you like not my company, you need only say so, and I will leave you this moment. But tell me, Beauty, do you not think me very ugly?"

"Why, yes," she said, "for I cannot tell a falsehood; but then I think you are very good."

"Am I?" sadly replied the Beast. "Yet, besides being ugly, I am also very stupid; I know well enough that I am but a beast."

"Very stupid people," said Beauty, "are never aware of it themselves."

At this kindly speech the Beast looked pleased and replied, not without an awkward sort of politeness, "Pray do not let me detain you from supper, and be sure that you are well served. All you see is your own, and I should be deeply grieved if you wanted for anything."

"You are very kind—so kind that I almost forgot you are so ugly," Beauty said earnestly.

"Ah, yes!" answered the Beast with a great sigh. "I hope I am good-tempered, but still I am only a monster."

"There is many a monster who wears the form of a man. It is better of the two to have the heart of a man and the form of a monster."

"I would thank you, Beauty, for this speech, but I am too stupid to say anything that would please you," returned the Beast in a melancholy voice. Altogether he seemed so gentle and so unhappy that Beauty, who had the tenderest heart in the world, felt her fear of him gradually vanish.

She ate her supper with a good appetite and talked in her own sensible and charming way, till at last, when the Beast rose to depart, he terrified her more than ever by saying abruptly, in his gruff voice, "Beauty, will you marry me?"

Now Beauty, frightened as she was, would speak only the exact truth: her father had told her that the Beast liked only to have the truth spoken to him. So she answered in a very firm tone, "No, Beast."

He did not go into a passion or do anything but sigh deeply and depart.

When Beauty found herself alone she began to feel pity for the poor Beast. "Oh," said she, "what a sad thing it is that he should be so very frightful, since he is so good-tempered!"

Beauty lived three months in this palace very well pleased. The Beast came to see her every night and talked with her while she supped; and though what he said was not very clever, yet she saw in him every day some new goodness. So, instead of dreading the time of his coming, she soon began continually looking at her watch, to see if it were nine o'clock, for that was the hour when he never failed to visit her. One thing only vexed her, which was that every night before he went away he always made it a rule to ask her if she would be his wife and seemed very much grieved when she firmly answered, "No."

At last, one night, she said to him, "You wound me greatly, Beast, by forcing me to refuse you so often. I wish I could take such a liking to you as to agree to marry you; but I must tell you plainly that I do not think it will ever happen. I shall always be your friend; so try to let that content you."

"I must," the Beast said with a sigh, "for I know well enough how frightful I am; but I love you better than myself. Yet I think I am very lucky in your being pleased to stay with me. Now promise me, Beauty, that you will never leave me."

Beauty would almost have agreed to this, so sorry was she for him, but she had that day seen in her magic glass, which she looked at constantly, that her father was dying of grief for her sake.

"Alas," she said, "I long so much to see my father that if you do not give me leave to visit him it shall break my heart."

"I would rather break mine, Beauty," answered the Beast. "I will send you to your father's cottage: you shall stay there and your poor Beast shall die of sorrow."

"No," said Beauty, crying, "I love you too well to be the cause of your death; I promise to return in a week. You have shown me that my sisters are married and my brothers are gone for soldiers, so that my father is left all alone. Let me stay a week with him."

"You shall find yourself with him tomorrow morning," replied the Beast. "But mind, do not forget your promise. When you wish to return you have nothing to do but to put your ring on a table when you go to bed. Good-bye, Beauty!" The Beast sighed as he said these words, and Beauty went to bed very sorry to see him so much grieved. When she awoke in the morning she found herself in her father's cottage. She rang a bell that was at her bedside, and a servant entered; but as soon as she saw Beauty the woman gave a loud shriek, upon which the merchant ran upstairs. When he beheld his daughter he ran to her and kissed her a hundred times. At last Beauty began to remember that she had brought no clothes with her to put on; but the servant told her she had just found in the next room a large chest full of dresses, trimmed all over with gold and adorned with precious stones.

Beauty, in her own mind, thanked the Beast for his kindness and put on the plainest gown she could find among them all. She then desired the servant to lay the rest aside, for she intended to give them to her sisters; but as soon as she had spoken these words the chest was gone out of sight in a moment. Her father then suggested that perhaps the Beast chose for her to keep them all for herself; and as soon as he had said this they saw the chest standing again in the same place. While Beauty was dressing herself a servant brought word to her that her sisters were come with their husbands to pay her a visit. They both lived unhappily with the gentlemen they had married. The husband of the eldest was very handsome, but was so proud of this that he thought of nothing else from morning till night, and did not care a pin for the beauty of his wife. The second had married a man of great learning; but he made no use of it, except to torment and affront all his friends, and his wife more than any of them. The two sisters were ready to burst with spite when they saw Beauty dressed like a princess and looking so very charming. All the kindness that she showed them was of no use, for they were vexed more than ever when she told them how happy she lived at the palace of the Beast. The spiteful creatures went by themselves into the garden, where they cried to think of her good fortune.

"Why should the little wretch be better off than we?" said they. "We are much handsomer than she is."

"Sister," said the eldest, "a thought has just come into my head: Let us try to keep her here longer than the week for which the Beast gave her leave; and then he will be so angry that perhaps when she goes back to him he will eat her up in a moment."

"That is a good idea," answered the other. "But to do this we must pretend to be very kind."

They then went to join her in the cottage, where they showed her so much false love that Beauty could not help crying for joy.

When the week was ended the two sisters began to pretend such grief at the thought of her leaving them that she agreed to stay a week more; but all that time Beauty could not help fretting for the sorrow that she knew her absence would give her poor Beast, for she tenderly loved him, and much wished for his company again. Among all the grand and clever people she saw she found nobody who was half so sensible, so affectionate, so thoughtful, or so kind. The tenth night of her being at the cottage she dreamed she was in the garden of the palace, that the Beast lay dying on a grass plot and with his last breath put her in mind of her promise, laying his death to her forsaking him. Beauty awoke in a great fright and burst into tears. "Am I not wicked," said she, "to behave so ill to a Beast who has shown me so much kindness? Why do I not marry him? I am sure I should be happier with him than my sisters are with their husbands. He shall not be wretched any longer on my account, else I shall blame myself all the rest of my life."

She then rose, put her ring on the table, got into bed again, and soon fell asleep. In the morning she with joy found herself in the palace of the Beast. She dressed herself very carefully, that she might please

him the better, and thought she had never known a day to pass away so slowly. At last the clock struck nine, but the Beast did not come. Beauty, dreading lest she might truly have caused his death, ran from room to room, calling out, "Beast, dear Beast." But there was no answer. At last she remembered her dream, rushed to the grass plot, and there saw him lying apparently dead beside the fountain. Forgetting all his ugliness, she threw herself upon him, and, finding his heart still beating, she fetched some water and sprinkled it over him, weeping and sobbing the while.

The Beast opened his eyes. "You forgot your promise, Beauty, and so I determined to die, for I could not live without you. I have starved myself to death, but I shall die content, since I have seen your face once more."

"No, dear Beast," cried Beauty passionately, "you shall not die; you shall live to be my husband. I thought it was only friendship I felt for you, but now I know it is love."

The moment Beauty had spoken these words the palace was suddenly lighted up, and all kinds of rejoicings were heard around them; she noticed none of this, but continued to hang over her dear Beast with the utmost tenderness. At last, unable to restrain herself, she dropped her head over her hands, covered her eyes, and cried for joy; and when she looked up again the Beast was gone. In his place she saw at her feet a handsome, graceful young prince, who thanked her with the tenderest expressions for having freed him from enchantment.

"But where is my poor Beast? I only want him, and nobody else," sobbed Beauty.

"I am he," replied the prince. "A wicked fairy condemned me to this form, and forbade me to show that I had any wit or sense till a beautiful lady should consent to marry me. You alone, dearest Beauty, judged me neither by my looks nor by my talents, but by my heart alone. Take it, then, and all that I have besides, for all is yours."

Beauty, full of surprise but very happy, suffered the prince to lead her to his palace, where she found her father and sisters, who had been brought there by the fairy lady whom she had seen in a dream the first night she came.

"Beauty," said the fairy, "you have chosen well, and you have your reward, for a true heart is better than either good looks or clever brains. As for you, ladies"—and she turned to the two elder sisters—"I know all your ill deeds, but I have no worse punishment for you than to see your sister happy. You shall stand as statues at the door of her palace, and when you repent of and have amended your faults you shall become women again. But, to tell you the truth, I very much fear you will remain statues forever."

JACK
THE GIANT-KILLER

I n the reign of King Arthur there lived in the county of Cornwall a worthy farmer, who had an only son named Jack.

Jack was a boy of a bold temper; he took pleasure in hearing or reading stories of wizards, conjurers, giants, and fairies. He was a leader in all the sports of youth, and hardly anyone could equal him at wrestling; or if he met with a match for himself in strength, his skill and cunning always made him the victor.

In those days there lived on St. Michael's Mount, off the coast of Cornwall, a huge giant. He was eighteen feet high and three yards around; and his fierce and savage looks were the terror of all his neighbors. He dwelt in a gloomy cavern on the very top of the mountain, and used to wade over to the mainland in search of his prey. When he came near, the people left their houses; and, after he had glutted his appetite upon their cattle, he would throw half a dozen oxen upon his back, tie as many sheep and hogs around his waist like a bunch of candles, and march back home. The giant had done this for many years, and all Cornwall was greatly hurt by his thefts, when Jack boldly resolved to destroy him.

Early in a long winter's evening Jack took a horn, a shovel, a pickax, and a dark lantern, and went over to St. Michael's Mount. There he fell to work at once, and before morning he had dug a pit twenty-two feet deep and almost as many feet broad. He covered it over with sticks and straw, and strewed some earth over them to make it look just like solid ground. He then put his horn to his mouth and blew such a loud and long tantivy that the giant awoke and came toward Jack, roaring like thunder, "You saucy villain, you shall pay dearly for breaking my rest. I will broil you whole for breakfast." He had scarcely spoken these words when he tumbled headlong into the pit, and his fall shook the very mountain.

GREG HILDEBRANDT

"Oho, giant!" said Jack. "Where are you now? Have you found your way so soon into Lob's Pound? Will nothing serve you now for breakfast this cold morning but broiling poor Jack?"

The giant now tried to rise, but Jack struck him a blow on the crown of the head with his pickax, which killed him at once.

Jack now made haste back, to rejoice his friends with the news of the giant's death. When the justices of Cornwall heard of this valiant action they sent for Jack and declared that he should always be called Jack the Giant-Killer; and they also gave him a sword and belt, upon which was written, in letters of gold:

> This is the valiant Cornishman
> Who slew the giant Cormoran.

The news of Jack's victory soon spread over all the west of England. Another giant, called Blunderbore, vowed to have revenge on Jack, if it should ever be his fortune to get him into his power.

Now, Blunderbore kept an enchanted castle in the midst of a lonely wood; and about four months after the death of Cormoran, as Jack was taking a journey into Wales, he passed through this wood. He was very weary, so he sat down to rest by the side of a pleasant fountain, and there he fell into a deep sleep. The giant came to the fountain for water just at this time and found Jack there. As the lines on Jack's belt showed who he was, the giant lifted him gently onto his shoulder, to carry him to his castle; but, as he passed through the thicket, the rustling of the leaves awakened Jack. He was sadly afraid when he found himself in the clutches of Blunderbore; yet this was nothing compared to his fright soon after. For when they reached the castle he beheld the floor covered all over with the bones of men and women. The giant quickly locked Jack up, while he went to fetch another giant, who lived in the same wood, to come to dinner with him. While he was away Jack heard dreadful shrieks, groans, and cries from many parts of the castle; and soon after he heard a mournful voice repeat these lines:

> Haste, valiant stranger, haste away,
> Lest you become the giant's prey.
> On his return he'll bring another,
> Still more savage than his brother.

Then Jack, looking out of the window, saw the two giants coming along arm in arm. This window was right over the gates of the castle. Now, thought Jack, either my death or freedom is at hand.

There were two strong ropes in the room. Jack made a large noose out of them, with a slipknot at both ends, and as the giants were coming through the gates he threw the ropes over their heads. He then made the other ends fast to a beam in the ceiling and pulled with all his might till he had almost strangled them. When he saw that they were both quite black in the face and had not the least strength left, he drew his sword and slid down the ropes; he then killed the giants and thus saved himself from a cruel death. Jack next took a great bunch of keys from the pocket of Blunderbore and went into the castle again. He made a search through all the rooms, and in them he found three ladies tied up by the hair of their heads, almost starved to death.

"Sweet ladies," said Jack, "I have killed the monster and his wicked brother, and now I set you free." He gave them the keys of the castle and bade them farewell.

Jack then went farther on his journey to Wales, traveling as fast as he could. At length he lost his way, and when night came on he was in a lonely valley between two lofty mountains, where at last he found a large house. He went up to it boldly and knocked loudly at the gate, when, to his surprise, there came forth a monstrous giant with two heads. He spoke to Jack very civilly, for he was a Welsh giant, and all the mischief he did was by private and secret malice, under the show of friendship and kindness. Jack told him that he was a traveler who had lost his way, upon which the huge monster made him welcome and led him into a room where there was a good bed in which to pass the night. But soon after he had gone to bed he heard the giant in the next room saying to himself:

> Though here you lodge with me this night,
> You shall not see the morning light;
> My club shall dash your brains outright.

"Say'st thou so?" quoth Jack. "Are these your Welsh tricks? But I hope to prove as cunning as you." Then, getting out of bed, he found a billet of wood; he laid it in his own place in the bed and hid himself in a corner of the room. In the middle of the night the giant came in with his club and struck many heavy blows on the bed, in the very place where Jack had laid the billet; then he left, thinking he had broken all the bones in Jack's skin. Early in the morning Jack put on a bold face and walked into the giant's room to thank him for his lodging.

"How have you rested?" quoth the giant. "Did you not feel anything in the night?"

"No," said Jack, "nothing but a rat, I believe, that gave me three or four slaps with his tail."

The giant wondered at this; yet he did not answer a word and went to bring two great bowls of hasty pudding for their breakfast.

Jack wished to make the giant believe that he could eat as much as himself; so he contrived to button a leathern bag inside his coat and slipped the hasty pudding into this bag, while he seemed to put it into his mouth. Then, telling the giant he would show him a trick, he took hold of the knife, ripped up the bag, and all the hasty pudding tumbled out upon the floor.

"Ods splutter hur nails," cried the Welsh giant, "hur can do that trick hurself." So he snatched up the knife, plunged it into his stomach, and fell down dead.

As soon as Jack had thus tricked the Welsh monster he went farther on his journey; and, a few days after, he met with King Arthur's only son, who had gotten his father's leave to travel into Wales to deliver a beautiful lady from the power of a wicked magician by whom she was held in enchantment.

When Jack found that the young prince had no servants with him he begged leave to attend him; the prince at once agreed to this and gave Jack many thanks for his kindness.

King Arthur's son was a handsome, polite, and brave knight, so good-natured that he gave money to everybody he met. At length he gave his last penny to an old woman, and then, as the sun began to grow low, he said, "Jack, since we have no money left, where can we lodge this night?"

"Master," said Jack, "be of good heart; two miles farther on there lives an uncle of mine. He is a huge and monstrous giant with three heads. He will fight five hundred men in armor and make them fly before him."

"Alas!" cried the king's son. "We had better never have been born than meet with such a monster."

"My lord, leave me to manage that; but tarry here till I return."

Then Jack rode on at full speed, and when he came to the gates of the castle he gave a loud knock. The giant, with a voice like thunder, roared out, "Who is there?"

Jack made answer, and said, "None but your poor Cousin Jack."

Quoth he, "What news with my poor Cousin Jack?"

"Dear Uncle," he replied, "heavy news, God wot!"

"Prithee!" said the giant. "What heavy news can come to me? I am a giant with three heads, and can fight five hundred men in armor and make them fly like chaff before the wind."

"Alas!" said Jack. "Here is the king's son coming with a thousand men to kill you and to destroy all that you have."

"Oh, Cousin Jack," said the giant, "this is heavy news indeed! But I have a large cellar underground, where I will hide myself, and you shall lock, bolt, and bar me in, and keep the keys till the king's son is gone."

Now when Jack had barred the giant fast in the vault he went back and fetched the prince, and they both made themselves happy while the poor giant lay trembling with fear in the cellar underground.

Early in the morning Jack gave the king's son gold and silver out of the giant's treasure and accompanied him three miles forward on his journey, by which time he was pretty well out of the smell of the giant. He then went back to let out his uncle, who asked him what he should give him for saving his castle.

"Why, good Uncle," said Jack, "I desire nothing but the old coat and cap, with the old rusty sword and slippers, which are hanging at your bed's head."

"Then," said the giant, "you shall have them, and pray keep them for my sake, for they are things of great use. The coat will keep you invisible, the cap will give you knowledge, the sword will cut through anything, and the shoes are of vast swiftness. They may be useful to you, so take them with all my heart."

Jack gave many thanks to the giant, and when he had caught up with the king's son they soon arrived at the dwelling of the lady who was under the power of a wicked magician. She received the prince very politely and made a noble feast for him. When it was ended she rose and, wiping her mouth with a fine handkerchief, said, "My lord, you must submit to the custom of my palace; I command you to tell me tomorrow morning on whom I bestowed this handkerchief, or lose your head." She then left the room.

The young prince went to bed very mournful, but Jack put on his cap of knowledge, which told him that the lady was forced, by the power of enchantment, to meet the wicked magician every night in the middle of the forest. Jack put on his coat of darkness and his shoes of swiftness, and he was there before her. When the lady came she gave the handkerchief to the magician. Jack, with his sword of sharpness, at one blow cut off his head; the enchantment was then ended in a moment, and the lady was restored to her former beauty and goodness. She was married to the prince on the next day, and they soon after went back to the court of King Arthur, where they were received with joyful welcomes; and Jack, for his many great deeds, was made one of the knights of the Round Table.

As Jack had been so lucky, he resolved not to be idle but still to do what he could for his king and country. He therefore begged His Majesty for a horse and money, that he might travel in search of new and strange exploits. "For," said he, "there are many giants yet living in the farthest parts of Wales, to the great distress of Your Majesty's subjects; therefore, if it please you, sire, to favor me in my design, I will soon rid your kingdom of these giants and monsters in human shape."

When the king heard this offer he gave Jack everything proper for such a journey. Taking with him his cap of knowledge, his sword of sharpness, his shoes of swiftness, and his invisible coat, the better to perform the great exploits that might come his way, Jack set off on his journey.

He went along over hills and mountains, and on the third day he came to a wide forest. He had hardly entered it when suddenly he heard dreadful shrieks and cries, and, forcing his way through the trees, he saw a monstrous giant dragging along by the hair of their heads a handsome knight and a beautiful lady. Their tears and cries melted the heart of honest Jack; he alighted from his horse and, tying him to an oak tree, put on his invisible coat, under which he carried his sword of sharpness.

When he came up to the giant he made several strokes at him; at length, putting both hands to his sword and aiming with all his might, he cut off both the giant's legs just below the garter, and the earth itself trembled with the force of his fall. At this the noble knight and the virtuous lady not only returned Jack hearty thanks for their deliverance, they also invited him to their house, to refresh himself after his dreadful encounter, as likewise to receive a reward for his good services.

"No," said Jack, "I cannot be at ease till I find out the giant's den."

The knight, on hearing this, grew very sorrowful and replied: "Noble stranger, it is too much to run a second hazard; this monster lived in a den under yonder mountain, with a brother fiercer and crueler than himself. Therefore, if you should go thither and perish in the attempt, it would be a heartbreaking thing to me and my lady. Let me persuade you to desist from any further pursuit and to go back with us."

"Nay," answered Jack, "if there be another, even if there were twenty more equal in hideous strength, not one of them should escape my fury.

But when I have finished this task I will come and pay my respects to you."

Jack had not ridden a mile and a half before he came in sight of the mouth of the cavern; and, near the entrance of it, he saw the other giant sitting on a huge block of timber, with a knotted iron club lying by his side, waiting for his brother. His eyes looked like flames of fire, his face was grim and ugly, his cheeks were like two flitches of bacon, the bristles of his beard seemed to be thick rods of iron wire, and his long locks of hair hung down upon his broad shoulders like curling snakes. Jack got down from his horse and turned him into a thicket; then he put on his coat of darkness, drew a little nearer, and said softly, "Oh! Are you there? It will not be long before I shall take you fast by the beard!"

The giant all this while could not see him, by reason of his invisible coat. Jack came quite close to him and struck a blow at his head with his sword of sharpness; but he missed his aim and only cut off his nose, which made the giant roar like loud claps of thunder. He took up his iron club and began to lay about him like one mad with pain and fury.

But Jack slipped nimbly behind him and drove his sword up to the hilt in the giant's back. This done, Jack cut off his head and sent it, with the head of his brother, to King Arthur, by a wagon he hired for that purpose. When Jack had thus killed these two monsters, he went into their cave in search of their treasure. He passed through many turnings and windings, which led him to a room paved with freestone. At the end of it was a boiling caldron, and on the right hand stood a large table, where the giants used to dine. He then came to a window that was secured with iron bars, through which he saw a number of wretched captives, who cried out when they saw Jack, "Alas! Alas! Young man, you are come to be one among us in this horrid den."

"Aye," said Jack, "but pray tell me what is the meaning of your being here at all?"

"Alas!" said one poor old man. "I will tell you, sir. We are persons that have been taken by the giants who hold this cave, and are kept till they choose to have a feast. Then one of us is to be killed and cooked to please their taste. It is not long since they took three for the same purpose."

"Say you so," quoth Jack, and immediately he unlocked the gate and set all the captives free. Then they searched the giant's coffers, and Jack divided among them all the treasures. The next morning they set off to their homes, and Jack journeyed to the knight's house, whom he had left with his lady not long before.

He was received with the greatest joy by the thankful knight and his lady, who, in honor of Jack's exploits, gave a grand feast, to which all the nobles and gentry were invited. They gave him also a fine ring, on which was engraved the picture of the giant dragging the knight and the lady by the hair, with this motto inscribed around it:

Behold in dire distress were we,
Under a giant's fierce command;
But gain'd our lives and liberty
From valiant Jack's victorious hand.

In the midst of their mirth a messenger brought the dismal tidings that Thunderdell, a savage giant with two heads, had heard of the death of his two kinsmen and was come to take his revenge on Jack. He was now within a mile of the knight's seat, the people flying before him like chaff. But Jack only drew his sword and said, "Let him come. I have here a tool to pick his teeth. Pray, ladies and gentlemen, do me the favor to walk into the garden, and you shall soon behold the giant's defeat and death."

The knight's house stood in the middle of a moat, thirty feet deep and twenty feet wide, over which lay a drawbridge. Jack set men to work to cut through the bridge on both sides, almost to the middle, and then dressed himself in his coat of darkness and went against the giant with his sword of sharpness. As he came close to him, though the giant could not see him for his invisible coat, yet he found some danger was near, which made him cry out:

Fee, fi, fo, fum,
I smell the blood of an Englishman!
Let him be alive, or let him be dead,
I'll grind his bones to make me bread!

"Say'st thou so?" said Jack. "Then thou art a monstrous miller indeed!"

"Art thou the villain who killed my kinsmen? Then I will tear thee with my teeth and grind thy bones to powder."

"You must catch me first," quoth Jack. Throwing off his coat of darkness and putting on his shoes of swiftness, he began to run, the giant following him like a walking castle, making the earth shake at every step.

Jack led him around and around the walls of the house, that the company might see the monster; then, to finish the work, he ran over the draw-bridge, the giant going after him with his club. When he came to the middle, where the bridge had been cut on both sides, the great weight of his body made it break, and he tumbled into the water, where he rolled about like a large whale. Jack stood by the side of the moat and laughed at him the while. The giant foamed to hear him scoff, and he plunged from side to side of the moat; but he could not get out to be revenged. At last Jack ordered a cart rope to be brought to him; he then cast it over his two heads, and by the help of a team of horses dragged him to the edge of the moat, where he cut off his heads and sent them both to the court of King Arthur.

After staying with the knight for some time, Jack set out again in search of new adventures. He went over hills and dales without meeting any, till he came to the foot of a very high mountain. Here he knocked at the door of a small and lonely house, and an old man, with a head as white as snow, let him in.

"Good father," said Jack, "can you lodge a traveler who has lost his way?"

"Yes," said the old man, "I can, if you will accept such fare as my poor house affords."

Jack entered, and the old man set before him some bread and fruit for his supper. When Jack had eaten as much as he chose the old man said: "My son, I know you are the famous conqueror of giants. At the top of this mountain is an enchanted castle, kept by a giant named Galligantus, who, by the help of a vile magician, gets many knights into his castle, where he changes them into the shape of beasts. Above all, I lament the hard fate of a duke's daughter, whom they seized as she was walking in her father's garden. They brought her hither through the air in a chariot drawn by two fiery dragons and turned her into the shape of a deer. Many knights have tried to destroy the enchantment and deliver her, yet none have been able to do it, by reason of two fiery griffins, who guard the gate of the castle and destroy all who come nigh. But as you, my son, have an invisible coat, you may pass by them without being seen; and on the gates of the castle you will find engraved by what means the enchantment may be broken."

Jack promised that in the morning, at the risk of his life, he would break the enchantment. After a sound sleep he arose early, put on his invisible coat, and got ready for the attempt. When he had climbed to the top of the mountain he saw the two fiery griffins; but he passed between them without the least fear of danger, for they could not see him because of his invisible coat. On the castle gate he found a golden trumpet, under which were written these lines:

JACK THE GIANT-KILLER

> Whoever can this trumpet blow
> Shall cause the giant's overthrow.

As soon as Jack had read this he seized the trumpet and blew a shrill blast, which made the gates fly open and the very castle itself tremble. The giant and the conjurer now knew that their wicked course was at an end, and they stood biting their thumbs and shaking with fear. Jack, with his sword of sharpness, soon killed the giant, and the magician was then carried away by a whirlwind. All the knights and beautiful ladies, who had been changed into birds and beasts, returned to their proper shapes. The castle vanished away like smoke, and the head of the giant Galligantus was sent to King Arthur. By then Jack's fame had spread through the whole country; and at the king's desire the duke gave him his daughter in marriage, to the joy of all the kingdom. After this the king gave him a large estate, on which he and his lady lived the rest of their days in joy and contentment.

RUMPELSTILTSKIN

here was once a miller who was very poor, but he had a beautiful daughter. Now, it fell out that he had occasion to speak with the king, and, in order to give himself an air of importance, he said: "I have a daughter who can spin gold out of straw."

The king said to the miller: "That is an art in which I am much interested. If your daughter is as skillful as you say she is, bring her to my castle tomorrow, and I will put her to the test."

Accordingly, when the girl was brought to the castle, the king conducted her to a chamber that was quite full of straw, gave her a spinning wheel and winder, and said, "Now, set to work, and if between tonight and tomorrow at dawn you have not spun this straw into gold you must die." Thereupon he carefully locked the door of the chamber, and she remained alone.

There sat the unfortunate miller's daughter, and for the life of her she did not know what to do. She had not the least idea how to spin straw into gold, and she became more and more distressed, until at last she began to weep. Then all at once the door sprang open, and in stepped a little manikin, who said: "Good evening, Mistress Miller, what are you weeping so for?"

"Alas!" answered the maiden. "I've got to spin gold out of straw, and don't know how to do it."

Then the manikin said, "What will you give me if I spin it for you?"

"My necklace," said the maid.

The little man took the necklace, sat down before the spinning wheel, and whir, whir, whir—in a trice the reel was full.

Then he fixed another reel, and whir, whir, whir—thrice around and that, too, was full.

So it went on until morning, when all the straw was spun and all the reels were full of gold.

Immediately at sunrise the king came, and when he saw the gold he was astonished and much pleased, but his mind became only the more avaricious. So he had the miller's daughter taken to another chamber, larger than the former one and full of straw, and he ordered her to spin it also in one night, as she valued her life.

The maiden was at her wit's end and began to weep. Then again the door sprang open, and the little manikin appeared and said, "What will you give me if I spin the straw into gold for you?"

"The ring off my finger," answered the maiden.

The little man took the ring, began to whir again at the wheel, and had by morning spun all the straw into gold.

The king was delighted at sight of the masses of gold but was not even yet satisfied. So he had the miller's daughter taken to a still larger chamber, full of straw, and said, "This must you tonight spin into gold, but if you succeed you shall become my queen." Even if she is only a miller's daughter, thought he, I shan't find a richer woman in the whole world.

When the girl was alone the little man came again and said for the third time, "What will you give me if I spin the straw for you this time?"

"I have nothing more that I can give," answered the girl.

"Well, promise me your first child if you become queen."

Who knows what may happen? thought the miller's daughter. She did not see any other way of getting out of the difficulty, so she promised the little man what he demanded, and in return he spun the straw into gold once more.

When the king came in the morning and found everything as he had wished, he celebrated his marriage with her, and the miller's daughter became queen.

About a year afterward a beautiful child was born, but the queen had forgotten all about the little man. However, he suddenly entered her chamber and said, "Now, give me what you promised."

The queen was terrified and offered the little man all the wealth of the kingdom if he would let her keep the child. But the manikin said, "No; I would rather have some living thing than all the treasures of the world." Then the queen began to moan and weep to such an extent that the little man felt sorry for her. "I will give you three days," said he, "and if within that time you discover my name you shall keep the child."

Then during the night the queen called to mind all the names that she had ever heard and sent a messenger all over the country to inquire far and wide what other names there were. When the little man came on the next day, she began with Caspar, Melchoir, Balzer, and mentioned all the names she knew, one after the other; but at every one the little man said: "No. That's not my name."

The second day she had inquiries made all around the neighborhood for the names of people living there, and suggested to the little man all the most unusual and strange names.

"Perhaps your name is Cowribs, Spindleshanks, or Spiderlegs?"

But he answered every time, "No. That's not my name."

On the third day the messenger came back and said: "I haven't been able to find any new names, but as I came around the corner of a wood on a lofty mountain, where the fox says good night to the hare, I saw a little house. In front of the house a fire was burning, and around the fire an indescribably ridiculous little man was leaping, hopping on one leg, and singing:

> Today I bake, tomorrow I brew my beer;
> The next day I will bring the queen's child here.
> Ah! Lucky 'tis that not a soul doth know
> That Rumpelstiltskin is my name, ho! ho!

You can imagine how delighted the queen was when she heard the name. When presently afterward the little man came in and inquired, "Now, Your Majesty, what is my name?" at first she asked:

"Is your name Tom?"

"No."

"Is it Dick?"

"No."

"Is it, by chance, Rumpelstiltskin?"

"The devil told you that! The devil told you that!" shrieked the little man. And in his rage he stamped his right foot into the ground so deep that he sank up to his waist.

Then, in his passion, he seized his left leg with both hands and tore himself asunder in the middle.

A TALE OF
THE TONTLAWALD

ong, long ago there stood in the midst of a country covered with lakes a vast stretch of moorland called the Tontlawald, on which no man ever dared set foot. From time to time a few bold spirits had been drawn by curiosity to its borders, and on their return had reported that they had caught a glimpse of a ruined house in a grove of thick trees, and around it were a crowd of beings resembling men, swarming over the grass like bees. The men were as dirty and ragged as gypsies, and there were besides a quantity of old women and half-naked children.

One night a peasant who was returning home from a feast wandered a little farther into the Tontlawald, and he came back with the same story. A countless number of women and children were gathered around a huge fire, and some were seated on the ground, while others danced strange dances on the smooth grass. One old crone had a broad iron ladle in her hand, with which every now and then she stirred the fire; but the moment she touched the glowing ashes the children rushed away, shrieking like night owls, and it was a long while before they ventured to steal back. And besides all this there had once or twice been seen a little old man with a long beard creeping out of the forest, carrying a sack bigger than himself. The women and children ran by his side, weeping and trying to drag the sack from off his back, but he shook them off and went on his way. There was also a tale of a magnificent black cat as large as a foal, but men could not believe all the wonders told by the peasant, and it was difficult to make out what was true and what was false in his story. However, the fact remained that strange things did happen there, and the king of Sweden, to whom this part of the country belonged, more than once gave orders to cut down the haunted wood; but there was no one with courage enough to obey his commands. At length one man, bolder than the rest, struck his ax into a tree, but his blow was followed by a stream of blood and shrieks as of a human creature in pain. The terrified woodcutter fled as fast as his legs would carry him, and after that neither orders nor threats would drive anybody to the enchanted moor.

A few miles from the Tontlawald was a large village, where dwelt a peasant who had recently married a young wife. As is common in such cases, she turned the whole house upside down, and the two quarreled and fought all day long.

By his first wife the peasant had a daughter called Elsa, a good quiet girl, who only wanted to live in peace; but this her stepmother would not allow. She beat and cuffed the poor child from morning till night, and as the stepmother had the whip hand of her husband there was no remedy, so for two years Elsa suffered this ill-treatment.

One day she went out with the other village children to pluck strawberries. Carelessly they wandered on, till at last they reached the edge of the Tontlawald, where the finest strawberries grew, making the grass red with their color. The children flung themselves down on the ground, and, after eating as many as they wanted, they began to pile up their baskets. Suddenly a cry arose from one of the older boys.

"Run, run as fast as you can! We are in the Tontlawald!"

Quicker than lightning they sprang to their feet, and rushed madly away, all except Elsa, who had strayed farther than the rest and had found a bed of the finest strawberries right under the tress. Like the others, she heard the boy's cry, but she could not make up her mind to leave the strawberries.

After all, what does it matter? she thought. The dwellers in the Tontlawald cannot be worse than my stepmother.

Looking up, she saw a little black dog with a silver bell on its neck come barking toward her, followed by a maiden clad all in silk. "Be quiet," said the maiden. Then, turning to Elsa, she added, "I am so glad you did not run away with the other children. Stay here with me and be my friend, and we will play delightful games together, and every day we will go and gather strawberries. Nobody will dare to beat you if I tell them not to. Come, let us go to my mother." And taking Elsa's hand, she led her deeper into the wood, the little black dog jumping up beside them and barking with pleasure.

Oh! What wonders and splendors unfolded themselves before Elsa's astonished eyes! She thought she really must be in Heaven. Trees and bushes loaded with fruit stood before them, while birds gayer than the brightest butterfly sat in their branches and filled the air with their song.

And the birds were not shy, but let the girls take them in their hands and stroke their gold and silver feathers. In the center of the garden was the dwelling house, shining with glass and precious stones, and in the doorway sat a woman clad in rich garments, who turned to Elsa's companion and asked:

"What sort of a guest are you bringing to me?"

"I found her alone in the wood," replied her daughter, "and brought her back with me for a companion. You will let her stay?"

The mother laughed but said nothing; she only looked Elsa up and down sharply. Then she told the girl to come near, and she stroked her cheeks and spoke kindly to her, asking if her parents were alive, and if she really would like to stay with them. Elsa stooped and kissed her hand, then, kneeling down, she buried her face in the woman's lap and sobbed out:

"My mother has lain for many years under the ground. My father is still alive, but I am nothing to him, and my stepmother beats me all the day long. I can do nothing right, so let me, I pray you, stay with you. I will look after the flocks or do any work you tell me; I will obey your lightest word; only do not, I entreat you, send me back to her. She will half kill me for not having come back with the other children."

And the woman smiled and answered, "Well, we will see what we can do with you." And, rising, she went into the house.

Then the daughter said to Elsa, "Fear nothing, my mother will be your friend. I saw by the way she looked that she would grant your request when she had thought it over." Telling Elsa to wait, she entered the house to seek her mother. Elsa meanwhile was tossed about between hope and fear, and felt as if the girl would never return.

At last Elsa saw her crossing the grass with a box in her hand.

"My mother says we may play together today, as she wants to make up her mind what to do about you. But I hope you will stay here always, as I can't bear you to go away. Have you ever been on the sea?"

"The sea?" asked Elsa, staring. "What is that? I've never heard of such a thing!"

"Oh, I'll soon show you," the girl answered, taking the lid from the box. At the very bottom lay a scrap of a cloak, a mussel shell, and two fish scales. Two drops of water were glistening on the cloak, and these the girl shook on the ground. In an instant the garden and lawn and everything else had vanished utterly, as if the earth had opened and swallowed them up; as far as the eye could see there was nothing but water, which seemed at last to touch Heaven itself. Only under their feet was a tiny dry spot. Then the girl placed the mussel shell on the water and took the fish scales in her hand. The mussel shell grew bigger and bigger, and turned into a pretty little boat, which could have held a dozen children. The girls stepped in, Elsa very cautiously, for which she was much laughed at by her friend, who used the fish scales for a rudder. The waves rocked the girls softly, as if they were lying in a cradle, and they floated on till they met other boats filled with men, singing and making merry.

"We must sing you a song in return," said the girl, but as Elsa did not know any songs, her companion had to sing by herself. Elsa could not understand any of the men's songs, but one word, she noticed, was repeated over and over again, and that was *Kisika.* Elsa asked what it meant, and the girl replied that it was her name.

It was all so pleasant that they might have stayed there forever had not a voice cried out to them, "Children, it is time for you to come home!"

So Kisika took the little box out of her pocket, with the piece of cloth lying in it, and dipped the cloth in the water, and lo! they were standing close to a splendid house in the middle of the garden. Everything around them was dry and firm, and there was no water anywhere. The mussel shell and the fish scales were put back in the box, and the girls went in.

They entered a large hall, where four and twenty richly dressed women were sitting around a table, looking as if they were about to attend a wedding. At the head of the table sat the lady of the house in a golden chair.

Elsa did not know which way to look, for everything that met her eyes was more beautiful than she could have dreamed possible. But she sat down with the rest and ate some delicious fruit, and thought she must be in Heaven. The guests talked softly, but their speech was strange to Elsa, and she understood nothing of what was said. Then the hostess turned around and whispered something to a maid behind her chair, and the maid left the hall; when she came back she brought a little old man with her, who had a beard longer than himself. He bowed low to the lady and then stood quietly near the door.

"Do you see this girl?" said the lady of the house, pointing to Elsa. "I wish to adopt her for my daughter. Make me a copy of her, which we can send to her native village instead of herself."

The old man looked Elsa all up and down, as if he were taking her measurements, bowed again to the lady, and left the hall. After dinner the lady said kindly to Elsa, "Kisika has begged me to let you stay with

her, and you have told her you would like to live here. Is that so?"

At these words Elsa fell on her knees and kissed the lady's hands and feet in gratitude for her escape from her cruel stepmother; but her hostess raised her from the ground and patted her head, saying, "All will go well as long as you are a good, obedient child, and I will take care of you and see that you want for nothing till you are grown up and can look after yourself. My waiting maid, who teaches Kisika all sorts of fine handiwork, shall teach you, too."

Not long after, the old man came back with a mold full of clay on his shoulders and a little covered basket in his left hand, He put down his mold and his basket on the ground, took up a handful of clay, and made a doll as large as life. When it was finished, he bored a hole in the doll's breast and put a bit of bread inside; then he drew a snake out of the basket and forced it to enter the hollow body.

"Now," he said to the lady, "all we want is a drop of the maiden's blood."

When she heard this, Elsa grew white with horror, for she thought she was selling her soul to the evil one.

"Do not be afraid!" the lady hastened to say. "We do not want your blood for any bad purpose, but rather to give you freedom and happiness."

Then she took a tiny golden needle, pricked Elsa in the arm, and gave the needle to the old man, who stuck it into the heart of the doll. When this was done, he placed the figure in the basket, promising that the next day they should all see what a beautiful piece of work he had finished.

When Elsa awoke the next morning in her silken bed with its soft white pillows, she saw a beautiful dress lying over the back of a chair, ready for her to put on. A maid came in to comb out her long hair and brought the finest linen for her use; but nothing gave Elsa as much joy as the little pair of embroidered shoes that she held in her hand, for the girl had hitherto been forced by her cruel stepmother to run about barefoot. In her excitement she never gave a thought to the rough clothes she had worn the day before, which had disappeared as if by magic during the night. Who could have taken them? Well, she was to know that by and by. But *we* can guess that the doll, which was to go back to the village in her place, had been dressed in them. By the time the sun rose, the doll had attained her full size, and no one could have told one girl from the other. Elsa started back when she met herself as she looked only yesterday.

"You must not be frightened," said the lady when she noticed her terror. "This clay figure can do you no harm. It is for your stepmother, that she may beat it instead of you. Let her flog it as hard as she will, it can never feel any pain. And if the wicked woman does not come one day to a better mind, your double will be able at last to give her the punishment she deserves."

From this moment, Elsa's life was that of the ordinary happy child, who has been rocked to sleep in her babyhood in a lovely golden cradle. She had no cares or troubles of any sort, and every day her tasks became easier and the years that had gone before seemed more like a bad dream. But the happier she grew the deeper was her wonder at everything around her, and the more firmly she was persuaded that some great unknown power must be at the bottom of it all.

In the courtyard stood a huge granite block about twenty steps from the house, and when mealtimes came around, the old man with the long beard went to the block, drew out a small silver staff, and struck the stone with it three times, so that the sound could be heard a long way off. At the third blow, a large golden cock sprang out and stood upon the stone. Whenever he crowed and flapped his wings, the rock opened and something came out of it. First a long table covered with dishes ready laid for the number of persons who would be seated around it flew into the house all by itself.

When the cock crowed for the second time, a number of chairs appeared and flew after the table; then wine, apples, and other fruit, all without trouble to anybody. After everybody had had enough, the old man struck the rock again, the golden cock crowed afresh, and back went dishes, table, chairs, and plates into the middle of the block.

When, however, it came to the turn of the thirteenth dish, which nobody ever wanted to eat, a huge black cat ran up and stood on the rock close to the cock, while the dish was on his other side. There they all remained, until they were joined by the old man.

He picked up the dish in one hand, tucked the cat under his arm, told the cock to get on his shoulder, and all four vanished into the rock. And this wonderful stone contained not only food but clothes and everything you could possibly want in the house.

At first, the language most often spoken at meals was strange to Elsa, but with the help of the lady and her daughter she began slowly to understand it, though it was years before she was able to speak it herself.

One day she asked Kisika why the thirteenth dish came daily to the table and was daily sent away untouched, but Kisika knew no more about it than she did. The girl must, however, have afterward told her mother

what Elsa had said, for a few days later she spoke to Elsa seriously:

"Do not worry yourself with useless wondering. You wish to know why we never eat of the thirteenth dish? That, dear child, is the dish of hidden blessings, and we cannot taste of it without bringing our happy life here to an end. And the world would be a great deal better if men, in their greed, did not seek to snatch everything for themselves but instead left something as an offering of thanks to the giver of the blessings. Greed is man's worst fault."

The years passed like the wind for Elsa, and she grew into a lovely woman, with a knowledge of many things that she would never have learned in her native village; but Kisika was still the same young girl that she had been on the day of her first meeting with Elsa. Each morning they both worked for an hour at reading and writing, as they had always done, and Elsa was anxious to learn all she could; but Kisika much preferred childish games to anything else. If the humor seized her, she would fling aside her tasks, take her treasure box, and go off to play in the sea, where no harm ever came to her.

"What a pity," she would often say to Elsa, "that you have grown so big you cannot play with me anymore."

Nine years slipped away in this manner, when one day the lady called Elsa into her room. Elsa was surprised at the summons, for it was unusual, and her heart sank, for she feared some evil threatened her. As she crossed the threshold, she saw that the lady's cheeks were flushed, and her eyes full of tears, which she dried hastily, as if she would conceal them from the girl. "Dearest child," she began, "the time has come when we must part."

"Part?" cried Elsa, burying her head in the lady's lap. "No, dear lady, that can never be till death parts us. You once opened your arms to me; you cannot thrust me away now."

"Ah, be quiet, child," the lady replied. "You do not know what I would do to make you happy. Now you are a woman, and I have no right to keep you here. You must return to the world of men, where joy awaits you."

"Dear lady," entreated Elsa again. "Do not, I beseech you, send me from you. I want no other happiness but to live and die beside you. Make me your waiting maid, or set me to any work you choose, but do not cast me forth into the world. It would have been better if you had left me with my stepmother, than first to have brought me to heaven and then send me back to a worse place."

"Do not talk like that, dear child," the lady replied. "You do not

159

know all that must be done to secure your happiness, however much it costs me. But it has to be. You are only a common mortal, who will have to die one day, and you cannot stay here any longer. Though we have the bodies of men, we are not men at all, though it is not easy for you to understand why. Some day or other you will find a husband who has been made expressly for you, and you will live happily with him till death separates you. It will be very hard for me to part from you, but it has to be, and you must make up your mind to it." Then she drew her golden comb gently through Elsa's hair and bade her go to bed; but little sleep had the poor girl! Life seemed to stretch before her like a dark, starless night.

Now let us look back a moment and see what had been going on in Elsa's native village all these years, and how her double had fared. It is a well-known fact that a bad woman seldom becomes better as she grows older, and Elsa's stepmother was no exception to the rule; but as the figure that had taken the girl's place could feel no pain, the blows that were showered on her night and day made no difference. If the father ever tried to come to his daughter's help, his wife turned upon him, and things were rather worse than before.

One day the stepmother had given the girl a frightful beating and then threatened to kill her outright. Mad with rage, she seized the figure by the throat with both hands, when out came a black snake from her mouth and stung the woman's tongue, and she fell dead without a sound. At night, when the husband came home, he found his wife lying dead upon the ground, her body all swollen and disfigured, but the girl was nowhere to be seen. His screams brought the neighbors from their cottages, but they were unable to explain how it had all come about. It was true, they said, that about midday they had heard a great noise, but as that was a matter of daily occurrence, they had not thought much of it. The rest of the day all was still, but no one had seen anything of the daughter. The body of the dead woman was then prepared for burial, and her tired husband went to bed, rejoicing in his heart that he had been delivered from the firebrand who had made his home unpleasant. On the table he saw a slice of bread, and, being hungry, he ate it before going to sleep.

In the morning he, too, was found dead and as swollen as his wife, for the bread he had eaten had been the piece placed in the body of the figure by the old man. A few days later he was placed in the grave beside his wife, but nothing more was ever heard of their daughter.

All night long after her talk with the lady, Elsa had wept and wailed at her hard fate in being cast out from her home that she loved for so long.

Next morning, when she got up, the lady placed a gold seal ring on her finger, strung a little golden box on a ribbon, and placed it around her neck; then she called the old man and, forcing back her tears, took leave of Elsa. The girl tried to speak, but before she could sob out her thanks the old man had touched her softly on the head three times with his silver staff. In an instant Elsa knew that she was turning into a bird: wings sprang from beneath her arms; her feet were the feet of eagles, with long claws; her nose curved itself into a sharp beak; and feathers covered her body. Then she soared high in the air and floated up toward the clouds, as if she had really been hatched an eagle.

For several days she flew steadily south, resting from time to time when her wings grew tired, for hunger she never felt. And so it happened that one day she was flying over a dense forest; below, hounds were barking fiercely because, not having wings themselves, she was out of their reach. Suddenly a sharp pain quivered through her body, and she fell to the ground, pierced by an arrow.

When Elsa recovered her senses, she found herself lying under a bush in her own proper form. What had befallen her, and how she got there, lay behind her like a bad dream.

As she was wondering what she should do next, the king's son came riding by, and seeing Elsa, he sprang from his horse and took her by the hand, saying, "Ah! It was a happy chance that brought me here this morning. Every night, for half a year, have I dreamed, dear lady, that I should one day find you in this wood. And although I have passed through it hundreds of times in vain, I have never given up hope. Today I was going in search of a large eagle that I had shot, and instead of the eagle I have found—you." Then he took Elsa on his horse and rode with her to the town, where the old king received her graciously.

A few days later the wedding took place, and as Elsa was arranging the veil upon her hair fifty carts arrived laden with beautiful things that the lady of the Tontlawald has sent to Elsa. And after the king's death Elsa became queen, and when she was old she told this story. But that was the last that was ever heard of the Tontlawald.

RAPUNZEL

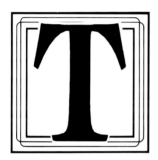

There was once a man and his wife who had long wished in vain for a child, when at last they had reason to hope that Heaven would grant their wish. There was a little window at the back of their house, which overlooked a beautiful garden, full of lovely flowers and shrubs. It was, however, surrounded by a high wall, and nobody dared to enter it, because it belonged to a powerful witch, who was feared by everybody.

One day the woman, standing at this window and looking into the garden, saw a bed planted with beautiful rampion. It looked so fresh and green that it made her long to eat some of it. This longing increased every day, and as she knew it could never be satisfied, she began to look pale and miserable, and to pine away. Then her husband was alarmed, and said: "What ails you, my dear wife?"

"Alas!" she answered. "If I cannot get any of the rampion from the garden behind our house to eat, I shall die."

Her husband, who loved her, thought, Before you let your wife die, you must fetch her some of the rampion, cost what it may. So in the twilight he climbed over the wall into the witch's garden, hastily picked a handful of rampion, and took it back to his wife. She immediately dressed it and ate it up very eagerly. It was so very, very nice that the next day her longing for it increased threefold. She could have no peace unless her husband fetched her some more. So in the twilight he set out again; but when he got over the wall he was terrified to see the witch before him.

"How dare you come into my garden like a thief, and steal my rampion?" she said with angry looks. "It shall be the worse for you!"

"Alas!" he answered. "Be merciful to me; I am only here from necessity. My wife sees your rampion from the window, and she has such a longing for it that she would die if she could not get some of it."

163

RAPUNZEL

The anger of the witch abated, and she said to him, "If it is as you say, I will allow you to take away with you as much rampion as you like, but on one condition. You must give me the child which your wife is about to bring into the world. I will care for it like a mother, and all will be well with it." In his fear the man consented to everything, and when the baby was born, the witch appeared, gave it the name of Rapunzel (rampion), and took it away with her.

Rapunzel was the most beautiful child under the sun. When she was twelve years old, the witch shut her up in a tower that stood in a wood. It had neither staircase nor doors, only a little window quite high up in the wall. When the witch wanted to enter the tower, she stood at the foot of it and cried:

"Rapunzel, Rapunzel, let down your hair."

Rapunzel had splendid long hair, as fine as spun gold. As soon as she heard the voice of the witch, she unfastened her plaits and twisted them around a hook by the window. They fell twenty ells downward, and the witch climbed up by them.

It happened a couple of years later that the king's son rode through the forest and came close to the tower. From thence he heard a song so lovely that he stopped to listen. It was Rapunzel, who in her loneliness made her sweet voice resound to pass away the time. The king's son wanted to join her, and he sought for the door of the tower, but there was none to find.

He rode home, but the song had touched his heart so deeply that he went into the forest every day to listen to it. Once, when he was hidden behind a tree, he saw a witch come to the tower and call out:

"Rapunzel, Rapunzel, let down your hair."

Then Rapunzel lowered her plaits of hair and the witch climbed up to her.

If that is the ladder by which one ascends, he thought, I will try my luck myself. And the next day, when it began to grow dark, he went to the tower and cried:

"Rapunzel, Rapunzel, let down your hair."

The hair fell down at once, and the king's son climbed up by it.

At first Rapunzel was terrified, for she had never set eyes on a man before, but the king's son talked to her kindly and told her that his heart had been so deeply touched by her song that he had no peace, and he was obliged to see her. Then Rapunzel lost her fear, and when he asked if she would have him for her husband, and she saw that he was young and handsome, she thought, He will love me better than old Mother Gothel. So she said, "Yes," and placed her hand in his. She said, "I

will gladly go with you, but I do not know how I am to get down from this tower. Every time you come, bring a skein of silk with you. I will twist it into a ladder, and when it is long enough I will descend by it, and you can take me away with you on your horse."

She arranged with him that he should come and see her every evening, for the old witch came in the daytime.

The witch discovered nothing, until suddenly Rapunzel said to her, "Tell me, Mother Gothel, how can it be that you are so much heavier to draw up than the young prince who will be here before long?"

"Oh, you wicked child, what do you say? I thought I had separated you from all the world, and yet you have deceived me." In her rage she seized Rapunzel's beautiful hair, twisted it twice around her left hand, snatched up a pair of shears, and cut off the plaits, which fell to the ground. She was so merciless that she took poor Rapunzel away into a wilderness, where she forced her to live in the greatest grief and misery.

In the evening of the day on which she had banished Rapunzel, the witch fastened the plaits that she had cut off to the hook by the window. Soon the prince came and called:

"Rapunzel, Rapunzel, let down your hair."

The witch lowered the hair and the prince climbed up; but there he found not his beloved Rapunzel but the witch who looked at him with angry and wicked eyes.

"Ah!" she cried mockingly. "You have come to fetch your lady love, but the pretty bird is no longer in her nest; and she can sing no more, for the cat has seized her, and it will scratch your own eyes out, too. Rapunzel is lost to you; you will never see her again."

The prince was beside himself with grief, and in his despair he sprang out of the window. He was not killed, but his eyes were scratched out by the thorns among which he fell. He wandered about blind in the wood and had nothing but roots and berries to eat. He did nothing but weep and lament over the loss of his beloved wife Rapunzel. In this way he wandered about for some years, until at last he reached the wilderness where Rapunzel had been living in great poverty with the twins who had been born to her, a boy and a girl.

He heard a voice that seemed very familiar to him, and he went toward it. Rapunzel knew him at once and fell weeping upon his neck. Two of her tears fell upon his eyes, and they immediately grew quite clear, and he could see as well as ever.

He took her to his kingdom, where he was received with joy, and they lived long and happily together.

THE MAGIC CARPET,
THE TUBE,
AND THE APPLE

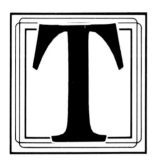here was once a sultan of India who had three sons and one niece, the ornaments of his court. The eldest of the princes was called Houssain, the second Ali, the youngest Ahmed, and the princess his niece Nouronnihar.

Princess Nouronnihar, having lost her father while she was still very young, had been brought up by the sultan. And now that she was grown to womanhood, the sultan thought of marrying her to some prince worthy of the alliance. She was very beautiful, and when the sultan's idea became known the princes informed him, singly, that they loved her and would fain marry her.

This discovery pained the sultan, because he knew that there would be jealousy among his sons. He therefore sent for each separately and spoke with him, urging him to abide permanently by the lady's choice, but none of them would yield without a struggle. As he found them obstinate, he sent for them all together and said:

"My children, since I have not been able to dissuade you from aspiring to marry the princess your cousin, and as I have no inclination to use my authority, to give her to one in preference to his brothers, I trust I have thought of an expedient which will please you all and preserve harmony among you, if you will but hear me and follow my advice. I think it would not be amiss if you were to travel separately into different countries, so that you might not meet each other; and as you know I am very curious, and delight in everything that is rare and singular, I promise my niece in marriage to him who shall bring me the most extraordinary rarity.

The three princes, each hoping that fortune would be favorable to him, consented to this proposal. The sultan gave them money, and early the next morning they started from the city, disguised as merchants. They departed by the same gate, each attended by a trusty servant, and for one day they journeyed together. They then halted at a khan, and having agreed to meet in one year's time at the same place, they said farewell and early the next morning started on their several journeys.

Prince Houssain, the eldest brother, who had heard wonders of the extent, power, riches, and splendor of the kingdom of Bisnagar, bent his course toward the Indian coast; after three months' traveling, sometimes over deserts and barren mountains, and sometimes through populous and fertile countries, he arrived at Bisnagar, the capital of the kingdom of that name, and the residence of its maharajah. He lodged at a khan appointed for foreign merchants; and having learned that there were four principal divisions where merchants of all sorts kept their shops—in the midst of which stood the maharajah's palace, surrounded by three courts, and each gate distant two leagues from the other—he went to one of these quarters the next day.

Prince Houssain marveled at the variety and richness of the articles exposed for sale. As he wandered from street to street, he wondered still more; for on all sides he saw the products of every country in the world. Silks, porcelain, and precious stones in abundance indicated the enormous wealth of the people.

Prince Houssain had finished his inspection when a merchant, perceiving him passing with weary steps, asked him to sit down in his shop. Before long a crier came past, carrying a piece of carpet for which he asked forty purses of gold. It was only about six feet square, and the prince was astonished at the price. "Surely," said he, "there must be something very extraordinary about this carpet which I cannot see, for it looks poor enough."

"You have guessed right, sir," replied the crier, "and will believe it when you learn that whoever sits on this piece of carpeting may be transported in an instant whithersoever he desires to be, without being stopped by any obstacle."

The prince was overjoyed, for he had found a rarity that would secure the hand of the princess. "If," said he, "the carpet has this virtue, I will gladly buy it."

"Sir," the crier replied, "I have told you the truth; and it will be an easy matter to convince you. I will spread the carpeting; and when we have both sat down, and you have formed the wish to be transported into your apartment at the khan, if we are not conveyed thither, it shall be no bargain."

On this assurance, the prince accepted the conditions and concluded the bargain. Then, having obtained the master's leave, they went into his back shop, where they both sat down on the carpeting; and as soon as the prince had formed his wish to be transported into his apartment at the khan, he in an instant found himself and the crier there. He needed no further proof of the virtue of the carpeting, so he immediately counted out the forty purses of gold and gave them to the crier, with an extra twenty pieces for himself.

For a time Prince Houssain tarried in the city, studying the manners and customs of the people. He gained much satisfaction and information from visiting the different buildings and witnessing the various ceremonies that took place. But he desired to be nearer to Princess Nouronnihar, whom he most ardently loved, and he considered that he could rely upon claiming her as his bride. Therefore, he paid his reckoning at the khan, spread the carpet upon the floor of his room, and he and his attendant were instantly transported to the meeting place from which he had set out.

Prince Ali, the second brother, joined a caravan. In four months he arrived at Shiraz, which was then the capital of the empire of Persia; and having in the way contracted a friendship with some merchants, he passed for a jeweler and lodged in the same khan with them.

On the morning after his arrival Prince Ali started to inspect the valuable articles that were exposed for sale in the quarter where the jewelers lodged. He was astonished by all the wealth he saw, and he wandered from street to street lost in admiration. But what surprised him most was a crier who walked to and fro carrying an ivory tube in his hand, for which he asked forty purses of gold. Prince Ali thought the man mad, but he was anxious to find out why the tube was so expensive. "Sir," said the crier, when the prince addressed him, "this tube is furnished with a glass; by looking through it, you will see whatever object you wish to behold."

The crier presented the tube for his inspection; and he, wishing to see his father, looked through it and beheld the sultan in perfect health, sitting on his throne, in his council chamber. Next he wished to see Princess Nouronnihar, and immediately he saw her sitting laughing among her companions.

Prince Ali wanted no other proof. He said to the crier, "I will purchase this tube from you for the forty purses." He then took him to the khan where he lodged, paid him the money, and received the tube.

Prince Ali was overjoyed at his purchase and persuaded himself that, as his brothers would not be able to meet with anything so rare and admirable, the Princess Nouronnihar must become his bride. When all was ready, he joined his friends and arrived at the meeting place, where he found Prince Houssain, and both waited for Prince Ahmed.

Prince Ahmed took the road of Samarcand, and the day after his arrival, as he went through the city, he saw a crier who had an artificial apple in his hand for which he asked thirty-five purses of gold. "Let me see that apple," said the prince, "and tell me what virtue or extraordinary property it possesses, to be valued at so high a rate."

"Sir," replied the crier, giving it into his hand, "if you look at the mere outside of this apple, it is not very remarkable; but if you consider its properties, and the great use and benefit it is to mankind, you will say it is invaluable, and that he who possesses it is master of a great treasure. It cures all sick persons of the most mortal diseases; and this merely by the patient's smelling it."

"If one may believe you," Prince Ahmed replied, "the virtues of this apple are wonderful, and it is indeed valuable; but what proof have you of what you say?"

"Sir," replied the crier, "the truth is known to the whole city of Samarcand."

While the crier was detailing to Prince Ahmed the virtues of the artificial apple, many persons came about them and confirmed what he declared. One amongst the rest said he had a friend dangerously ill, whose life was despaired of, which was a favorable opportunity to make the experiment; upon which Prince Ahmed told the crier he would give him forty purses for the apple if it cured the sick person by smelling it.

The crier said to Prince Ahmed, "Come, sir, let us go and make the experiment, and the apple shall be yours."

The experiment succeeded; and the prince, after he had counted out forty purses to the crier and had received the apple from him, waited with the greatest impatience for the departure of a caravan for the Indies.

When Prince Ahmed joined his brothers, they embraced with tenderness and expressed much joy at meeting again. Then Prince Houssain said: "Brothers, let us postpone the narrative of our travels, and let us at once show each other what we have bought as a curiosity that we may do ourselves justice beforehand, and judge to which of us our father may give the preference. To set the example, I will tell you that the rarity which I have brought from the kingdom of Bisnagar is the carpeting on which I sit. It looks but ordinary and makes no show; but it possesses wonderful virtues. Whoever sits on it, and desires to be transported to any place, is immediately carried thither. I made the experiment myself, before I paid the forty purses, which I most readily gave for it. I expect now that you should tell me whether what you have brought is to be compared with this carpet."

Prince Ali spoke next and said: "I must own that your carpet is very wonderful; yet I am as well satisfied with my purchase as you can possibly be with yours. Here is an ivory tube which also cost me forty purses. It looks ordinary enough; yet on looking through it you can behold whatever you desire to see, no matter how far distant it may be. Take it, brother, and try for yourself."

Houssain took the ivory tube from Prince Ali, with the intention of seeing the Princess Nouronnihar. Ali and Prince Ahmed, who kept their eyes fixed upon him, were extremely surprised to see his countenance change in such a manner as expressed extraordinary alarm and affliction. He cried out, "Alas! Princes, to what purpose have we undertaken such long and fatiguing journeys, with but the hope of being recompensed by the possession of the charming Nouronnihar, when in a few moments that lovely princess will breathe her last. I saw her in her bed, surrounded by her women all in tears, who seem to expect her death. Take the tube, behold yourselves the miserable state she is in, and mingle your tears with mine."

Prince Ali took the tube out of Houssain's hand and, after he had seen the same object, presented it with sensible grief to Ahmed, who took it, to behold the melancholy sight that so concerned them all.

When Prince Ahmed had taken the tube out of Ali's hands and had seen that the Princess Nouronnihar's end was so near, he addressed himself to his two brothers. "Brothers, the Princess Nouronnihar is indeed at death's door; but provided we lose no time, we may preserve her life." He then took the artificial apple out of his bosom and resumed, "This apple cost me as much as the carpet or tube, and has healing properties. If a sick person smells it, though in the last agonies, it will restore him to perfect health immediately. I have made the experiment and can show you its wonderful effect on the person of Princess Nouronnihar, if we hasten to assist her."

"We cannot make more dispatch," said Prince Houssain, "than by transporting ourselves instantly into her chamber by means of my carpet. Come, lose no time! Sit down; it is large enough to hold us all."

Ali and Ahmed sat down by Houssain, and as their interest was the same, they all framed the same wish and were transported instantaneously into Princess Nouronnihar's chamber.

The presence of three princes, who were so little expected, alarmed the princess's women, who could not comprehend by what enchantment three men should be among them; for they did not know them at first.

Prince Ahmed no sooner saw himself in Nouronnihar's chamber, and perceived the princess dying, than he rose off the carpet, went to the bedside, and put the apple to her nostrils. The princess instantly opened her eyes and asked to be dressed, with the same freedom and recollection as if she had awakened out of a sound sleep. Her women presently informed her that she was obliged to the three princes, her cousins, and particularly to Prince Ahmed, for the sudden recovery of her health. She immediately expressed her joy at seeing them and thanked them all together, but afterward Prince Ahmed in particular.

While the princess was dressing, the princes went to throw themselves at their father's feet; but when they came to him, they found he had been previously informed of their unexpected arrival, and by what means the princess had been so suddenly cured. The sultan received and embraced them with the greatest joy, both for their return and for the wonderful recovery of the princess his niece, who had been given over by the physicians.

After the usual compliments, each of the princes presented the rarity that he had brought: Prince Houssain his carpet, Prince Ali his ivory tube, and Prince Ahmed the artificial apple. After each had commended his present and put it into the sultan's hands, they together begged of him to pronounce their fate and declare to which of them he would give the Princess Nouronnihar, according to his promise.

The sultan of the Indies, having heard all that the princes had to say, remained some time silent, considering what answer he should make. At last he said to them in terms full of wisdom, "I would declare for one of you, my children, if I could do it with justice; but consider whether I can? As for you, Houssain, the princess would be very ungrateful if she did not show her sense of the value of your carpet, which was so necessary a means toward effecting her cure. But consider, it would have been of little use if you had not been acquainted with her illness by Ali's tube, or if Ahmed had not applied his artificial apple. Therefore, as neither the carpet, the ivory tube, nor the artificial apple has the least preference to the other articles, I cannot grant the princess to any one of you; and the only fruit you have reaped from your travels is the glory of having equally contributed to restoring her to health. As this is the case, you see that I must have recourse to other means to determine the choice I ought to make; and as there is time enough between this and night, I will do it today. Go and procure each of you a bow and arrow, repair to the plain where the horses are exercised. I will soon

172

join you, and will give Princess Nouronnihar to him who shoots the farthest.''

The three princes had no objection to the decision of the sultan. When they were dismissed, each provided himself with a bow and arrow, and they went to the plain appointed, followed by a great concourse of people.

The sultan did not make them wait long for him; as soon as he arrived, Prince Houssain, as the eldest, took his bow and arrow and shot first. Prince Ali shot next, and much beyond him. Prince Ahmed shot last of all, but it happened that nobody could see where his arrow fell; and notwithstanding the search made by himself and all the spectators, it was not to be found. Though it was believed that he had shot the farthest, still, as his arrow could not be found, the sultan determined in favor of Prince Ali and gave orders for preparations to be made for the solemnization of the nuptials, which were celebrated a few days after with great magnificence.

Prince Houssain would not honor the feast with his presence; he could not bear to see Princess Nouronnihar wed Prince Ali, who, he said, did not deserve her better or love her more than himself. In short, his grief was so extreme that he left the court and renounced all right of succession to the crown, to turn dervish and put himself under the discipline of a famous sheikh, who had gained a great reputation for his exemplary life.

Prince Ahmed, urged by the same motive, did not attend the wedding; yet he did not renounce the world as Houssain had done. He could not imagine what could have become of his arrow, and resolved therefore to search for it, that he might not have anything to reproach himself with. With this intent he went to the place where Houssain's and Ali's arrows were gathered up and, proceeding straightforward thence, looked carefully on both sides as he advanced. He went so far that at last he began to think his labor was in vain; yet he could not help proceeding till he came to some steep craggy rocks, which completely barred the way.

To his great astonishment he perceived an arrow, which he recognized as his own, at the foot of the rocks. Certainly, said he to himself, neither I, nor any man living, could shoot an arrow so far. Perhaps fortune, to make amends for depriving me of what I thought the greatest happiness of my life, may have reserved a greater blessing for my comfort.

There were many cavities, into one of which the prince entered. Looking about, he beheld an iron door, which he feared was fastened; but it opened as he pushed against it and disclosed an easy descent, which he walked down with his arrow in his hand. At first he thought he was going into a dark place, but presently a light quite different from that which he had quitted succeeded; and entering into a spacious square, he beheld a magnificent palace. At the same instant, a lady of majestic air and of remarkable beauty advanced, attended by a troop of ladies, all magnificently dressed.

As soon as Ahmed perceived the lady, he hastened to pay his respects; and the lady, seeing him, said, "Come near, Prince Ahmed; you are welcome."

Prince Ahmed was surprised at hearing himself addressed by name, but he bowed low and followed into the great hall. Here she seated herself upon a sofa and requested the prince to sit beside her. Then she said: "You are surprised that I know you, yet you cannot be ignorant, as the Koran informs you that the world is inhabited by genies as well as men. I am the daughter of one of the most powerful and distinguished of these genies, and my name is Perie Banou. I am no stranger to your loves or your travels, since it was I myself who exposed to sale the artificial apple, which you bought at Samarcand; the carpet, which Prince Houssain purchased at Bisnagar; and the tube, which Prince Ali brought from Shiraz. You seemed to me worthy of a happier fate than that of possessing the Princess Nouronnihar; and that you might attain it, I carried your arrow to the place where you found it. It is in your power to avail yourself of the favorable opportunity which presents itself to make you happy."

Ahmed made no answer but knelt to kiss the hem of her garment; but she would not allow him, and presented her hand, which he kissed a thousand times and kept fast locked in his.

"Well, Prince Ahmed," said she, "will you pledge your faith to me, as I do mine to you?"

"Yes, madam," replied the prince in an ecstasy of joy. "What can I do more fortunate for myself, or with greater pleasure?"

"Then," answered the fairy, "you are my husband, and I am your wife. Our fairy marriages are contracted with no other ceremonies, and yet are more indissoluble than those among men, with all their formalities."

The fairy Perie Banou then conducted Prince Ahmed around the palace, where he saw much that delighted him, and showed him its wealth. At last she led him to a rich apartment in which the marriage feast was spread. The fairy had ordered a sumptuous repast to be prepared; the prince marveled at the variety and delicacy of the dishes, many of which were quite strange to him. While they ate there was music; and after dessert a large number of fairies and genies appeared and danced before them.

THE MAGIC CARPET, THE TUBE, AND THE APPLE

Day after day new amusements were provided, each more entrancing than the last, and every day he grew more and more in love with the beautiful Perie Banou.

At the end of six months he bethought him of his father and asked permission to visit him; but the genie persuaded him not to go. "Only harm would come of it, my love," she told him.

Meantime his father, the sultan of the Indies, grieved over the loss of his two sons. He had learned of Houssain and of his place of retreat, but there was no trace of Ahmed. He called to his aid a sorceress, but she was unable to find the missing prince.

As the days went by, Prince Ahmed did not renew his request for permission to visit his father; but the fairy, Perie Banou, saw that the desire was in his mind and at last said to him, "Prince, I can see you are grieving for a sight of your father and I am willing to let you go, but you must promise that your absence shall not be long. Do not speak of your marriage or of the place of our residence. Let your parent be satisfied with the knowledge that you are happy."

Prince Ahmed was greatly pleased at this; and, accompanied by twenty horsemen, he set out on a charger, which was most richly caparisoned and as beautiful a creature as any in the sultan of the Indies' stables. It was no great distance to his father's capital; when Prince Ahmed arrived, the people received him with acclamations and followed him in crowds to the palace. The sultan embraced him with great joy, complaining at the same time, with a fatherly tenderness, of the affliction his long absence had occasioned.

"Sir," replied Prince Ahmed, "when my arrow so mysteriously disappeared, I wanted to find it; and returning alone, I commenced my search. I sought all about the place where Houssain's and Ali's arrows were found, and where I imagined mine must have fallen, but all my labor was in vain. I proceeded along the plain in a straight line for a league and, to my dismay, found nothing. I was about to give up my search, when I found myself drawn forward against my will; and after having gone four leagues, to that part of the plain where it is bounded by rocks, I saw an arrow. I ran to the spot, took it up, and immediately knew it to be the same which I had shot. Then I knew that your decision was faulty, and that some power was working for my good. But as to this mystery I beg you will not be offended if I remain silent, and that you will be satisfied to know that I am happy and content with my fate. Nevertheless, I was grieved lest you should suffer in uncertainty; but I beg you to allow me the honor of coming here occasionally to visit you."

"Son, I wish to penetrate no further into your secrets. Your presence has restored to me the joy I have not felt for a long time, and you shall always be welcome when you can come."

Prince Ahmed stayed three days at his father's court, and on the fourth he returned to the fairy, Perie Banou, who received him with great joy.

Once every month Ahmed visited his father and was received by the sultan with the same joy and satisfaction. For several months he constantly paid him visits, and always with a richer and more brilliant equipage.

At last the sultan's favorites, who judged of Prince Ahmed's power by the splendor of his appearance, contrived to make him jealous of his son. He sent for the sorceress and bade her watch where his son went. The sorceress was more successful this time; she followed Ahmed to the beautiful palace and by feigning sickness had herself carried within. The fairy Perie Banou, taking pity on the woman, directed two of her ladies-in-waiting to conduct the sorceress to a splendid apartment. She was laid on a luxurious bed, and one of the attendants brought her a cup, full of a certain liquor. "Drink this," she said. "It is the water of the fountain of lions and a potent remedy against fevers. You will feel the effect of it in less than an hour's time."

The attendants then left her and returned at the end of an hour. When she saw them open the door of the apartment, she cried out, "Oh, the admirable potion! It has wrought its cure, and I have waited with impatience to desire you to conduct me to your charitable mistress, as I would not lose time but prosecute my journey."

The two women conducted her through several apartments, all more superb than that wherein she had lain, into a large hall, the most richly and magnificently furnished in all the palace.

Perie Banou was seated in this hall upon a throne of massive gold, enriched with diamonds, rubies, and pearls of an extraordinary size; she was attended on each hand by a great number of beautiful fairies, all richly dressed. At the sight of so much splendor, the sorceress was not only dazzled but so struck, that after she had prostrated herself before the throne she could not open her lips to thank the fairy, as she had proposed. However, Perie Banou saved her the trouble and said, "Good woman, I am glad that you are able to pursue your journey. I will not detain you; but perhaps you may like to see my palace. Follow my women, and they will show it you."

The old sorceress, who had not power or courage to say a word, prostrated herself once more, with her head on the carpet that covered the foot of the throne, took her leave, and was conducted by the two fairies through the palace. Afterward they conducted her to the iron gate through which she had entered, and let her depart, wishing her a good journey.

On her return the sorceress related to the sultan how she had succeeded in entering the fairy's palace, and told him all the wonders she had seen there. When she had finished her narrative, the sorceress said: "I shudder when I consider the misfortunes which may happen to you, for who can say that the fairy may not inspire him with the unnatural design of dethroning Your Majesty and seizing the crown of the Indies? This is what Your Majesty ought to consider as of the utmost importance."

The sultan of the Indies had been consulting with his favorites, when he was told of the sorceress's arrival. He now ordered her to follow him to them. He acquainted them with what he had learned might happen. Then one of the favorites said: "In order to prevent this, now that the prince is in your power, you ought to put him under arrest; I would not take away his life, but make him a close prisoner." This advice all the other favorites unanimously applauded.

But the sorceress said, "No. The fairy would work some spells on us if we imprisoned her husband. A better way is to make demands on his filial love, and if he refuses, then we will have just cause for complaint. For example, ask him to procure you a tent which can be carried in a man's hand but is large enough to shelter your whole army."

The sultan agreed and made this request to his son on his next visit.

Prince Ahmed was greatly embarrassed but said he would present the request to Perie Banou. He returned to the palace, shamefaced; but to his surprise, the fairy only laughed. "It is but a trifle," she told him. "I will gladly give your father what he desires."

She then sent for her treasurer, to whom she said, "Noor-Jehaun, bring me the largest pavilion in my treasury."

Noor-Jehaun returned presently with a pavilion, which could not only be held but concealed in the palm of the hand, and he presented it to her mistress, who gave it to Prince Ahmed to look at.

When Prince Ahmed saw the pavilion, which the fairy called the largest in her treasury, he fancied she had a mind to jest with him, and his surprise soon appeared in his countenance. Perie Banou perceived this and laughed. "What! Prince," cried she, "do you think I jest with you? You will see that I am in earnest. Noor-Jehaun," she said to her treasurer, "go and set it up, that he may judge whether the sultan will think it large enough."

The treasurer went out immediately with it from the palace and set it up. The prince found it large enough to shelter two armies as numerous as his father's. "You see," said the fairy, "that the pavilion is larger than your father may have occasion for; but you are to observe that it has one special property—it becomes larger or smaller, according to the extent of the army it has to cover, without applying any hands to it."

The treasurer took down the tent again, reduced it to its first size, brought it, and put it into the prince's hands. He took it, and the next day he mounted his horse and rode off to the sultan his father.

The sultan was greatly surprised at the prince's speedy return. He took the tent; but after he had admired its smallness, his amazement was so great that he could not recover himself when he had it set up in the great plain before mentioned and found it large enough to shelter an army twice as large as he could bring into the field.

The sultan expressed great obligation to the prince for so noble a present, desiring him to return his thanks to the fairy; and to show what a value he set upon it, he ordered it to be carefully laid up in his treasury. Within himself, however, he felt greater jealousy than ever of his son; therefore, more intent upon his ruin, he went to consult the sorceress again, who advised him to engage the prince to bring him some of the water of the fountain of lions.

In the evening, when the sultan was surrounded as usual by all his court, and the prince came to pay his respects among the rest, he put forward his request for a bottle of the curative water.

Again Ahmed returned to the fairy Perie Banou and unwillingly tendered his father's second request.

"I do not ask this of myself," he said hesitantly. "I do but repeat the words of my father, the sultan; and I am grieved that he was not content with what you did for him before. I leave it to your own pleasure whether you will gratify or reject this new desire. It shall be as you please."

"No, no," replied the fairy. "I will satisfy him, and whatever advice the sorceress may give him (for I see that he hearkens to her counsel), he shall find no fault with you or me. There is much wickedness in this demand, as you will understand by what I am going to tell you. The fountain of lions is situated in the middle of a court of a great castle, the entrance into which is guarded by four fierce lions, two of which sleep alternately, while the other two are awake. But let not that frighten you. I will supply you with means to pass by them without danger."

The fairy Perie Banou was at work with her needle. She took up one of several clews of thread and, presenting it to Prince Ahmed, said, "First take this clew of thread; I will tell you presently the use of it. In the second place you must have two horses. One you must ride yourself; the other you must lead, loaded with a sheep cut into four quarters, which must be killed today. In the third place you must be provided with a bottle, which I will give you, to bring the water in. Set out early tomorrow morning, and when you have passed the iron gate, throw before you the clew of thread, which will roll till it reaches the gates of the castle. Follow it, and when it stops, as the gates will be open, you will see the four lions. The two that are awake will, by their roaring, wake the other two. Be not alarmed, but throw each of them a quarter of the sheep, and then clasp spurs to your horse and ride to the fountain. Fill your bottle without alighting and return with the same expedition. The lions will be so busy eating they will let you pass unmolested."

Prince Ahmed set out the next morning at the time appointed him by the fairy, and he followed her directions punctually. When he arrived at the gates of the castle, he distributed the quarters of the sheep among the four lions and, passing through the midst of them, reached the fountain, filled his bottle, and returned safely. When he had gotten a little distance from the castle gates, he turned about; and perceiving two of the lions coming after him, he drew his saber and prepared himself for defense. But as he went forward, he saw one of them turn out of the road at some distance; he knew then by his head and tail that he had not come to do him any harm but only to go before him, and that the other had stayed behind to follow. He therefore put his sword again into its scabbard. Guarded in this manner, he arrived at the capital of the Indies; the lions never left him until they had conducted him to the gates of the sultan's palace. After that, walking gently and showing no signs of fierceness, they returned the way they had come, though not without alarming the populace, who fled or hid themselves to avoid them.

A number of officers came to attend the prince while he dismounted and conduct him to the sultan, who was at that time conversing with his favorites. He approached the throne, laid the bottle at the sultan's feet, kissed the carpet that covered the footstool, and, rising, said, "I have brought you, sir, the salutary water which Your Majesty so much desired; but at the same time I wish you such health as never to have occasion to make use of it."

After the prince had concluded, the sultan placed him on his right hand, and said, "Son, I am much obliged to you for this valuable present; but I have one thing more to ask of you, after which I shall expect nothing more from your obedience, nor from your interest with your wife. This request is to bring me a man not above a foot and a half high, whose

beard is thirty feet long, who carries upon his shoulders a bar of iron of five hundredweight, which he uses as a quarterstaff, and who can speak."

The next day the prince returned to Perie Banou, to whom he related his father's new demand, which, he said, he looked upon to be a thing more impossible than the first two. "For," he added, "I cannot imagine there is or can be such a man in the world."

"Do not alarm yourself, prince," replied the fairy. "You ran a risk in fetching the water of the fountain of lions for your father, but there is no danger in finding this man. He is my brother Schaibar, who is far from being like me, though we both had the same father. He is of so violent a nature that nothing can prevent his giving bloody marks of his resentment for a slight offense; yet, on the other hand, he is so liberal as to oblige anyone in whatever they desire. I will send for him; but prepare yourself not to be alarmed at his extraordinary figure."

"What! My queen," replied Prince Ahmed, "do you say Schaibar is your brother? Let him be ever so ugly or deformed, I shall love and honor him as my nearest relation."

The fairy ordered a gold chafing dish to be set with a fire in it under the porch of her palace. She took some incense and threw it into the fire when there arose a thick cloud of smoke.

Some moments after, the fairy said to Prince Ahmed, "Prince, there comes my brother. Do you see him?"

The prince immediately perceived Schaibar, who looked at the prince with fierce eyes and asked Perie Banou, "Who is that man?"

She replied, "He is my husband, brother. His name is Ahmed and he is a son of the sultan of the Indies. On his account I have taken the liberty now to call for you."

At these words, Schaibar, looking at Prince Ahmed with a favorable eye that diminished neither his fierceness nor his savage look, said, "It is enough for me that he is your husband. I will do for him whatever he desires."

"The sultan his father," said Perie Banou, "is curious to see you, and I desire that he be your guide to the sultan's court."

"He needs but lead the way, I will follow him," replied Schaibar.

The next morning Schaibar set out with Prince Ahmed to visit the sultan. When they arrived at the gates of the capital, several people, as soon as they saw Schaibar, ran and hid themselves in their shops and houses, shutting their doors. Others, taking to their heels, communicated their fear to all they met, who stayed not to look behind them. Thus Schaibar and Prince Ahmed, as they went along, found all the streets and squares desolate, until they came to the palace, where the porters, instead of preventing Schaibar from entering, ran away, too. As a result, the prince and Schaibar advanced without any obstacle to the council hall, where the sultan was seated on his throne, giving audience.

Schaibar went fiercely up to the throne, without waiting to be presented, and addressed the sultan thus: "You have asked for me. Speak!"

The sultan turned his head away to avoid the sight of so terrible an object. Schaibar was so much provoked at this rude reception that he instantly lifted up his iron bar and let it fall on the sultan's head, killing him, before Prince Ahmed could intercede in his behalf.

Schaibar then smote all the favorites who had given the sultan bad advice; he spared the grand vizier, who was a just man. When this terrible execution was over, Schaibar came out of the council hall into the courtyard with the iron bar upon his shoulder, and, looking at the grand vizier, said, "I know there is here a certain sorceress, who is a greater enemy of the prince my brother-in-law than all those base favorites I have chastised; let her be brought to me immediately."

The grand vizier instantly sent for her, and as soon as she was brought, Schaibar slew her with his iron bar.

"After this," he said, "I will treat the whole city in the same manner, if they do not immediately acknowledge Prince Ahmed, my brother-in-law, as sultan of the Indies."

Then all who were present made the air ring with repeated acclamations of "Long Life to Sultan Ahmed!" Schaibar caused him to be clothed in the royal vestments, installed him on the throne, and made all swear homage and fidelity. Then he returned home and brought back his sister Perie Banou, whom he made sultana of the Indies.

Prince Ali and Princess Nouronnihar were given a considerable province, with its capital, where they spent the rest of their lives. Afterward he sent an officer to Houssain to acquaint him with the change and make him an offer of any province he might choose; but that prince thought himself quite happy in his solitude. He desired the officer to return to his brother with thanks for the kindness he proposed, but the only favor he desired was to be indulged with leave to retire to the palace he had chosen for his retreat.

THE ELVES
AND THE SHOEMAKER

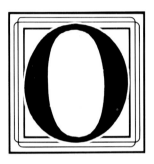nce there lived a kindly old shoemaker and his wife. They were a hardworking couple who labored every day from dawn till dusk, joining lovely pieces of leather together to make ladies' shoes and gentlemen's boots. Then they would close their little shop and dine on a humble repast of cheese and warm milk, for they were very poor. Still and all, they were happy together and loved each other very much.

At the end of a day like all others, the old shoemaker cut the leather into shoes and set the pieces on his workbench to be sewn tomorrow. But this day, he cut just enough leather for one pair of shoes, for the shoemaker and his wife had not a scrap left to make even a baby's bootie.

"Dear husband, what shall we do?" said the shoemaker's wife. "We have no money to buy more leather, and even if we could sell this last pair of shoes tomorrow, the money would scarcely buy a loaf of bread."

The gentle shoemaker tried to comfort his wife, but within he was greatly concerned. Together, they climbed the narrow stair and went to bed, and each prayed in his heart that tomorrow would bring better fortune.

The following morning, the shoemaker kissed his wife and went down alone to their small shop, for two people were certainly not required to sew one pair of shoes.

To his amazement, he discovered a lovely pair of brand-new shoes where he had left the leather pieces the night before.

"Come, good wife, and see these wondrous shoes!" shouted the old shoemaker with glee. The old woman hurried down the stairs and husband and wife marveled at the fine craftsmanship of the shoes.

"My husband, it would surely take us a week if it took a day to make such shoes as these. Only a magical being could sew shoes as exquisite as this pair in just one night!" the shoemaker's wife exclaimed.

Later that morning, a very prosperous lady came into the shop and, upon seeing the wonderful shoes, purchased them instantly for a generous sum.

"Hurrah!" shouted the old shoemaker. "Now we can afford to buy leather for two more pairs of shoes!"

With that the old couple hurried to the market before sunset and purchased just enough fine leather for two additional pairs of shoes. Then the shoemaker cut the leather into pieces and left them on his workbench just as he had done the night before, and he and his wife went to bed.

The next day brought a wonderful surprise to the old couple: two splendid pairs of shoes as finely sewn as the first were waiting for them just where the shoemaker had left the leather pieces the evening before. So beautiful were the shoes that as soon as the shoemaker placed them in the window, two rich gentlemen came in and immediately purchased them for a generous price. The shoemaker and his wife were overjoyed; with the money earned from the sale of these two pairs, the shoemaker bought leather for four more pairs, and so it continued. Every evening, the shoemaker cut the pieces of leather and left them on his workbench for sewing, and each morning, he and his wife awoke to behold pairs of brand-new shoes, lined up in rows, each more splendid then the next. Soon the entire shop was filled with shoes, shoes, and more shoes, and elegant men and women from near and far came to purchase a pair at any cost. But the shoemaker and his wife were honest folk and never asked for more than the fairest price; their honesty and kindness were well rewarded, for neither did they want for food or coal anymore.

One day, the shoemaker's wife said, "Good husband, oughtn't we stay up one night and see who it is that sews such fine stitches and makes such exquisite shoes for us?"

But the shoemaker was reluctant to do so. "Wife, no doubt we are the blessed recipients of some good fairy's benefactions. Let us not tamper with our good fortune, lest we dispel the magic."

The shoemaker's wife went on to explain that it would be unfair to accept the kindness of this magical helper without repaying it for its efforts, and at last the shoemaker agreed to stay up that night and see who it was that sewed the wondrous shoes.

When night fell, the shoemaker prepared the leather pieces for sewing and the couple climbed the narrow stair as they did each evening. But after a few moments, they sneaked back into the shop, quiet as mice, and hid to watch and wait. Hours passed, and at last the clock struck midnight. All at once, just as the final chime was rung, two little men

slipped in through the window as silent as moonlight, hopped up onto the workbench, and began to sew. Their elfin fingers flew like spindles as they sewed the leather pieces together with the neatest of stitches. They labored long but happily, humming a little tune as they worked in the dim moonlight. At last their task was completed; a dozen new pairs of shoes lined the workbench. With that, the two little men danced with joy and vanished just as the last star left the sky.

The good shoemaker and his wife rubbed their eyes in silent disbelief. At last the wife spoke. "Truly, husband, we have witnessed the most marvelous magic. But I can't help feeling sorry for those poor little men; they must be cold, without any clothes to cover themselves!"

All at once the old shoemaker had an idea. "My wife," he said, "I think I know the perfect gift that we could make the elves. Let us sew them tiny suits to protect them from the night chill."

The following day, the shoemaker and his wife purchased a bolt of the finest velvet and tiny brass buttons and set to work, sewing elfin jackets, britches, and caps. And when the outfits were complete, the shoemaker sewed two tiny pairs of slippers out of the softest suede, small enough to fit a child's thumb.

That evening, instead of laying out fresh pieces of leather on the workbench to be sewn into shoes, the shoemaker and his wife left the little outfits and tiny slippers behind, as well as two elfin-sized helpings of stew. Then they climbed the narrow stair and went to bed.

At midnight, the elves slipped through the window and nimbly scampered up the workbench. But instead of finding the leather pieces waiting for them, they discovered to their delight the gifts of the shoemaker and his wife. With a hum and a giggle, they donned the jackets, britches, and caps, and slipped their tiny feet into the suede slippers. Then they sat down to their supper, and when they were through, they danced an elfin jig and slipped out into the moonlight, never to return.

Though the good shoemaker and his wife were never to be visited by the elves again, the magical beings must have sprinkled fairy dust in the corners of the workshop, for the kindly couple lived out their days in happiness and plenty, never to know poverty again.

THE STORY OF IUBDAN,
KING OF THE LEPRA
AND THE LEPRACAUN

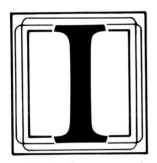n the kingdom of the Lepra and the Lepracaun, which lies in the far, fair north, the saying was, at the time, "A noble king is Iubdan, one whose form undergoes no change, and who has no need to strive for wisdom." Alone, of all the people of Lepra, their king had jet-black hair. His skin was as white as the foam on the wave, and like the blood-red rowanberry were his cheeks. His eyes were as bland as a stream of mead. He wore a cloak of pure purple over his white embroidered tunic, a fillet of gold and silver filigree held back the dark ringlets from his brow, and on his feet he wore white-bronze sandals; of marvelous virtue they were, for whosoever wore them, fairy or mortal, could travel alike on land or sea.

On the day of the Great Feast the king was in the midst of his yellow-haired host. The guests were placed according to their quality and precedence at two long, narrow tables that stretched the whole length of the hall on either side. On each of the tables were nine wrought-gold candlesticks, and set in the ceiling was a gem of precious stone that gave a soft clear radiance to all the house.

Bebo the queen, loveliest of the women of Lepra, whose goodly talk held nothing of arrogance, though much of mischief and play, sat on the king's right hand. She called her husband "the Dark Man." Her own yellow-gold hair hung to her ankles in thick braids threaded with jewels.

To the left of Iubdan, Eshirt, the chief poet of the Lepracaun, had his chair. He wore a scarlet cloak of varied patterns, all fringed with gold, and he carried his poet's rod. Glomar, son of Glas, the greatest warrior in the land, whose feat it was to hew down a thistle at a single stroke, stood guard at the doorpost of the hall.

When the deep notes of the timpan echoed around the pillars that gleamed copper-gold in the light, and the horn-blowers blew a mellow blast on their silver horns, the carvers stood up to carve, the servers stood ready with their silver platters, and the spigots were drawn from the dusky-red vats of hewn wood. Feror, tall and slender and bold of eye, cupbearer to the king, led his men to pour the aged ale for the whole company, and the storytelling began. The poets lauded the warriors of the Lepracaun and praised the beauty of the women. There was reciting of the ancient tales, the singing of poems, and concerted minstrelsy, while the cupbearers kept each goblet ever full of the ale, compelling and delicious, so that on one side of the hall and the other there was huge noise of mirth.

Merry and affable indeed, with the *corn breac,* the jeweled drinking horn of Mag Faithleinn in his hand, and inclined to talk, the king stood up.

"Have you," he said, looking about him, "ever seen a king better than myself?"

"We have not!" They spoke with one accord.

"Men of battle, who ride a bridle-wearing army of strong, headlong horses, have you ever seen better than those here tonight?"

"By our word! We never have!"

"I, too, Iubdan, your king, give my word"—he raised the *corn breac*— "that it would be hard, indeed, forcibly to take out of this house tonight either captives or hostages"—and he gave a toast to Glomar on guard at the doorway—"so surpassing are its heroes and its men of might. So great the number of its fierce and haughty ones . . ." The chief poet burst out laughing, and his poet's wand made a merry, scornful sound. Surprised and angered, the king turned to him. "Eshirt!" There was silence in the hall. "Eshirt, why do you laugh?"

"Because I know of a province in Ireland, one man of which could take us all hostages and captive."

"Lay the poet by the heels." The king spoke with quiet voice. "Glomar! Seize him. Let vengeance be taken on him for his bragging speech." Glomar made to do his bidding, but Eshirt asked respite to speak. "It is your right," Iubdan said. "So be it."

Glomar released his gentle hold on his friend and Eshirt spoke.

"This seizure of me will bear evil fruit, O King, for in return, you, Iubdan, king of the Lepra and the Lepracaun, will yourself spend five years captive of this same man of whom I speak."

Iubdan, well aware of the foreknowing and the wisdom of his poet, asked:

"Who is this man?"

"Fergus mac Leide. He is king at Emain Macha, in Ulster, and you shall not escape him till you have given to him, as a gift, and at his pleasure, the rarest of your treasures."

"What proof have you that what you say is true?"

"Grant me now, Iubdan," Eshirt said, "three days and three nights respite, that I may travel to Emain Macha, to the house of Fergus mac Leide. If I find evidence there to prove I speak the truth, I will bring it to you. If not, do with me as you will."

Iubdan thought for a while, then said, "So be it," and Eshirt, calling to his wife to join him, left the feast and went to prepare for his journey.

He set out, choosing the shortest way and the straightest course to Emain Macha, and when he came to the court of Fergus mac Leide, he stood at the huge gateway and shook his poet's rod.

The doorkeeper heard a sound so piercingly clear and sweet that he crept forth, full of wonder, to find the cause of it. When he saw there a man comely and of the most gallant carriage, but so tiny that the short-cropped grass of the castle green reached up to the thick of his thigh, his wonder grew apace; and asking Eshirt to wait, he hurried inside to tell Fergus mac Leide and the assembled nobles and warriors of Ulster of the strange, courageous, and tiny man who was at their gates.

"Is he smaller than Aed?" the king asked. Aed was the chief poet of Ulster, and a dwarf.

"He could stand, and have room, on Aed's palm, as Aed stands on your own, I give you my word."

There was pealing laughter among the Ulster warriors, and none there could wait to see Eshirt, and to speak with him. When he was brought into the hall, they crowded around him, both men and women, but Eshirt cried out:

"Huge men that your are! Let not your infected breaths play so closely to me." Then he saw Aed. "Let the small man approach me, I pray you," he said, and Aed came. Taking Eshirt gently in the palm of his hand, he bore him to the king.

Fergus mac Leide looked down at the tiny man standing on the table before him.

"Who are you, little man?" All there assembled waited, breathless, for the answer.

"I am Eshirt, chief poet of the Lepra and the Lepracaun."

"Give wine to the guest that is come to us," the king said.

But the man of Lepra refused. "Neither your wine nor your food will I accept."

"By my faith! You are a flippant and a mocking wee fellow," Fergus said, "and it is but fitting to drop you into this beaker; then at least you shall impartially, and on all sides, quaff my wine."

And the cupbearer to the king closed his hand on Eshirt and dropped him into the goblet. He struggled for a moment, then swam to the jeweled rim, and, holding on to it, he said to the king:

"You allow me to drown, you nobles and poets of Ulster, when, upon my conscience, there is much desirable knowledge and instruction I have to impart to you."

The king laughed, but Aed came closer.

"Let him speak, O King," he pleaded.

"We would not let him drown, Aed," Fergus said, and Eshirt was taken from the beaker, and with fair satin napkins and fabrics of silk he was gently dried and made clean again.

"Why will you not eat of our food, nor drink with us?" the king asked.

"I will tell you the impediment." Eshirt reached for his poet's rod, which was lying on the base of the goblet, and holding it in his hand, he spoke. "With a poet's sharp words never be angered, O King. Let my words not make you angry."

"On my word, O wee man, I will not."

"Judgments lucid and truthful are mine," said Lepra's poet, "and I here pronounce that you, Fergus mac Leide, trifle with your steward's wife, the while your own foster son ogles the queen. But have no fear, for women fair-haired and accomplished do not let their humor dwell on chieftains, however excellent the form of them, when they are wife to the king."

Fergus sat silent. The nobles and warriors, the poets and the harpers, the women and the maidens, the cupbearers and the pages scarce breathed, and there was no sound in the hall at Emain Macha.

After a while, the king said, "Eshirt, you are, in truth, no child, but an approved man of verity." Those assembled breathed again. "You are devoid of reproach, and no wrath of mine shall hurt you." Eshirt bowed. "For what you have said of my share in the matter, it is true. The steward's wife is, indeed, my pastime. Therefore all the rest I believe more readily to be true."

"Now," said Eshirt, "I will gladly partake of your food and wine." And he bowed again. "And if it be your pleasure, O King, I will recite a poem I have made upon my own lord."

And with Fergus's consent, he began his lay:

IUBDAN, KING OF THE LEPRA AND THE LEPRACAUN

> Renowned and pleasant is he, Iubdan,
> King of the Lepra and the Lepracaun.
> Over that land's noble multitude,
> He of the truthful utterance holds sway.
>
> Brave men he brings to death;
> When he sets himself in motion
> Rushing torrentlike, is he,
> In beauty and in cattle he is rich.

Eshirt turned to Fergus. "However great the love women are reputed to bear you, O King, when Iubdan touches a single string of his timpan it is sufficient to delight all the women of the universe." This, and more, Eshirt declaimed for the hosts of Ulster, and when the lay ended, the poet of the Lepracaun was showered with an abundance of treasures and of good things. He was feasted in Emain Macha for three days and three nights, and when he took his leave, Aed approached his friend.

"I will go with you to the kingdom of the Lepra and the Lepracaun," he said.

Joyfully Eshirt embraced him and replied, "I will not invite you, Aed, so that the kindness you receive will not be on my account and therefore of more consequence to you."

The two poets bade farewell to Fergus mac Leide and the nobles and warriors of Ulster, and went on their way. Though Aed could stand on the palm of an Ulsterman, beside Eshirt he was a giant, and his step being the longer, he said:

"Eshirt, you are indeed a poor walker." Eshirt laughed, then he ran so swiftly that he was an arrow's flight in front of his companion. "Between these two extremes," Aed said, "there is a golden mean." And they traveled on in harmony and good talk until they came to the White Strand of the Strong Men. Seeing no boat awaiting them, Aed asked, "What must we do now?"

"Travel the sea to her depths," answered Eshirt.

"I shall never come safely out of that."

"Seeing that I accomplish the task, it would be strange if you should fail."

"In the vast sea, what shall I do?" Aed asked, and then he said, "O generous Eshirt, though I mount upward on the merciless waves, the wind will bear me down. In the end I shall perish."

Eshirt laughed at his friend, and answered, "Fair Iubdan's horse will

carry you across the stammering sea. He is an excellent horse, a king's valued treasure. Trust yourself to him, Aed, sit on him, and be not troubled." And as he finished speaking they saw, out across the sea, something careering swiftly toward them on the crests of the waves.

"On itself be the evil it brings," Aed said, and he raised his poet's rod.

"What do you see?"

"A russet-clad hare, I see."

"Not so, Aed. The king's golden-yellow horse it is that comes to fetch you."

As he spoke, the animal came ashore and galloped toward them, and it had four green legs, and a long tail that floated away in wavy crimson curls. Two red flashing eyes and an exquisite pure crimson mane, and on its head was a golden jewel-encrusted bridle.

"Come up beside me, Aed," Eshirt said as he leapt astride the horse.

"Never!" Ulster's poet stood on the Strand. "To carry even you, wee man, is beyond its powers."

"Oh, Aed! Cease from fault-finding. Though your wit is heavy, yet he will carry both of us."

Aed mounted behind his friend, and Iubdan's golden-yellow horse carried them over the roiling seas and under the ocean's great profound until, without mishap and undrowned, they came to Mag Faithleinn, and there they were greeted by the hosts of Lepra, assembled on the shore. A huge cry arose as they emerged from the waves and dismounted.

"Eshirt! Eshirt! He comes, and a giant bears him company."

Then Iubdan and Bebo, and the poet's wife, came forward and they all embraced and kissed.

"But Eshirt!" Bebo said. "I knew you were not pleased, but why do you bring this great giant to destroy us?"

"Bebo, no giant is he, and"—he turned and bowed to Iubdan—"my renowned and pleasant king, he is Ulster's poet, and a dwarf. In the land from whence we came Aed is the very least, and he can stand on the palm of an Ulsterman's hand, as I on his." And he jumped upon Aed's outstretched hand and stood there.

Iubdan and his queen welcomed Aed, but the hosts of Lepra said:

"Alas! He is huge indeed." And they were afraid.

But soon Aed was as admired and beloved in Mag Faithleinn as Eshirt had been in Emain Macha, and when at last the customary feasting had come to an end, Eshirt turned to his king and spoke.

"On you, O Iubdan, I now put, for the unjust seizure you made upon me, the taboo which no true warrior breaks. This night, you will go to Emain Macha and taste the king's porridge, which is at this moment being prepared." And he bowed.

Iubdan and Bebo were grieving and faint of spirit.

"When you had Eshirt seized, you did unjustly, Dark Man," she said, "but I will come with you."

"So be it," said Iubdan, and together, mounted on the king's golden horse, that same night, they made their way to Emain Macha.

"Iubdan," said Bebo, "let us search the town for the porridge and depart before the people of this huge place awaken."

They gained the inside of the castle, and there in the huge kitchen hung the great caldron of Emain Macha, and inside it was what was left of the porridge. Iubdan drew near. He looked up. He could by no means reach it from the ground.

"Get up on the horse," said Bebo, "and then from his back leap to the rim."

This Iubdan did, but the porridge was in the bottom of the caldron and he could not reach the handle of the ladle. He made a great effort, stretching his arm downward; his foot slipped, and he was up to his navel in the porridge, fettered and tethered as though with gyves.

"Long will you tarry there, Dark Man," Bebo said, and she laughed and said again, teasing him, "Long will you tarry here, and dire is the strait you are in."

And Iudban called from the depths of the caldron; "O fair-haired woman of desire, gyves hold me in this viscous mass. Bebo! Fly from here. Dawn is at hand. My leg sticks in the doughy remnant. If you stay here, you are foolish, Bebo. Fly now, to the land of the Lepracaun. Take back my horse."

But Bebo called to him, "Never! I will surely not depart until I see what turn events shall take for you."

The dwellers in Emain Macha awakened, and they soon found Iubdan in the caldron. When they saw his size and the plight he was in, they set up a mighty roar of laughter, picked him up out of the porridge, and took him to Fergus mac Leide.

"By my conscience," said the king, "this is not the same wee man who was here before. That one had fair hair. This one has a black thatch." He looked down on Iubdan. "Who are you at all? And from whence do you come?"

"I am the king of the Lepra folk, and"—Bebo, unseen till now, leapt up beside him—"this is my wife, Bebo, queen over the Lepra and the

Lepracaun. I have never told a lie."

"Let this king be taken out and put with the rabble of the household," Fergus said. "Guard him well." He looked down at Bebo, her golden braids shining with tiny jewels. "This wee woman with the yellow hair I will entertain awhile."

After three days and three nights Bebo said, "May it please you to show me some favor?"

"It pleases me." Fergus mac Leide held her up in his palm and looked on her with joy.

"Then let my husband come before you."

"It shall be done," he said, and Iubdan was brought again before the king.

"Suffer me no longer to be among those kitchen varlets, for their breaths do offend my nostrils," he said. "On my word! I pledge to stay with you till you and Ulster free me."

"Could I believe you, no more would you be with common varlets."

"Never have I—nor ever will I—transgress my plighted word."

Fergus mac Leide believed Iubdan and trusted him, and he had a fair chamber prepared for him, and he set Ferdiad, a trusted servant, to minister to him.

When Bebo saw that her husband was well housed, she did his bidding, and mounting the yellow horse, she rode to the White Strand of the Strong Men and down through the depths of the sea to Mag Faithleinn.

Iubdan stayed at Emain Macha, and to the poets and scholars and the warriors of Ulster, and to the women and the maidens, he was a source of joy, and it was for them a recreation to look at him and to listen to his voice, which was as sweet as copper's resonance. They would gather each day, at the hour before the noonday feasting, and listen to his words, and to his teaching of the fairy wisdom. He taught them the knowledge of healing herbs, and of the habits of the animals and birds, and of the languages they spoke.

On a day in winter, when he had been in Ulster for three years of his exile, he was talking to Fergus mac Leide and the people of his court, when Ferdiad came to the great stone fireplace, carrying a huge pile of wood of every kind. The first log that he threw onto the fire had a woodbine twined around it.

"Ferdiad! No, Ferdiad! Burn not the king of trees—the pliant woodbine—for he should not be burnt." He turned to his guests. "And would you, noble men and women of Ulster, but act upon my counsel, then neither by sea, by land, nor from the prey birds in the air would you be in danger." And Iubdan uttered an ancient lay:

> O Fergus mac Leide, of the Feasts,
> Whose fires burn, welcoming
> Whether afloat or ashore,
> Never burn the king of woods.
> Monarch of all Ireland's forests,
> None may hold him captive. . . .

Iubdan spoke to the king. "O Fergus," he said, "well you should know that it is no feeble sovereign's feat to hold all great tough trees in his embrace." And he returned to the telling of his lay:

> And if you burn the pliant woodbine,
> Wailings and misfortune will abound.
> Dire extremity at weapon's point
> And drowning in great waves.

"Withdraw from the fire that log so royal-embedded," Fergus mac Leide said, and Ferdiad obeyed, and propped it up against the stone wall.

> Nor burn the precious apple tree,
> Of spreading and low-sweeping bough,
>
> A wanderer, the surly blackthorn,
> The artificer burns him not.
>
> Burn not the noble willow,
> A tree sacred to poems. . . .
> The company was silent, listening.
>
> The graceful tree with berries,
> The wizard's tree, the rowan, burn!
>
> Dark is the color of the ash,
> Timber that makes the wheels to go.
>
> Tenterhook among the woods, the spiteful brier, is,
> Burn him by all means, who is so keen and green,

IUBDAN, KING OF THE LEPRA AND THE LEPRACAUN

Fiercest to give heat is the green oak,
And by his acrid embers, the eye is made to water.

Both the alder and the white-thorn,
Burn at your discretion.

And holly! Burn it green, and burn it dry,
Of all trees whatsoever, the best is holly.

Elder, that hath tough bark,
Burn till he is charred.

Patriarch of long-lasting woods, the yew,
Sacred to feasts, of him build dark-red vats of goodly size. . .

His lay ended, Iubdan turned to the king. "O Fergus," he said, "if you would but do as I say, for your soul and body it would work advantage."

These and many other wise and hidden things he told to the poets and the scholars of Ulster, and he was honored, and the people loved him. But he longed for Bebo, as she longed for him, and when the people of the Lepracaun, impatient to see their king, sent Glomar and the chief warriors to talk with the queen, she urged them on and aided them in all their plans, and one day seven battalions of the Lepracaun came to Emain Macha.

Fergus mac Leide and the Ulster warriors came out to parley with them.

"Bring us our king that we may ransom him," they said.

"What ransom?" Fergus mac Leide asked.

"Every year, and that without sowing or ploughing, we will cover this vast plain with a mass of corn."

"I will not give up your king."

"Then tonight we will do you a mischief."

"What mischief?" Fergus asked.

"That all the calves shall drink from their dams, and there shall not, by morning, be left on the whole of Ulster one babe's portion of milk."

"So much you will have gained, but not Iubdan."

The Lepracaun took vengeance on Fergus mac Leide seven times, and at last they threatened to shave the hair on both the men and the women so that the kingdom of Ulster should be forever shamed. At this, Iubdan

went to Fergus.

"This is not right at all," he said. "Let me speak with them."

"It shall be so," Fergus said, and Iubdan came out onto the green. Seeing him, his people thought him free and raised a mightly shout of triumph. When they were silent again, Iubdan said:

"My trusted people, depart now. I am not, in honor, able to go with you."

The Lepracaun, on hearing their king, became gloomy and dejected, and a poet among them made a lay and recited it before Fergus, Iubdan, and the nobles of Emain Macha:

> O Fergus, owner of many strong places,
> From whose standing corn we have snipped the ears,
> We have burnt your kilns,
> Your mill streams we have defined,
> Your calves we have accurately, and universally,
>   admitted to their dams.
> Yet may no inward flux ever seize you
> Nor eye distemper reach you,
> Nor heat inordinate assail you
> During all your life. But, Fergus,
> This is not for love of thee.
> Were it not for Iubdan here,
> The manner of our going would have shown full well
> That your refusal was an evil one.

But Iubdan said, "Depart now, for Eshirt has put it upon me that before I leave this kingdom I must give his choice of my possessions to the king of Ulster, at whatever time he chooses."

So the seven battalions of the Lepracaun returned to their country, and when the five years that Eshirt had said his king must remain in Emain Macha were almost over, Iubdan said to Fergus:

"Of all my treasures now choose a single one. It is your due."

To delay the matter, Fergus said, "I know not all your treasures, Iubdan."

"Then you shall," the king said, and Fergus mac Leide and the hosts of Ulster gathered to hear the lay of Iubdan, on his treasures.

> Take my spear, Fergus, take my spear.
> Who has enemies in number,

199

IUBDAN, KING OF THE LEPRA AND THE LEPRACAUN

In battle it is match for a hundred.
The king who holds it fears not hostile spear points.

My sword! Oh, my sword,
There is not in a prince's hand
Throughout the lands
A more excellent thing.

Take my cloak. Oh, take my cloak.
It will be forever new.
My mantle is good, Fergus,
For thy son and grandson it will endure.

My belt, in gold and silver wrought,
Oh, take my belt.
Sickness will not touch him who is encircled by it,
Nor skin erupt, encompassed by my girdle.

My helmet, take my helmet, Fergus.
No man that on his scalp shall put it
Will suffer the reproach of baldness.

Take my tunic. Oh, my tunic take,
Well-fitting, silken garment.
Though it were worn a hundred years
Yet its crimson were none the worse.

My caldron, my caldron. Oh, Fergus,
A rare thing in its daily use.
Should it be fed with stones,
Yet it will turn out meat for princes.

My vat, my life-giving vat.
By any that shall bathe in it,
Though he be a hundred,
Life's stage is traversed thrice.

My horse rod. Oh, Fergus, my horse rod.
Rod of the yellow horse so fair to see.
Let the whole world's women look on thee

IUBDAN, KING OF THE LEPRA AND THE LEPRACAUN

With that rod in thy hand, their hottest love will center on thee.

> My timpan. Oh, my timpan,
> Endowed with string-sweetness from the Red Sea's borders.
> Within its wires is minstrelsy
> To delight all women in the universe.

Then he added, speaking to the king alone, "Whosoever should, in the matter of tuning my timpan, be suddenly put to the test, if he had never hitherto been a man of art, yet would the instrument itself perform the minstrel's function. Oh, Fergus," Iubdan said, "how melodious is its martial strain; its low cadence. Without a finger on a single string of all its strings, by itself it plays." And turning again to the people of the court at Emain Macha, he resumed his lay:

> Of my swine two porkers take,
> They will last you to your dying day.
> Though every night they are killed and eaten
> By morning they will live again.

> My sandals. Oh, my sandals, Fergus,
> Brogues of the white bronze, of virtue marvelous.
> Alike they travel on land or sea.
> Happy the king whose choice shall fall on these.

The lay ended. Fergus mac Leide turned away.

"Fergus," said Iubdan, "from these treasures choose now. Choose one precious thing and let me go."

But Fergus, for love of Iubdan's presence, refused to make his choice, and at this hour Aed returned from the kingdom of the Lepracaun, and a great welcoming and feasting began at Emain Macha. The sages and the scholars gathered around their chief poet, to greet him, to hear of his adventures and his travels, and to examine him about the house of Iubdan, his household, and of the land of the Lepracaun. Aed, forthwith, made a lay concerning all these things:

"A wondrous enterprise it was that took me away from you, to a populous fairy palace with a great company of princes and little men. Smooth are its terraces. Its roof is thatched with yellow bird feathers, and there are crystal pillars there, and columns of silver and copper."

The company listened, spellbound, to their poet.

"There was every day in that land the reciting of tales and the singing of poems, the mellow blast of trumpet horns, and concerted minstrelsy. Women are there. They bathe in a pure lake, and each one has a chain of gold. Their bodies are pure white, and their locks reach to their ankles. Bebo"—he bowed to his friend—"Iubdan's queen, an object of desire. Eshirt was there, and the poet's wife, a lovely woman. She could sleep in my rounded glove. The king's cupbearer, Feror, I loved him. He could lie in my sleeve, and Glomar, stern doer of doughty deeds, he could fell a thistle at one stroke.

"Seventeen lovely girls lay in my sleeves, and four of the men of Lepra in my belt, and unbeknown to me, among my beard would be another; and they—the fighting men of that land and the scholars of that fairy mound—would say to me, the public acclamation ever was, 'Oh, Aed! Enormous Aed! Oh, very giant!'" He turned to Fergus mac Leide. "Such, my king, is my adventure. In truth wondrous things have befallen me in the land of Iubdan."

Then the king of the Lepra embraced Aed and said to him, "It is our country's loss that you have returned to your own." And they embraced.

Fergus stood tall above his two friends and, looking down at them, said, "Now I will make my choice." And he was sad. He chose the white-bronze sandals that would travel on land or sea. "That I, too, may travel where Aed has been," he said, and he lifted Iubdan onto the palm of his hand and embraced him.

And Iubdan took leave of the nobles and warriors of the court and of the women and the maidens. And he bade farewell to Ferdiad, who had ministered to him, and to Aed, his friend, and to Fergus mac Leide. And the hosts of Ulster gave him escort to the White Strand of the Strong Men, where his yellow-gold horse was waiting for him, and the whole kingdom of Emain Macha was grieved at the departure from their land of Iubdan, king of the Lepra and the Lepracaun.

THE STORY OF PERSEUS

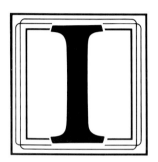n the ancient land of Argos, there lived a king by the name of Acrisius. Though he enjoyed all the power and wealth of his eminent status, he was deeply unhappy because he possessed no heir. His only child was a beautiful daughter named Danae, whose magnificent skin and dark eyes could lure Zeus himself from his Olympian throne. Still, the king could take no pleasure in his daughter's beauty, so consumed was he in his desire for a son. At last, and in despair, he journeyed to Delphi to consult the Oracle. There, he was told that it was not his fate to have a son, and what was worse, that the son of his daughter would slay him. King Acrisius left Delphi understandably much shaken but determined to thwart the prophecy. Though his love for his daughter was not great, her murder was beyond consideration; King Acrisius knew only too well that the shedding of familial blood was the gravest of offenses in the eyes of the gods. Rather than have her put to death, he had built a subterranean house of bronze, which would admit only light and air. There, King Acrisius reasoned, Danae could live out her days, beyond the reach of prospective suitors.

And so Danae was shut up in her bronze prison, doomed to a life of solitude, and King Acrisius was rid of his problem; or so he thought. The king had failed to consider that no prison, however isolated and secure, could bar the entry of the mighty Zeus, whose eye for feminine beauty was renowned among men and gods alike. And so it happened that one day, while Danae was sitting in her bronze chamber watching the clouds pass overhead, she was visited by the god himself in the form of a mysterious shower of gold; the birth of a son, named Perseus, resulted from this strangest of unions.

Try as she might, Danae could not keep her child a secret from his grandfather for long. When at last Acrisius discovered the baby in his daughter's chamber, he was astonished and outraged.

"Who is the father of this child?" he demanded.

Danae answered truthfully that it was the ruler of Olympus himself, but Acrisius scoffed at her answer and accused her of lying. Nonetheless, he was once again presented with the problem of disposing of his daughter and, now, her young son. The wrath of the Furies was enough to turn his thoughts from murder a second time, but the prospect of his own death at the hands of his grandson dissuaded him from behaving in a merciful fashion toward either mother or son. Hoping to orchestrate their destruction in such a way that blame would not fall on his head, Acrisius had a sturdy chest built and ordered that the two unfortunates be locked inside. He then had the chest plunged into the foaming sea.

Danae spent long hours adrift in her strange vessel with her tiny son curled up asleep on her lap, the interminable sound of the waves his only lullaby. When all hope of rescue seemed to be spent, the chest at last came to rest on solid land with a thump that fell like music on Danae's ears. However, delivery from the waves was not enough; it still remained for Danae and Perseus to be rescued from the trunk that had been their home and prison for so many days. Despair returned, as overwhelming as the pounding of the waves, and Danae wept at her misfortune. But fate—or divine intervention—came to her rescue; a kindly fisherman named Dictys stumbled upon the chest, heard the young woman's cries, and released her and her small son from their bondage. Taking pity upon the forlorn pair, he invited them to come live with him and his wife as their own kin. And so the two lived the simple life of fishing-folk and were happy for many years. However, fate would deal another cruel blow to mother and son. Polydictes, the ruler of the small island on which Danae and Perseus were living, all at once took notice of the still beautiful Danae and wished to marry her. However, he had no desire to adopt Perseus, now grown to manhood, and so the king set about getting rid of the young man.

One day, when Polydictes and Perseus were talking together, the king seized an opportunity to mention that more than anything else he wished to possess the head of one of the Gorgons, those three monstrous sisters with hair of living snakes. Shortly thereafter, the king arranged for a prenuptial celebration and invited the most wealthy and prestigious citizens of the kingdom. As was the custom of the land, each presented the couple with a wedding gift—glittering silver urns bedecked in jewels and lavish golden ornaments; only Perseus had nothing to give. Being young and impetuous, Perseus acted upon Polydictes' suggestion and proudly announced that as his wedding gift he would obtain the head of one of the Gorgon sisters. Polydictes smiled to himself; the young man had played perfectly into his hands. No one could survive an encounter with the Gorgons, for it was reputed that the monsters had the ability to turn anyone who looked upon them instantly to stone. Perseus' youthful ambition and pride would surely be his undoing.

But even before Perseus could meet the challenge of the Gorgons head-on, he must first discover where they lived. Without so much as a farewell to his mother—for no doubt she would try to dissuade him from his task—he left for Greece in the hope of there discovering the Gorgons' whereabouts. His quest took him to consult the Oracle of Delphi; travel to the land of Dodona, land of the talking oak trees; and venture to the domain of the Selli, who made their bread with acorns.

But Perseus' journey brought no answers to his questions, and he wandered on, in much despair, until the gods Hermes and Athena came to his aid. One day on the open road, he met an exquisite youth dressed in a winged hat and sandals and carrying a golden wand with wings at one end. Recognizing this divine personage as none other than the god Hermes himself, Perseus was greatly heartened. The god informed the young man that in order to vanquish one of the fearsome Gorgons, he must be properly outfitted for the fight; only the nymphs of the North could provide him with the necessary equipment. But before he could visit the nymphs, Hermes explained, Perseus must seek out the Gray Women, those ashen-colored hags who dwelt in the land of perpetual twilight, and who shared the vision of a single eye, passed in turns between them; they alone could reveal to Perseus the whereabouts of the nymphs of the North. Brave lad that he was, Perseus must have trembled at the thought of entering that dimly lit domain, but Hermes allayed his fears with the reassurance that he would accompany him in his quest. He further counseled Perseus, saying that he must remain hidden until he spied one of the women in the act of passing on the eye; at that moment, all three of the women would be blind. Perseus must seize that opportunity to get hold of the eye and, once it was in his possession, threaten not to return it unless the Gray Women disclosed the dwelling place of the nymphs of the North.

In the meantime, Hermes presented Perseus with a sword of such sturdy mettle that it could cut through the Gorgons' scales as though they were made of butter. Perseus thanked the god for his most valuable gift, but he could not help voicing a doubt.

"Divine herald," he began, "forgive the impertinence of my question, but how shall I use this wonderful sword if the Gorgons' glances may turn the mortal onlooker to stone?''

Perseus' question was answered by the sudden and resplendent appearance of the goddess Palla Athena. Standing beside the astonished youth, she removed her shield of glowing bronze and held it out to him, saying, "With this shield you will be immune to the Gorgons' deadly glances. Use it as a mirror, so that your mortal eye may never meet their petrifying gaze."

Perseus accepted the goddess's gift graciously and set out under the divine aegis of Hermes for the dwelling place of the Gray Women. The journey was a long and perilous one, but at last Perseus arrived in the twilight country where the eclipsed sun shone, and he beheld the Gray Women. They had the appearance of human-headed swans but with arms and hands beneath their wings. Perseus did just as Hermes had instructed him: he waited, unseen, in the shadows, until one of the women had removed the eye from her forehead and proceeded to pass it along. At that moment, the lad rushed forward, seized the eye, and ransomed it in return for the knowledge he required. The Gray Women were eager to oblige, as long as their precious eye was returned to them. They set Perseus on the right road, and he and Hermes embarked on the next leg of their journey, his destination the land of the Hyperboreans, at the back of the North Wind. His arrival in that land of joy was greeted with much hospitality and merriment; a banquet was set before Perseus and the rejoicing was interrupted only to fetch those remaining items he required to conquer one of the Gorgons: winged sandals, an enchanted purse that assumed the size and shape required of anything it carried, and a special cap that rendered the wearer invisible. At last, Perseus was prepared to meet the Gorgons, and Hermes led the way.

It was most auspicious that the monstrous trio was asleep when Hermes and Perseus arrived at their island; it also permitted Perseus the uneasy luxury of surveying the creatures, reflected in the mirrored surface of Athena's shield. They were grotesque beyond description, with large, feathered wings, scaly torsos, and a knot of slimy snakes for hair. Athena and Hermes stood beside Perseus and informed him that only one of the monsters, Medusa, was vulnerable to the sword; the other two were immortal.

Armed with this important information and the gifts bestowed on him by the gods, Perseus flew above the heads of the sleeping monsters, held aloft by his winged sandals, and poised his sword over Medusa's neck, all the while looking into his shield. Then, with Athena's guidance, he lopped off the monster's head with a single blow, quickly caught up the head by its snaky hair, and slipped it into the enchanted purse provided by the Hyperboreans. Just then, the two remaining Gorgons awoke and, upon discovering their sister's headless corpse, filled the air with their shrieks of vengeance. But Perseus was safe from their wrath, for he wore the cap of invisibility; even the petrifying glances of the Gorgons could not penetrate his cloak of darkness.

Perseus sped toward home and victory on his winged sandals, with Hermes beside him to guide the way. Upon reaching the land of Ethiopia, Hermes departed and Perseus landed upon that shore for a brief respite from his adventures. But he would not find rest there; instead, he discovered Andromeda, the lovely daughter of Queen Cassiopeia, chained to a cliff, awaiting her death. Perseus would later discover that the unfortunate girl was being offered as a sacrifice to a ferocious sea monster because her mother had dared to boast that her own beauty surpassed that of the sea god's daughters. As punishment for her arrogance, it was ordained by the Oracle that the Ethiopian nation's only salvation from a ravaging serpent decimating their numbers would be the offering up of young Andromeda to the monster. But the gods were not without their mercy: they decreed that Andromeda, manacled to her cruel fate by the transgressions of her mother, would be delivered by a young stranger from a distant land. Perseus looked upon the maiden and fell in love with her at first sight. There, at the water's edge, he remained by her side, sword drawn, until the serpent appeared to claim his prize. Then he slew the monster with a single blow and flew with Andromeda to the house of her father to ask for her hand in marriage, which he was quick to grant with joy and appreciation.

But Perseus' homecoming with his bride was not a happy one. In the time that he was gone, Dictys' kind wife, who had acted as a second mother to him, had died, and Dictys and Danae were driven into hiding by Polydictes when Danae refused to marry him. Perseus soon learned that the kindly fisherman and his mother had taken refuge in the temple, just as Polydictes was reveling at a banquet attended by his supporters. Perseus first made his way to the palace and burst in on the festivities. He was a splendid figure to behold, dressed in Athena's gleaming shield and carrying the purse containing the monstrous head; all eyes looked with astonishment at the lad they were certain had met his death long ago. Before any of the company could so much as blink an eye, Perseus reached into the enchanted purse and pulled out Medusa's head, holding it high so that he would not look directly at it. Instantly, every reveler

was turned to stone; even in death, the Gorgon's head had not lost its deadly potency.

Once free of Polydictes' tyranny, the island folk were quick to disclose the whereabouts of Danae and Dictys. Perseus had Dictys made king, and he and his mother decided to return to Argos to see whether Acrisius had not mellowed with the passing years and would not embrace his daughter and grandson to his bosom.

Upon arriving in Argos, however, Perseus and Danae learned that the king had been driven into exile and that his whereabouts were a secret. Shortly after their arrival in Argos, Perseus learned that the king of Larissa was holding an athletic competition, and he journeyed to that northern land to participate. As fate would have it, when it was Perseus' turn to throw the discus, he missed the mark and sent the weight hurtling into the crowds of onlookers. One of the spectators was Acrisius himself, in Larissa on a visit; the discus, guided by the hand of divine prophecy, struck the exiled king of Argos in the head, killing him instantly.

With Acrisius' death, an unhappy chapter in the lives of Danae, Perseus, and Andromeda came to a close. All lived long and happy lives, but the memory of their suffering—the severed head of the Gorgon Medusa—forever after emblazoned on Athena's shield, serves to remind all who come after of the immortal tale of Perseus.

HANSEL AND GRETHEL

lose to a large forest there lived a woodcutter with his wife and his two children. The boy was called Hansel and the girl Grethel. They were always very poor and had very little to live on; and at one time, when there was famine in the land, the woodcutter could no longer procure their daily bread.

One night he lay in bed worrying over his troubles, and he sighed and said to his wife: "What is to become of us? How are we to feed our poor children when we have nothing for ourselves?"

"I'll tell you what, husband," answered the woman. "Tomorrow morning we will take the children out quite early into the thickest part of the forest. We will light a fire and give each of them a piece of bread; then we will go to our work and leave them alone. They won't be able to find their way back, and so we shall be rid of them."

"Nay, wife," said the man. "We won't do that. I could never find it in my heart to leave my children alone in the forest; the wild animals would soon tear them to pieces."

"What a fool you are!" she said. "Then we must all four die of hunger. You may as well plane the boards for our coffins at once."

She gave him no peace until he consented. "But I grieve over the poor children all the same," said the man.

The two children could not go to sleep for hunger either, and they heard what their stepmother said to their father.

Grethel wept bitterly and said: "All is over with us now!"

"Be quiet, Grethel!" said Hansel. "Don't cry; I will find some way out of it."

When the old people had gone to sleep, he got up, put on his little coat, opened the door, and slipped out. The moon was shining brightly, and the white pebbles around the house shone like newly minted coins.

Hansel stooped down and put as many into his pockets as they would hold.

Then he went back to Grethel and said: "Take comfort, little sister, and go to sleep. God won't forsake us." And then he went to bed again.

When the day broke, before the sun had risen, the woman came and said: "Get up, you lazybones; we are going into the forest to fetch wood."

Then she gave them each a piece of bread and said: "Here is something for your dinner, but mind you don't eat it before, for you'll get no more."

Grethel put the bread under her apron, for Hansel had the stones in his pockets. Then they all started for the forest.

When they had gone a little way, Hansel stopped and looked back at the cottage; he did the same thing again and again.

His father said: "Hansel, what are you stopping to look back at? Take care, and put your best foot foremost."

"Oh, Father!" said Hansel. "I am looking at my white cat. It is sitting on the roof, wanting to say good-bye to me."

"Little fool! That's no cat, it's the morning sun shining on the chimney."

But Hansel had not been looking at the cat, he had been dropping a pebble on the ground each time he stopped. When they reached the middle of the forest, their father said:

"Now children, pick up some wood, I want to make a fire to warm you."

Hansel and Grethel gathered the twigs together and soon made a huge pile. Then the pile was lighted, and when it blazed up, the woman said: "Now lie down by the fire and rest yourselves while we go and cut wood. When we have finished we will come back to fetch you."

Hansel and Grethel sat by the fire, and when dinnertime came they each ate their little bit of bread, and they thought their father was quite near because they could hear the sound of an ax. It was no ax, however, but a branch that the man had tied to a dead tree, and that blew backward and forward against it. They sat there such a long time that they got tired, their eyes began to close, and they were soon fast asleep.

When they woke up it was night. Grethel looked around her and cried: "How shall we ever get out of the wood!"

Hansel comforted her and said: "Wait a little till the moon rises, then we will soon find our way."

When the full moon rose, Hansel took his little sister's hand, and they walked on, their footsteps guided by the pebbles, which glittered like newly minted coins in the silvery light. They walked the whole night long, and at daybreak they found themselves back at their father's cottage.

HANSEL AND GRETHEL

They knocked at the door, and when the woman opened it and saw Hansel and Grethel, she said: "You bad children, why did you sleep so long in the wood? We thought you did not mean to come back anymore."

But their father was delighted, for it had gone to his heart to leave them behind alone.

Not long after they were again in great destitution, and the children heard the woman at night in bed say to their father: "We have eaten up everything again but half a loaf, and then we are at the end of everything. The children must go away. We will take them farther into the forest so that they won't be able to find their way back. There is nothing else to be done."

The man took it much to heart and said: "We had better share our last crust with the children."

But the woman would not listen to a word he said, she only scolded and reproached him. Anyone who once says "A" must also say "B," and as he had given in the first time, he had to do so the second as well. The children were again wide awake and heard what was said.

When the old people went to sleep Hansel again got up, meaning to go out and get some more pebbles, but the woman had locked the door and he couldn't get out. But he consoled his little sister and said:

"Don't cry, Grethel; go to sleep. God will help us."

In the early morning the woman made the children get up and gave them each a piece of bread, but it was smaller than the last. On the way to the forest Hansel crumbled it up in his pocket and stopped every now and then to throw a crumb onto the ground.

"Hansel, what are you stopping to look about you for?" asked his father.

"I am looking at my dove, which is sitting on the roof and wants to say good-bye to me," answered Hansel.

"Little fool!" the woman said. "That is no dove; it is the morning sun shining on the chimney."

Nevertheless, Hansel strewed the crumbs from time to time on the ground. The woman led the children far into the forest where they had never been in their lives before. Again they made a big fire, and the woman said:

"Stay where you are, children, and when you are tired you may go to sleep for a while. We are going farther on to cut wood, and in the evening when we have finished we will come back and fetch you."

At dinnertime Grethel shared what little bread she had with Hansel, for he had crumbled his up on the road. Then they went to sleep, and the evening passed, but no one came to fetch the poor children.

It was quite dark when they woke up, and Hansel cheered his little sister, saying: "Wait a bit, Grethel, till the moon rises. Then we can see the bread crumbs which I scattered to show us the way home."

When the moon rose they started, but they found no bread crumbs, for all the thousands of birds in the forest had pecked them up and eaten them.

Hansel said to Grethel: "We shall soon find the way."

But they could not find it. They walked the whole night, and all the next day from morning till night, but they could not get out of the wood.

They were very hungry, for they had nothing to eat but a few berries that they found. They were so tired that their legs would not carry them any farther, and they lay down under a tree and went to sleep.

When they woke up in the morning, it was the third day since they had left their father's cottage. They started to walk again, but they only got deeper and deeper into the wood, and if no help came they must perish.

At midday they saw a beautiful snow-white bird sitting in a tree. It sang so beautifully that they stood still to listen to it. When it stopped, it fluttered its wings and flew around them. They followed the bird till they came to a little cottage; there, on the roof, the bird settled itself.

When they got quite near, they saw that the little house was made of bread; its roof was cake and its windows were transparent sugar.

"This will be something for us," said Hansel. "We will have a good meal. I will have a piece of the roof, Grethel, and you can have a bit of the window. It will be nice and sweet."

Hansel stretched up and broke off a piece of the roof to try what it was like. Grethel went to the window and nibbled at that. A gentle voice called out from within:

Nibbling, nibbling like a mouse,
Who's nibbling at my little house?

The children answered:

The wind, the wind doth blow
From heaven to earth below.

They went on eating without disturbing themselves. Hansel, who found the roof very good, broke off a large piece for himself; and Grethel

pushed a whole round pane out of the window and sat down on the ground to enjoy it.

All at once the door opened and an old, old woman, supporting herself on a crutch, came hobbling out. Hansel and Grethel were so frightened that they dropped what they held in their hands.

But the old woman only shook her head and said: "Ah, dear children, who brought you here? Come in and stay with me; you will come to no harm."

She took them by the hand and led them into the little house. A nice dinner was set before them: pancakes and sugar, milk, apples, and nuts. After this she showed them two little white beds into which they crept and felt as if they were in Heaven.

Although the old woman appeared to be friendly, she was really a wicked old witch who was on the watch for children, and she had built the bread house on purpose to lure them to her. Whenever she could get a child into her clutches, she cooked it and ate it, and considered it a grand feast. Witches have red eyes and can't see very far, but they have keen scent like animals and can perceive the approach of human beings.

When Hansel and Grethel came near her, she laughed wickedly to herself, and said scornfully: "Now I have them, they shan't escape me."

She got up early in the morning, before the children were awake, and when she saw them sleeping, with their beautiful rosy cheeks, she murmured to herself: "They will be dainty morsels."

She seized Hansel with her bony hand and carried him off to a little stable, where she shut him up with a barred door; he might shriek as loud as he liked, she took no notice of him. Then she went to Grethel, shook her till she woke up, and cried:

"Get up, little lazybones, fetch some water and cook something nice for your brother; he is in the stable and has to be fattened. When he is nice and fat, I will eat him."

Grethel began to cry bitterly, but it was no use; she had to obey the witch's orders. The best food was now cooked for poor Hansel, while Grethel had only the shells of crayfish.

The old woman hobbled to the stable every morning and cried: "Hansel, put your finger out for me to feel how fat you are."

Hansel put out a knucklebone, and the old woman, whose eyes were dim, thought it was his finger and was much astonished that he did not get fat.

When four weeks had passed, and Hansel still kept thin, she became very impatient and would wait no longer for the boy to fatten.

"Now then, Grethel," she cried, "bustle along and fetch the water. Fat or thin, tomorrow I will kill Hansel and eat him."

Oh, how his poor little sister grieved! As she carried the water, the tears streamed down her cheeks.

"Dear God, help us!" she cried. "If only the wild animals in the forest had devoured us, we should, at least, have died together."

"You may spare me your lamentations; they will do you no good," said the old woman.

Early in the morning Grethel had to go out to fill the kettle with water, and then she had to kindle a fire and hang the kettle over it.

"We will bake first," said the old witch. "I have heated the oven and kneaded the dough."

She pushed poor Grethel toward the oven and said: "Creep in and see if it is properly heated, and then we will put the bread in."

She meant, when Grethel had got in, to shut the door and roast her.

But Grethel saw her intention and said: "I don't know how to get in. How am I to manage it?"

"Stupid goose!" cried the witch. "The opening is big enough; you can see that I could get into it myself."

She hobbled up and stuck her head into the oven. But Grethel gave her a push that sent the witch right in, and then she banged the door and bolted it.

"Oh! Oh!" she began to howl horribly. But Grethel ran away and left the wicked witch to perish miserably.

Grethel ran as fast as she could to the stable. She opened the door and cried: "Hansel, we are saved. The old witch is dead."

Hansel sprang out like a bird out of a cage when the door is set open. How delighted they were! They fell upon each other's necks, and kissed each other, and danced about for joy.

As they had nothing more to fear, they went into the witch's house; there they found chests in every corner full of pearls and precious stones.

"These are better than pebbles," said Hansel as he filled his pockets.

Grethel said: "I must take something home with me, too." And she filled her apron.

"But now we must go," said Hansel, "so that we may get out of this enchanted wood."

Before they had gone very far, they came to a great piece of water.

"We cannot cross," said Hansel. "I see no stepping stones and no bridge."

"And there are no boats, either," answered Grethel. "But there is a duck swimming. It may help us over if we ask it."

So she cried:

> Little duck, that cries quack, quack,
> Here Grethel and here Hansel stand.
> Quickly, take us on your back,
> No path nor bridge is there at hand!

The duck came swimming toward them; Hansel got on its back and told his sister to sit on his knee.

"No," answered Grethel, "it will be too heavy for the duck; it must take us over one after the other."

The good creature did this, and when they had got safely over and walked for a while, the wood seemed to grow more and more familiar to them, and at last they saw their father's cottage in the distance. They began to run and rushed inside, where they threw their arms around their father's neck. The man had not had a single happy moment since he had deserted his children in the wood, and in the meantime his wife had died.

Grethel shook her apron and scattered the pearls and precious stones all over the floor, and Hansel added handful after handful out of his pockets.

So all their troubles came to an end, and they lived together as happily as possible.